LITTLE FOXBURY

OMNIBUS EDITION

ELIZABETH LEYDIN

ISBN 978-1-923418-10-3

Improbable Fictions
PO Box 283
Annandale NSW 2038
Australia
contact@improbablefictions.com

LITTLE FOXBURY

Under the wide skies of Norfolk, the market town of Little Foxbury is a charming and historic place.

It boasts a ruined abbey, a sixteenth century church, a famous coaching inn, a monument to Boudicca's rebellion, and an entry in the Domesday book. Ownership of the pile of stones that used to be a castle is disputed with the village of Wymond, a few miles to the east, in a mild feud that persists to this day.

The town is home to a varied and (mostly) congenial assortment of inhabitants from farriers to farmers, blacksmiths to brewsters, and tradesmen and merchants of all descriptions. The self-described gentry usually go off to London for the Season, but everyone is home for haymaking and, in case of trouble, they will rally behind each other.

Little Foxbury is a wonderful place to look for love…and to bring love home for good.

THE RELUCTANT COUNTESS

CHAPTER 1

"Why do we have to wear black, Aunt Diana?" Victoria asked. It was a fair question, Diana admitted. The custom of children—of anyone—wearing black for mourning was just tradition. It had no reason behind it. Certainly not reasons a six year old would care about.

"It's to show people that we're sad, so they won't expect us to be happy," she said. She laid the small black dresses on the bed, her heart twisting in her chest.

"*I'm* not happy." Dorothy—Dora—two years younger than Vicky, clung to Diana's leg. She bent and picked her niece up, cuddling her comfortingly.

"I know, sweetheart. None of us is happy." The news of the shipwreck of her sister and brother-in-law, the girls' parents, had come so unexpectedly, they were all still in shock. Diana sat down on the bed, and Vicky sat beside her, holding her free hand.

"Will we live here with you now?" Vicky was so like her mother, Catherine. She always liked to pin everything down and have it organised and under control.

"Yes, you will." At least Catherine and Sebastian had left the girls to her care. She couldn't have borne it if they'd been whisked off to some relative of Sebastian's. "Now, you can go down to the kitchen and see the cat's new kittens."

Thank God for kittens! The girls' faces brightened immediately and they ran out of the room and clattered down the servants' stairs. She had better go and write some letters to all their relatives, informing them of Catherine and Sebastian's deaths.

A PEREMPTORY KNOCK at the door made Diana sit up from her desk in indignation. Couldn't this person see they had crepe over the doorknocker? The house was in mourning!

She dabbed tears from her cheeks. Mr Gunnel would deal with this ill-mannered intruder.

A few moments later, Mr Gunnel opened the drawing room door with an apologetic expression on his face.

"Lord Hindmouth, madam," he said.

The words jolted her as if she had been kicked under the heart. Sebastian! It was all a mistake! They were alive!

Then a tall, dark-haired man walked through the door. Another kick. How stupid she was. It was the *new* earl, not her brother-in-law. Of course Gunnel would have let him in. She pushed down tears and swallowed around the lump in her throat.

She rose to greet him, and curtseyed as he bowed.

"Miss Tilney," he said with a scowl, "why have you kidnapped my wards?"

"I beg your pardon! I have done no such thing!"

"Then where are they?"

"Upstairs, in the nursery, where they belong!"

"They belong at Swanstead and you had no right to remove them."

She glared at him. How *dare* he!

"I think you will find, my lord, that I have *every* right. You may have been appointed their guardian, but my sister and brother-in-law's wills will make it very clear that *I* was to have the raising of them."

He pursed his mouth. "While true, that was not well considered."

"It's best if they are raised by someone who loves them." The poor lambs. They were so bewildered and sorrowful, she hadn't hesitated to scoop them up and take them away from that echoing, empty house as soon as she'd been informed of their parents' death.

Looking around the admittedly modest room, he lifted an eyebrow. "It's best if they are raised to fit their station in life."

Gunnel interrupted, bringing in the tea tray. With embarrassment, she realised she hadn't asked the earl to sit.

"Please, my lord." She waved him to a chair and he took it as she sat on the sofa.

The ceremony of pouring and handing over completed, she sipped at the welcome warmth of her tea. She *had* to explain herself well enough that this man would leave them alone to grieve together.

"The girls need security. Their world has been, has been *smashed*. I felt very strongly that they needed me with them."

He nodded. "In the short term, you may have a case. Not in the long term, Miss Tilney." He hesitated. "I'm not sure what you know about their inheritance."

"I know that Swanstead Abbey was entailed, and goes to you as the next earl."

"Yes." He put down the cup on a side table, and leaned forward, his pale blue eyes intent. "However, your brother-in-law Sebastian knew that, of course, and so he purchased estates for both of Victoria and Dorothy, to be part of their dowry. They are very wealthy young women in their own right. I am their trustee." He cast another glance around the room. "Forgive me, Miss Tilney, but they will not learn how to run a large household here. They will not learn the skills and knowledge which will be expected of them when they marry. You are doing them harm by keeping them here. You must understand that. You yourself were raised on a large estate, were you not?"

Leftwich. Gone to a distant cousin because of entails. The whole system was barbaric.

"Yes. Which means that I *can* teach them what they need to know."

"Can you? With a staff of, what? Four or five?"

"Six counting Mary, the girls' nursemaid."

"And Swanstead has thirty or so inside servants and probably another twenty outside." He just *looked* at her.

Damn him! "I *will* raise my nieces."

"Certainly. But not *here*. Little Foxbury, while fine in its way, does not offer them enough." He tapped his index finger on his knee. "The best plan," he continued thoughtfully, "would be for you to live at Swanstead."

"As your pensioner? I think not! I prefer my independence."

He sighed, and ran a hand through his hair. "You could bring your chaperone with you, and establish a more or less separate life there."

How much to tell him? Only honesty would do. "I don't have a chaperone yet."

"Yet?"

"My sister Emma and I lived here together until her marriage a few months ago. Mrs Torbett. I haven't—I haven't found anyone suitable yet."

"The deuce! You're living here *alone*?" He looked appalled.

"I'm quite capable of managing my own affairs," she snapped. "And I have no desire to be an unwanted relative in another woman's house."

Why did he make her so *angry*? She was normally far calmer.

"You wouldn't *be* in another woman's house!" He was no calmer than she. How could pale blue eyes look so fiery? "I'm not married. And if you're alone in this house, this meeting is most improper. You could be compromised."

"Don't worry, I'm not about to trick you into marriage. I have no intention of ever marrying."

Dumbfounded, he surged to his feet and took a few paces around the room, which seemed even smaller than usual. She loved this house, but it wasn't designed for men this tall and energetic. He whirled and stared at her incredulously.

"*Never*?"

"Never. Marriage is a form of slavery for women, and I want no part of it."

"Don't be ridiculous! It's anything but slavery."

"Indeed, my lord? What would you call it, when a married woman has no say over where she lives, no control over her own money, no ability to earn her own living, and if she dares to leave, the sheriff's officers can, on the simple say-so of her husband, drag her back to him, and allow him to beat her as much as he pleases with no fear of reprisals! That sounds like slavery to me."

His mouth opened but he was lost for words. Good. Men never even *thought* about marriage from the legal standpoint for women. Let him think that over, the conceited know-it-all! He rallied.

"But children?"

A qualm ran through her. Still, she had the girls now.

As though called, Dora and Vicky ran into the room and stopped, wary of the visitor. Then they saw who he was.

"Uncle Ned!" They dropped very creditable curtseys for a six and four year old.

At her questioning look, he shrugged. "Sebastian and I were close friends. I'm no stranger to them."

The girls both ran to Diana, climbing into her lap like puppies.

"We need a hug!" Dora said.

She looked at the earl over their heads as she cuddled them. His lips tightened.

"Mr Courtenay has organised the memorial service for Thursday morning at eleven," he said. Mr Courtenay was the local vicar. Highly regarded for his sermons, he was generally regarded as a very holy man; although Diana had observed wryly that it was Mrs Courtenay who actually ran the parish. "Children would not normally attend a funeral, but a simple service should be acceptable for them. And for you and your sister Mrs Torbett."

Women didn't attend funerals either; at least, not women of their social class. It was quite broad-minded of him to have them there.

"I'll have them ready. The dressmaker is already making their new clothes." She didn't want to say the words "mourning clothes" in front of them. In the first sign of delicacy he had shown, he simply nodded.

"After the service, people will be invited back to Swanstead. There will be the reading of the wills. At that point, we can come to an understanding." Again he showed delicacy by not allowing the girls to know their futures would be decided then.

"Very well, my lord."

"Why are you calling Uncle Ned "my lord"?" Vicky asked, sitting up. "He's not a lord. He's Mr Faulkes."

Diana pulled both of them back to lie against her. "He's the new earl, my loves, now that your father is gone."

Their little bodies stiffened and then they burrowed into her like newly-whelped puppies with their dam. Dora trembled.

She stroked their backs and hugged them tighter, and slowly they relaxed.

"You see, my lord?"

He nodded, his face inscrutable.

"I'll remove myself before we become a scandal in Little Foxbury." He stood and bowed, and went out.

She wouldn't let him take these darlings away from her. She would *not*, not if she had to spend every penny she owned in Chancery Court!

CHAPTER 2

*D*amn the woman!

No chaperone, no intention to marry, and no *need*, either. The Tilneys were famous for their wealth, and Catherine, the eldest sister and principal heir, had settled ten thousand pounds on each of her sisters before her own marriage. It had even been reported in the newspapers.

Diana Tilney had been reading too much of Mary Wollstonecraft's *Vindication of the Rights of Woman.* Never marrying indeed!

He walked along the charming High Street of Little Foxbury, scowling. It was a nice enough place, a market town filled here at the centre with the brown and cream of half-timbered Tudor buildings. Their diamond window panes shone, and behind them were goods laid out for sale, everything from boots to bobbins to horse brasses.

The livery stable was on the next street over, by a monument to Boudicca's rebellion against the Romans. He walked briskly, driving cape under one arm, his Hessian boots tapping firmly on the cobblestones. There were people everywhere, and carts and even a hackney. A number of men tipped their hats, their wives curtseying, so who he was had become common knowledge. He nodded back or bowed, as appropriate.

Everything he did would be under scrutiny from now on, including what happened to the girls.

Damn woman. What had Sebastian been thinking, giving her custody of the children?

Although…those little girls clearly knew and loved her. They would need someone they loved and who loved them. He couldn't imagine how hard it was for them, to lose both parents at once. The shipwreck which had taken them had upended all their lives, including Miss Diana Tilney's.

His groom—Sebastian's groom, really—had the horses ready. He headed his phaeton out of Little Foxbury, onto the road to Swanstead, thinking hard. He had to admit she had a point about marriage.

His own wife, before her death, had complained that he had control of her dowry and all of her actions. It had not been the case in the Languedoc of her childhood, in southern France, where married women could own their own property and run their own businesses, no matter what their husbands thought: "Until that monster Bonaparte came and took away all our rights!"

He missed Petrona. She'd married him to stay out of France, but had been quite open about it, and he had married her…why? Because it was what one did, and none of the simpering English misses he'd met at Almack's had raised the slightest interest in him. He hadn't exactly loved her, but by God he'd liked her! She'd been funny and witty and slightly outrageous. He'd never known what to expect from day to day.

Her death in childbed three years ago, and the child with her, had killed any desire he'd had for an heir of his body. As he drove along the elm-lined road, images of her in the lying-in bed crowded his mind, making him sick and clammy. So much blood. So much pain.

His brother and his brother's brood were enough heirs for any man.

The vast Norfolk sky arched over him, clouds gathering on the horizon. He clicked his tongue to his greys and they picked up the pace. The weather swept in here like a charging bull, and he wanted to get them into shelter before the pelting Autumn rain came down.

Diana Tilney was a problem. Whoever had named her Diana had chosen well. She'd been a veritable goddess, eyes spitting fire, defending her little ones and denouncing marriage.

Unlike most of the current batch of debutantes, she hadn't cropped her strawberry-blonde hair, but wore it in a simple bun. He was six foot, and she was tall enough to barely tilt her head to look him in the eyes. *Glare* at him, rather, with those fine blue eyes.

He chuckled. She was definitely a problem. Without a chaperone…the girls could continue where they were until she had one, but have one she must, or he could never visit. And once that was settled…Even with a chaperone, the gossip would be vicious if she came to live at Swanstead.

Perhaps the Dower House, which currently held his senile old cousin Bosworth who cared only about the warmth of his fire and the quality of his whisky. Perhaps they could swap? Bosworth to her house in Little Foxbury, and she to the Dower House?

That might work. The girls could live with him at the big house, but they could see their aunt daily, and she could teach them what they needed to know about running the house; and supervise their dancing practice and their music and painting lessons, show them how to embroider…

He turned into the gates of Swanstead, laughing. He

couldn't quite see Diana Tilney sitting quietly, embroidering a fichu.

The butler, Mr Haley, let him. He missed his own butler, Sutton, who had been his valet in his green years, but Sutton was back in Hampshire at what had been his main residence, before he came into this blasted earldom.

"Mrs Keach has been asking for a word," Mr Haley said, taking his driving coat, hat and gloves.

The housekeeper. Yes, he had to talk to her about Thursday.

"I'll see her in the library," he told Mr Haley.

He'd set up his papers on a desk there. Partly a matter of delicacy—one didn't want to just ride roughshod over the old ways of doing things. And partly so that Sebastian's solicitor could go over all the paperwork in Seb's office with him, to make sure he knew the state of the estate and of his inheritance.

The solicitor would be here either today or early tomorrow, for the reading of the will after the service, and staying for a couple of days. Ned sighed. He'd far rather be at home in Hampshire. Norfolk was as flat as a pancake, and about as interesting. Humbug country.

He'd never expected to inherit the earldom. Seb had already had two children, so there was no reason to think he wouldn't have more, and one of them be a boy. *And* he'd had a younger brother, Trevor, but Trevor had died at Waterloo without ever being married. At the beginning of June, the peerage hadn't even crossed Ned's mind. Now it was the end of September, and here he was, Earl of Hindmouth and richer than he'd ever expected to be.

Some men he knew would be cock-a-hoop, but Ned missed Sebastian, and missed his old home. He'd put Petrona's death behind him, finally. He'd worked his way back to being *all right*, dammit!

Mrs Keach sidled in as if he were going to shout at her.

He smiled. "Yes, Mrs Keach?"

"After the service, my lord…" Another thing he had to get used to. My lord this and my lord that. His brows twitched together and she gasped.

"I'm so glad you've come to discuss that, Mrs Keach," he reassured her. "I was about to tell Humphreys that the workers on the estate will have time off to go to the memorial, if they'd like to."

"Oh, yes, sir, they'd all like to. So would we in the house, but of course that won't be possible, with everyone coming back here straight after."

No doubt Miss Diana Tilney would point out the unfairness of women's time being at everyone else's mercy.

He grimaced apologetically. "I'm afraid there's no way around that, Mrs Keach."

"Oh, no, sir! I mean, my lord. I was just wanting some instructions."

"Instructions?"

Her eyes sharpened. "About whether we're putting on a spread in the main barn for our own workers, and which china to use if we are, and which china to use for the guests to the house, and if we should order in from Norwich to get the best ham from that butcher her ladyship liked…"

Perhaps his face wasn't encouraging, because she faltered to a stop. "Surely you can make these decisions, Mrs Keach?" His own housekeeper certainly would have, without a qualm.

She gasped. "Oh no, my lord. I wouldn't want to overstep. Her ladyship always decided everything. She liked to keep a firm hand on the reins, she said, so she'd always know what was happening."

Blast. And he couldn't criticise that as damnably managing, because Catherine was dead.

This was why the girls needed someone who could train

them up in how to run a big household. He had no idea what the answers were to any of these questions.

Floundering, he grabbed onto a lifeline. "I'll ask Miss Tilney to come up and speak to you this afternoon. I'm sure she'd know what Lady Hindmouth would have wanted."

"*Thank* you, m'lord! Oh, that would be perfect! Miss Tilney is such an accomplished young lady, and, and, very decisive."

He almost laughed aloud, but that would have been unkind. Decisive. Indeed she was! He rather liked that about her, although it was going to cause him a deuced amount of trouble.

CHAPTER 3

The note sounded almost plaintive. It made her laugh. Poor man. Pitchforked into managing a new estate, and no wife to help him.

At least he had sent the carriage to bring her to Swanstead. Slightly overbearing, as it implied she would jump to do his bidding, but then he would know she *would* do whatever she could to honour Catherine and Sebastian's memory. Diana gathered up the girls and Mary their nurse-maid, and they set off.

The girls' good mourning clothes had arrived not long after Lord Hindmouth had left, so they were appropriately dressed in black dresses with white collars, and black ribbons in their hair. Their fair prettiness shone out from the sombre clothes, and it made her heart catch. They looked so much like Catherine!

Her own mourning clothes were still being finished, but she had a dress. Not the height of fashion, but not shaming. It was a couple of years old, from when an uncle had died and they'd all gone into black for six weeks.

So she got down from the carriage with composure, was

escorted into Catherine's old office by Mr Haley while the girls were taken up to their rooms by Mary to gather more of their things, and greeted Mrs Keach with warmth.

"Now, Mrs Keach, what needs to be done?"

"Oh, thank goodness you're here, miss! His lordship has no idea! We all just want everything to be perfect!"

The woman was actually wringing her hands, and curt-seying with every other sentence.

"Please, sit down, Mrs Keach, and we'll just work our way down the list of what needs to be done. Let's start with the outdoor workers and the minor tenants. Is the big barn emptied out ready for their gathering?"

"No, miss. We didn't know…"

"Well, that's the first thing to be done, because I *know* that this house is already perfect. You keep it so well."

That settled her.

An hour later, there was a knock at the door. Ned Faulkes. It was hard to think of him as Lord Hindmouth, but she had to. Mrs Keach practically levitated off her chair and into a curtsey. The woman needed to calm down.

"My lord?" Diana raised her brows.

"Just wanting to see how you're getting on. Mrs Keach, er, seemed to think a good many things had to be decided today."

"Indeed they did, but we're finished, now, I think. Use your own judgement on the flowers for the hall, Mrs Keach." Panic flicked across the older woman's face, and Diana felt a jab of combined annoyance and pity. "My sister loved—" What was in season now? Not much. "—chrysan-themums."

"Oh, yes, she did!" Of course she did. They were both pretty and fashionable. "Very good, miss." Mrs Keach scur-ried off, actually making an arc around the earl as if he were a rabid dog. Diana bit her lip to stop smiling.

"Well may you laugh," he said, dropping into a chair. "That woman is terrified of me, and I have no idea why!"

"She's afraid you'll replace her."

"It's tempting. My own housekeeper would have sorted that business out in two shakes of a lamb's tail."

Diana laughed out loud, and then covered her mouth in mortification. Laughter was out of place in this house of mourning.

"Oh, don't stop!" he begged. "Everyone is so Friday-faced. I know we're all in mourning, but we don't have to go around looking like professional mourners following a tricked-out hearse."

That made her go still. Part of her agreed, but the other, rawer, part, shied away from the words.

He leant forward, his eyes intent. "I'm sorry. My blasted tongue runs away with me sometimes. My wife complained about it."

"Your wife?" She knew that he'd been married. Sebastian had mentioned it. Perhaps the wife was back at his old estate.

"Dead," he said succinctly. "Three years now." His voice was tight. "Enough about me. I was all at sea with Mrs Keach, and why?"

She knew exactly where he was going. Cutting him off, she sighed. "I know. You didn't know what to do because you'd never been trained to run a large household."

He grinned. "In the gold!"

A reference to archery, where the centre circle was gold. She had hit the mark.

"Even if I grant that the girls need that kind of instruction–"

"Ah, but I've had a brilliant idea!" He outlined his plan about the Dower House.

That shook her. It *might* work. But again, she'd be his pensioner. And the gossip...

"I doubt that would stop the old tabbies of Little Foxbury from thinking the worst."

The door opened and two little heads peeped in.

"They're here!" Dora cried. The two of them came in, followed by their nursemaid Mary, a young girl with flyaway mousy hair and large ears.

"Mary's had a wonderful idea!" Vicky announced.

"Now, miss, there's no need to repeat–"

"You two should get married!" Dora and Vicky spoke together, cutting Mary off. "Then you can be our, our–" She turned to Mary. "What was it you said?"

"Adoptive parents," Mary mumbled. "But really, m'lord, I was just passing the time of day with your valet and, and, it was just a thing to say."

"So it's not *exactly* the same as parents," Vicky explained earnestly. "But it's just *like* that. And then we can all live here together and be happy!"

She beamed, and Dora beamed, and Mary hid her face in her apron.

What could one say to that?

God help them all, Ned thought.

He scrambled to find a response, but Diana got there before him.

She came around the desk and crouched down in front of the girls.

"It's lovely that you want us for your parents." She smoothed their hair back. "And we *are* in a way already your parents. We are your guardians. You are our wards, which is like adoption."

"But we want to live *here*," Dora said in a very small voice. "With our ponies."

Ponies! Yes, that was another good reason he should have

thought of that they should live at Swanstead. Ponies, and dogs, and room to ride and play. From Diana's face, she was thinking of all that now. He should be pleased, but he had a small spike of guilt. They were putting unfair pressure on her.

For the girls' sake.

He wanted her to live on the estate.

Would he be prepared to marry her to make that happen?

A companionate marriage, a marriage of convenience?

Something in his gut warned him away, but it would solve so many problems! He could turn his attention to the estate and financial matters, take his seat in the House of Lords, not worry about the girls or the house or the servants or…or anything!

Women really were essential to the life of the *ton*.

"You can visit and ride the ponies still, if you live with me," Miss Tilney said.

Both girls started to cry; big, fat tears brimmed and fell. His heart twisted.

Would it be so bad? It wasn't as though it would be a *real* marriage, where he'd have to court her.

Or bed her.

That twist in his gut got tighter, but he ignored it.

"Your aunt and I will discuss it, and let you know what we decide later."

Tears disappeared as if by magic.

"Oh, *thank* you, Uncle Ned! You'll be a very good papa." Vicky grabbed Dora by one hand and Mary by the other and dragged them out. "Let them *talk*!" she whispered loudly.

Miss Tilney stood slowly and turned to regard him with narrowed eyes.

"Don't even think about it."

"It's a good idea. It would solve everything."

"I've already told you I have no intention of ever marrying."

He marshalled his arguments, and took a step nearer her. Those dark blue eyes were a stormy grey now, but they were reddened by days of tears. Sighing, he spread his hands.

"It wouldn't be a real marriage."

"Real in the eyes of the law, and it's the law that I object to."

He nodded, thinking it through.

"Seb's solicitor is coming tomorrow. I could discuss it with him. See what avenues there are to maintain your independence. Secure your own income. Control over your own life." He gestured to the door. "You saw those girls. They need *both* of us, here. And this is the only way we can do it without causing a massive scandal—which would, I have to point out, hurt them too."

IT WAS TRUE. Any scandal about the two of them would seriously hurt the girls' chances later in life. Diana blinked, suddenly exhausted.

"I'm going home," she said. "I'll see you tomorrow at the service."

He took her hand, and kissed it formally as he bowed. "Thank you for your help today. We'd have been in queer stirrups without you."

She smiled as though she couldn't help it. "Your use of slang in front of a lady is shocking, you know."

He chuckled. Keep it light. "Surely not to a woman of independent mind?"

She actually snorted at that.

"Hah. I'll see you tomorrow, my lord."

"Oh, for Heaven's sake call me Ned. We're family now."

She looked sideways at him, and he had no idea what she was thinking.

"Perhaps."

The door closed behind her. He stood there for a full minute, just thinking.

It would have to be a private wedding, given that Diana, at least, would be in full mourning for six months, and half mourning another six. They couldn't wait that long. Those girls needed them both *now*.

Mr Haley coughed at the door and he came back from wool-gathering.

"Mr Tompkins, my lord."

The solicitor johnny. Excellent.

They shook hands and Tompkins, an extremely tall, narrow person with spaniel eyes, accepted a brandy before laying his despatch case on the desk.

Ned put up a hand.

"Now, before we discuss the estate," he said, "there's another matter I need your advice on."

IMPOSSIBLE. Ridiculous. *Stupid*. She should have just said no, the minute that idea came out of Vicky's mouth. But they'd looked so *hopeful*. They'd still looked hopeful when they'd gone up to their room, after a nice tea in the kitchen of her High Street house.

Damn. The problem was…this was the answer to their problems. So simple. Become the countess. (Oh, Lud, a countess. She'd have to be so *proper*!) Become their legal mother, not just their aunt.

It would give her rights to the girls that she wouldn't have otherwise. Although Catherine and Sebastian had named her as the one to raise them, Hindmouth still had the final say. He was their guardian and their trustee. No court would give an unmarried women rights over her sister's children, because they wouldn't be considered her *sister's* children, but their father's. And, in turn, his heir's. She suspected that if she were Ned's *wife*, he'd be far more likely to just let her get on with it.

That was the way in their world. Men's lives and women's lives were separate.

As countess, she'd be expected to entertain—

"The Dowager Countess Merryam, madam," Mr Gunnell announced.

Phoebe Merryam swept in, looking sumptuous in pale green velvet, and waved Diana down as she began to rise. "Oh, Mr Gunnell, *please* don't use that word! I refuse to be a dowager until my son marries."

"Very good, my lady." Gunnell hid a smile and went off, no doubt to order tea.

Phoebe kissed Diana on the cheek and gave her a swift embrace. She smelled sumptuous too.

Although she was *just* old enough to be Diana's mother, the countess moved and acted like a woman far younger. She was beautifully blonde and impeccably dressed, always. Diana had long ago concluded that her shining tresses were natural rather than dyed. Phoebe Merryam, one felt, would scorn any artifice. She'd been a stalwart friend upon the death of Diana's mother two years ago.

"My dear, I know I'm not supposed to pay visits of condolence without sending in my card and being accepted, but I did so want to see you. I told Gunnell it would do you good, and I must say I think I was right! Have you been sitting here in the dark alone?"

Diana hadn't even realised it was getting dark. What on Earth was the countess doing here at this hour? She'd be late for dinner.

"No. I've been sitting here wondering how *not* to marry Ned Faulkes!"

"Now this I *must* know about!"

Her usually mischievous eyes were concerned. Diana was overwhelmed with gratitude that she had Phoebe to talk to; an experienced woman of the world who knew exactly what being a countess entailed.

She poured out the whole story.

"That man has rag manners!" Phoebe said indignantly. "Honestly, what kind of proposal was that? There wasn't even a ring!"

"An honest one, I suppose? He's not offering romance."

Phoebe fell silent.

"If you weren't several years older than Tony, I'd have matchmade the two of you years ago, you know," she said absently. "You're what he needs. Someone independent minded, who won't be swept away by his good looks. And perhaps that's what Ned Faulkes needs too."

"You think I should marry him?"

Gunnel came in with the tea tray and Diana poured while Phoebe nibbled a shortbread.

"Yes. Yes, I think I do." She held up a hand. "Hear me out. I know you're reluctant, but I'm concerned about the girls. Ned will have to take his seat in the Lords. He has an estate near Hampshire, and he'll also be administering the estates that Sebastian bought for the girls." She took a good sip of tea, and went on. "The point is, Ned will have a multitude of duties as the earl. He *will* need a wife, to keep Swanstead organised and running smoothly. Swanstead, and the house in Grosvenor Square. Sooner or later, he'll marry."

"That's true." Thoughtfully, she ate a shortbread. The first thing she'd wanted to eat since the news of Catherine's death.

"The minute he marries, he will take the girls, and no judge in the country will give custody of minors to an unmarried woman over a married couple where the man is already their guardian."

Diana could feel the blood drain from her face. Phoebe was right. Dear God, of course he would marry! And of course he would take the girls! He was already convinced it was in their best interests to live at Swanstead. She would have *no* legal recourse. She would lose them.

"Think about it."

Nodding, Diana took more tea. "I will." Would he really marry so quickly? If the girls had been living with her for years at that point, would a judge actually hand them over? She needed legal advice. That steadied her. Yes. She could find out where she stood legally before she took action.

"Marriage with Ned would secure the girls' future." Phoebe smiled at her. "And even if he goes back on his word and makes it a real marriage…well, my dear, would that be such a hardship? He's an attractive man!"

"Phoebe!" Blushing and laughing, Diana slapped Phoebe's arm.

"Oh, tosh! You're not a green miss. And although I shouldn't say this, you're wasted on the old biddies of Little Foxbury. As Ned's countess, you'd be mixing with a different kind of person entirely."

"Such as yourself?"

"Exactly!" Phoebe batted her eyelashes so plaintively that Diana had to laugh. "Or, even better, some young women your own age and education! You know you've been lonely since Emma married."

She had been, since Emma now lived in the next town over, although she'd seen more of her since Captain Torbett had been posted to the Continent last month.

It would be nice to have more friends.

"I can't go to parties or anything for at least six months."

"Not *formal* parties. But a quiet nuncheon here and

there…a dinner with a few guests. Rides with friends. There's nothing improper about that."

A single woman couldn't invite anyone but other women to their house. Dinner parties were impossible.

Riding…she hadn't kept her own horse since her father died and Mama had bought this house. It was more than big enough for her needs, but it had no stables, being right in the main street of Little Foxbury. She could ride Mercy, Catherine's chestnut mare. Catherine wouldn't mind. Ned wouldn't mind.

When had she started thinking of him as Ned?

"My dear, I hate the thought of you dwindling away to an old maid with no one but old biddies like Mrs Shepherd and Mrs Birch for company."

Shuddering, Diana nodded. Good women in their way, those two, but…not congenial company.

"Just think about it." Phoebe pressed her hand. "I think you'd make a delightful countess, and how much fun it would be, going in to dinner before Lady Yarbury!"

She twinkled at Diana and, oddly, the thought of being higher in precedence than Lady Yarbury, a noted keeper of score, made the idea of being Lady Hindmouth more real.

More possible.

CHAPTER 4

The memorial service was well attended. Ned was pleased with the turn-out. More for the girls' sake than his own, but he thought that the entire population of Little Foxbury had attended, including all his recently-acquired tenants.

He sat with the girls next to him, and Diana on the other side, in the front left hand pew; the Hindmouth pew. Diana had been going to sit in her normal pew, but Vicky had clung to her hand so fiercely that she had stayed with them.

It was odd, sitting there with a woman and children. As though they were already married.

They had both Mr Courtenays concelebrating: the vicar and his son Thomas, the curate. They formed a picture of Youth and Age: two tall men, alike with bushy hair and long, expressive hands, but one's hair was brown and the other white.

The vicar gave a short opening prayer in his magnificently mellow voice, and then it was Ned's turn. The eulogy.

How Ned hated speaking in public! The thought of

having to make his maiden speech in the House of Lords was daunting; this only just a little less so.

He edged past the girls and Diana and went to the altar, Thomas Courtenay patting him on the back as he stepped up to the pulpit. Nerves rose in his stomach like moths. He fixed his eyes on Diana. She nodded gravely. Swallowing, he began to read, his knees weak.

It was hard. Sebastian and he had been at school together. They had chummed up on the first day, and stayed friends through university and young manhood. Seb had been his best man when he married Petrona.

He missed him. His throat blocked up with unshed tears, and he had to keep his eyes on Diana's face; if he looked at the girls he'd be undone.

He spoke about Sebastian and Catherine's generosity, their charitable actions (which got quite a few heads nodding), their excellence as stewards of Swanstead, their love for each other and for their children. The girls cried. Diana blinked back tears; she'd moved to sit in between the girls, and had an arm around each of them. Thank God she wasn't giving them the 'ladies don't show emotions in public' lecture.

Ned kept it short, and returned to the pew with relief. Diana and the children moved along for him and he sat with Dora's hand in his for the rest of the mercifully brief service.

Thomas Courtenay finished with the prayer for those in peril on the sea, a nod to the shipwreck which had taken Seb and Catherine from them, and then the vicar gave the general invitation for everyone to go to Swanstead for refreshments.

As he processed down the aisle to the front door, Dora whispered to Ned, "Is that all? Is that all there is?"

"Yes, sweetheart. Now we go back home and have cakes." He was grateful that there was no graveside service. How he had hated throwing those clumps of earth into his father's grave and hearing the thump and clatter as they landed on the coffin.

Dora brightened a little, and whispered, "Cakes!" to Vicky, so the girls weren't crying as they went out, curtseyed to the vicar, and headed for the carriage. He shook both Courtenays' hands and thanked them, and invited them both to the wake. The vicar refused; no surprise, he hardly ever came to public events. Thomas agreed.

"That was a good eulogy," he said. Of course, he and Sebastian had been friends too.

Done. It was over.

Now there was just the wake to get through, and he could start to look ahead, and plan for this new life which had been dumped on him.

As he got into the Swanstead carriage, he was absurdly grateful that Diana was there too.

THE GIRLS WEREN'T EXPECTED to stay for the wake. Diana sent them upstairs to the nursery with Mary and a plate of cakes and sandwiches, then stiffened her spine and turned to face the ordeal of sympathy.

Before she could greet anyone she knew, Mrs Keach was at her side with a question about the order in which to serve the food.

Five minutes later, when she was in polite conversation with Meg Deveny—a tall young woman whom she knew mainly through church—and the curate Mr Courtenay, Mrs Keach was back again, asking her to check on the buffet before the doors were opened to the dining room.

She excused herself and went to look. There were some things which needed to be changed: not large issues, but there was a particular way that her mother had always laid out a buffet, and she suspected that Catherine would have followed that model. She felt instinctively that everything should be as if Catherine had ordered it.

"Thank you so much, Miss!" Mrs Keach said as they regarded the perfect, laden table. "I knew it wasn't exactly as my lady would do it, but…" She reached into her pocket and drew out a handkerchief, blotting her eyes.

Diana patted her shoulder. "She'd be very pleased with this, Mrs Keach." She gave the footmen the nod to open the doors for the guests, and moved back along the wall to give them room. She couldn't eat anything. It felt as though her heart was in her throat, blocking her gullet. As though she were lucky to be able to breathe.

Mrs Keach had another question about the ratafia glasses and whether older gentlemen should be offered ratafia as well as the women.

"No. Men should be offered tea, coffee, or claret if they wish for wine."

There were so many decisions. A truly competent house-keeper would make most of them herself, but Catherine always had liked being in charge, and she'd clearly chosen a housekeeper who wouldn't object to that. Still, even a competent housekeeper would have had to ask direction for some of the decisions Diana had made on Catherine's behalf in the last week.

Phoebe was right. Ned was going to have to marry.

He couldn't possibly run this enormous house and the house in London, along with the kitchen garden and dairy staff, *and* sit in the House and run his multiple estates. He would need help, and the traditional helpmeet was a wife.

There was no reason for him *not* to be married, and a hundred reasons for him to be, even if he didn't want or need another heir.

Any woman he married would have the raising of her nieces.

As the guests filtered in, speaking quietly to one another in the subdued tones appropriate to a wake, she made her decision.

She *could not* risk losing Vicky and Dora.

There he was, at the back where the host should be, gesturing to a footman to bring the decanter of claret over to Anthony, Phoebe's son, Lord Merryam. His lands stretched east from Little Foxbury, whereas Swanstead stretched west. She watched the two men for a moment. Both tall, Lord Merryam was blondly, classically handsome, whereas Ned's face was rugged, his hair black. Irish blood somewhere in the background, with that black hair and blue eyes?

Both attractive, but Lord Merryam seemed young and less *solid*. She hadn't really looked at Ned as a man before. If she married him...he *said* it would be a marriage of convenience, but if he decided otherwise, the law was on his side.

How much would she risk to be with the girls and raise them as Catherine would have wanted?

Unbidden, she remember Phoebe's voice saying, "...would that be such a hardship? He's a handsome man!" A blush forced its way up; she could feel it reddening her cheeks.

No. Best not to even think that way. It was embarrassing enough that she'd have to, in effect, *propose* to him.

She made her way over to Ned and Lord Merryam. They both greeted her.

"Everything all right?" Ned asked her.

"Yes. Mrs Keach just had some questions." She paused. This was the moment everything changed. "I'd appreciate a moment of your time later. To discuss the girls' future."

"After the reading of the wills." He nodded.

Mrs Keach signalled her from the hall doorway, and Diana sighed.

"Excuse me, my lords."

THE READING of the wills was straightforward. Catherine had left some bequests to her sisters, both monetary and jewellery, and some to servants. Sebastian had left the unentailed property to his daughters, with Ned as trustee, plus the normal pensions and gifts to servants. Both of them commended the girls to Diana's care.

No wiggle room there, but surely she could see that it was, well, *awkward*?

Diana sat unmoving, head high, like the goddess she was named for. He was learning to know her face, though, and could see the tension in her jaw and the tight hold she had on her grief.

His heart twisted. He mourned Seb, but he'd be in a much worse case if something happened to Jonathan, his own brother. Diana was admirable in so many ways.

Her sister Emma, Mrs Torbett, cried openly. Diana moved to comfort her.

Afterwards, he and the solicitor took Diana and Mrs Torbett up to Catherine's room to collect the jewellery. Technically they should wait until probate, but there would be no one contesting this will.

Catherine's room had been cared for by her maid after the death, but only tidied. It had been a supposed pleasure trip to Newcastle on a friend's yacht which had ended in an early Autumn storm; the only thing to be thankful for was that they hadn't taken the maid or valet, there being no room for them on board.

Her maid stood stiffly by, taking out the jewel cases reluctantly. A new hire, she hadn't been mentioned in the will, which would have wounded her, especially since she was now out of work. He'd have to organise something to see her re-employed.

Diana spoke to her quietly. Whatever she said brightened the woman's mood.

As the solicitor and Mrs Torbett went over the inventory from the will, Diana drew him aside.

"A moment, my lord?"

"Of course."

Her face coloured, as if she were embarrassed. "I've been thinking…"

"About the Dower House?" Excellent.

She took a deep breath in, and let it out in a rush. "No. About…about the other thing."

That *was* embarrassment! Oh, Lord, she was hinting about marriage. For a devilish moment, he wanted to make her say it. If she were so independent, let *her* propose! But that was a nasty attitude.

"Let me save you the bother of proposing to me. Or of me proposing formally, given the circumstances. Just say "yes"."

That annoyed her. How he loved to see her eyes flash! He grinned at her and she relaxed, looking away and then back with a very small smile of her own. She understood he was only teasing. Had any woman understood him like that before?

"Yes." She said it baldly, bluntly, definitely. "As long as we can organise the legalities so I still have my own income."

He'd expected it, and yet…that "Yes" knocked him off balance.

Married to this Amazon.

It wasn't as though he hadn't been married before. He'd not felt this uncertain of himself when Petrona had accepted him, for equally practical reasons.

"Excellent," he managed to say. "Let's talk to the vicar about timing."

"Let's talk to his son. *He'll* get it organised."

Ned laughed at that, which made Mrs Torbett glare at him with reproach.

"I'll go into Norwich for a bishop's licence tomorrow." She stiffened at that, but nodded. Yes, it was quick, but if they were going to do it, it should be quick, for the girls' sake. At least, this way, people would understand he hadn't courted her while she was mourning.

MORTIFYING. Embarrassing. Honestly worse than she had expected.

On the other hand…a man who could laugh at a moment like that would be easy to live with, no matter how shocking it would be if people knew why he laughed.

He really was *not* fit for polite society.

Her stomach was in turmoil; tears not far away, especially when the solicitor handed her one of Catherine's jewellery cases with her share of the bequests inside.

How she wished Catherine was here to advise her! They'd fought, often, because as the older sister, Catherine had believed she had the right to give advice. Especially about marriage. She'd welcome that advice now, before she did something irreversible.

Emma came over to her and handed her another small case. She had a jewellery pouch in her other hand.

"Will you keep these for me in your wall safe, please, Di? I don't have anywhere secure enough in our house."

"Of course."

Oh Lord, she had to say it. Emma needed to know.

"I'm marrying Hindmouth," she blurted out. Emma's eyes widened and her mouth formed an O. Diana hurried on. "To make sure I can raise the girls. If he marries someone else, he'll take them. He thinks they should be raised at Swanstead."

"He's *blackmailing* you?"

"No, no! He's never mentioned marrying someone else. But you must admit, it's likely. And the courts…"

She didn't need to say more. They all knew how the courts treated women.

Emma nodded. "I see. Yes." Her eyes lit with mischief. "And you were so certain you'd never marry!"

Here it was. Diana sighed. She knew she'd be in for an avalanche of jokes from her friends once the news was out. Her own fault for spouting off so often, perhaps.

Touching her arm, Emma said quietly, "He seems like a good man, a *kind* man. And kindness is what counts, in a marriage."

That sounded like hard-won wisdom. Diana's heart twisted. Captain Torbett was been charming, but perhaps kindness wasn't one of his obvious virtues. It was hard to know. He'd been sent to the Continent with his regiment only weeks after their marriage.

"I'm here if you need me," she said. Emma nodded, but briskly, as if the conversation was over.

"So, when's the wedding?"

TALK to the solicitor and set it up so Diana kept her financial independence. Done.

A bishop's licence. Acquired.

Tell the staff. Done.

Notice for next Saturday's *Norfolk Chronicle* for the "Marriages" section: "The Earl of Hindmouth to Miss Tilney, daughter of Sir Raymond Tilney, deceased, in a private ceremony." Mailed.

Next: ask Thomas Courtenay about that private ceremony.

Ned found the curate at the vicarage, going over some accounts in the dining room. His father, of course, had the study and Ned gathered that he only came out for services and meals. A charming way to live for his family.

Thomas greeted him with pleasure and invited him to sit and have coffee, which the maid brought in almost immediately. Well trained staff.

"What can I do for you, my lord?"

"It used to be "Ned", before I acquired the earl's coronet."

Thomas grinned. "Just being polite. What can I do for you, Ned?"

"You can marry me to Diana Tilney."

Nodding, Thomas sat back in his chair, his face grave. "I see." He thought for a moment. "Of course, I'll be happy to do it—at the Swanstead chapel?"

"Yes. It has to be a private ceremony."

"Naturally." He paused, and then said, as if compelled, "I can see why *you* have chosen this, but Miss Tilney has always been quite forthright about her intention to never marry."

"The needs of her nieces have overcome that reluctance."

"Yes. I see." Another pause. What was the man thinking? "May I involve my mother in this conversation?"

His *mother*? Good Lord, why?

"Certainly."

Thomas went out for a moment, and came back in with Mrs Courtenay. Ned rose and bowed, and she curtseyed perfunctorily. No great respecter of rank, Mrs Courtenay was a tall, handsome woman of middle years, who Ned knew ran the parish with compassion and common sense. Sebastian had often laughed over the reputation the vicar had as "holy", when his wife was the one who acted on Christian principles.

"Mrs Courtenay."

She smiled grimly. "You're wondering why Thomas brought me in, aren't you?' She sat and they followed suit. "You've found a way out of your difficulty with the girls, but it's Miss Tilney who will bear the brunt of gossip. We need to make sure that doesn't happen."

Ah. Yes.

"This marriage…you talked her into it?"

He nodded. "It was by far the best solution. Miss Tilney's house wasn't a suitable place for them to be raised. They need to learn how to manage a big house and staff, and they couldn't learn that in the High Street of Little Foxbury. Since I'm not married, there was no one to instruct them if they lived at Swanstead, and obviously Miss Tilney couldn't live there with them."

She pursed her lips. "You're lucky she loves those girls so much. I doubt anything else would have pushed her into marriage." She got up, dusting her hands off. "Leave it with me. Give me a few days to start the ball rolling, and then *stay at home* for the wedding calls. Show yourselves to be calm and concerned only with the girls. We want you to smell of October and November, not of April and May!"

Ned couldn't help but laugh. "You're a wise, wise woman, Mrs Courtenay. Tell me, is there any little thing you need for the church which I could give to show my appreciation?"

She narrowed her eyes, but her lips twitched. "Yes. You can give Molly Hicken's husband a job. She's got three children and another on the way. The man's not a fool, but he'd be best stuck in a field watching sheep, not near any machinery."

Ned bowed comically deeply. "It shall be done."

At the door, she looked back seriously. "Diana seems strong, but you could hurt her a great deal. Don't expect her to be made of steel."

That sobered him. "I will take the very best care of her I can."

One sharp nod, and she was gone.

Thomas smiled ruefully at him. "I can marry the two of you, but Mother will save you from yourself."

"I can see that. Thank you for thinking of it."

Then they got down to planning the ceremony.

Next: a ring.

WHEN MR GUNNEL showed Mrs Courtenay into the parlour where Diana was teaching the girls their letters, Diana wasn't surprised. No doubt Ned had been to the vicarage.

Mrs Courtenay was an old friend. She had been a source of great comfort when their mother had died, and Diana sang in the choir she led. Would she have to give that up? No, she decided, she wouldn't. Apart from anything else, it was a place where she could see Emma.

Of course, she hadn't been to practice; a month of seclusion was expected after such a loss.

They sat and Mrs Gunnel brought in refreshments and chivvied the girls out to the kitchen for milk and cake.

"Well…" Mrs Courtenay said.

Diana threw up a hand in a fencer's salute.

"I know! I said I'd never marry, but…" She looked towards where the girls had gone out, and shrugged.

"Yes. For what it's worth, I think you're doing the right thing."

That was balm to the soul.

"I'm glad," she said simply.

"Ned Faulkes is a good man, but he's not ready to take on a family without help. And those girls need you there."

Something settled in her mind. Mrs Courtenay always knew what was best.

"I think it will be all right," Diana said.

Taking a sip of tea, Mrs Courtenay paused with the cup still in her hand. "Your mother died two years ago now."

"Yes. And my father, ten years ago. He was a baronet, as you know, and the title went to his nephew, so Mother decided to move us all here to be near Catherine. And then, she died."

"Quite. Er…" She had never seen Mrs Courtenay hesitate before.

"Yes?"

"Did your mother ever discuss, hem, marital relations with you?" A faint trace of colour appeared on Mrs Courtenay's cheeks, and Diana was sure there was red on her own.

"No…but it's all right, Mrs Courtenay. This will be a marriage in name only."

"Will it? I see." She put the cup down with a snap. "Still. It's only right that you know, as a married woman."

Mrs Courtenay spoke for a minute or two, simply and plainly. Some of what she said, Diana already knew. Other parts…not. Good Lord, it seemed it was rather more complicated than the animals in the fields!

"There's just one more thing…" Mrs Courtenay paused, for once looking uncertain. Whatever this was, it must be daring!

"Yes?"

"If it *is* a marriage in name only, you must expect your husband to seek… companionship…elsewhere. And if it's *your* choice to keep it in name only, then you must accept that with complaisance and dignity. It's unfair to keep a man in the prime of life celibate when it's not really his choice."

That seemed reasonable, although surprising when coming from a vicar's wife. So why did the thought of Ned having a mistress make her heart hurt? She had no right to be angry or feel betrayed when they weren't going to be properly married. As always, she kept her emotions under control, as a lady should.

"I understand."

Mrs Courtenay cleared her throat. "You may also find that *you* have difficulties with celibacy. Women do, you know. If that becomes the case, I urge you to approach your husband, rather than a stranger."

That was…unexpected.

"I have no intention of betraying my wedding vows, I assure you." A bit stiff, but what else could she say? The very thought of "approaching" Ned made her sick with nerves.

Mrs Courtenay smiled, and suddenly Diana could see the pretty young woman she had been. Someone far lighter of heart than she was now. "My dear, I have every confidence in you. Remember, I'm always here if you need an older female's advice."

She was so kind! "Thank you. I do appreciate that. Especially now, with Catherine gone."

And just like that, the grief was back, gripping her heart with a claw.

"Don't worry about the town gossip; I'll make sure everyone understands it happened for the right reasons," Mrs Courtenay said as she got up to leave.

Diana saw her out and Gunnel closed the door behind her.

There was only one remedy for this wave of grief. She went to the kitchen to find the girls.

CHAPTER 5

The wedding took place three days later in private, in the Swanstead chapel, with Thomas Courtenay presiding, and only Emma and Ned's brother, Jonathan, in attendance. And her nieces, who were trembling with excitement.

Diana had never imagined what her wedding would be like. Her decision not to marry had been with her a long time, since childhood turned into girlhood and she began hearing, "Ladies don't, ladies can't, ladies shouldn't..." along with "When you're married..."

It was good that she hadn't had some airy-fairy romantic idea of a wedding in her head, because being married in funereal black with no guests, no wedding breakfast and no honey- moon was...flat.

There *was* one moment. When Ned looked into her eyes and said, "With this ring I thee wed, with my body I thee worship..." she had trembled. But then came "with all my worldly goods I thee endow" which was just a straight out lie. *And* she had to promise to obey him!

Dora and Vicky, she told herself. *It's all for Dora and Vicky.*

Afterwards, they had luncheon, including the children.

Ned sat at the other end of the table in the family dining room, his face calm but his fingers tapping on the arm of his chair. She wished she knew what he was thinking. Perhaps about the wedding night which wouldn't happen?

She knew so little of him, and yet now she was his legally, to do with as he pleased. A shiver ran down her spine, mingled terror and foreboding, but that was ridiculous. Catherine had liked Ned. She'd mentioned him often, when he visited Sebastian. It was odd, in a way, that they hadn't met before. She had a vague memory of him at Catherine's wedding, as best man, but that was all.

She didn't know him at all.

Without discussing it, she had left her house untouched, only bringing her personal items to Swanstead. Despite the legal truths, she knew that if she ran away to Little Foxbury, Ned wouldn't pursue her. It was some comfort to know she had a bolthole if she needed one.

And it also solved the problem of what to do with Mr and Mrs Gunnell, who were too old to be looking for a new situation, especially since many employers didn't like to hire a married couple.

So they stayed, the yard boy stayed, the housemaid stayed…only the scullery maid asked if she could have a position "at the big house, please, miss". Which Mrs Keach, pathetically grateful that Diana would be her new mistress, happily organised.

After luncheon, Emma excused herself, citing 'household duties' but clearly wanting to give them privacy. Diana kissed her goodbye, grateful she lived so near. Ned provided a carriage to take her home.

So many privileges were suddenly available to her.

The girls went with her up to Catherine's room while Ned said goodbye to Jonathan. This was her own room, now, although that seemed positively horrible. It even smelled like Catherine. Diana opened all the windows wide, despite the cloudiness of the day.

It was the countess's room, however, and it would be thought very strange if she didn't take it.

The nobility were ruthless like that. Inheritance was taken for granted. Often, the old earl or duke or viscount died in the same bed their father and grandfather and great-grandfather had died in. The same bed they'd been born in.

That sense of continuity underpinned the entire way the country was run. Gentry, like her and her family, had some of the same, but it was less…less in the blood and bone. Gentry cared what other people thought. Nobility did as it liked, generation after generation.

Well, she was nobility now, and she would do as she liked, which was to totally redecorate Catherine's room as soon as she could. And buy new linens.

The drapes and bed hangings were in a particular cream which had suited Catherine's fair prettiness, but which washed Diana out. Blue, perhaps, or turquoise.

She sat with her nieces on the bed and let them go through her jewellery boxes.

"Would you girls mind if I put up new drapes and hangings? You could help me choose them."

Perhaps they would be hurt if she changed *anything*. But, like their mother, it appeared they loved to shop.

"Ooh, yes!" Vicky squealed, jumping up. "We can go to Norwich! It has the best stores, Mama says." She stopped and her whole body drooped. "Said."

Diana hugged her.

"Mama liked shopping," Dora said. She looked around at the bedroom assessingly. "I like red!"

"Red might be a little hard to live with." Diana smiled gently. "Let's see what's in the shops."

"Tomorrow?"

So soon? The morning callers would flood in tomorrow, and they should be home for them.

"Perhaps next week."

"We have to ask Uncle Ned," Vicky said wisely. "Mama always asked Papa before *she* went shopping."

Good Lord! Did she have to get his permission for *everything*? That would be unsupportable.

Ned came in not long after, and Dora informed him that they'd be going to Norwich shopping, but, "We'll let you come if you want to."

He laughed.

"How kind! Thank you."

"Tomorrow?" Vicky asked hopefully.

"We'll need to leave a few days for callers, but after that."

No doubt there'd be calls this very afternoon. Mrs Courtenay had said she would make sure everyone put the "right" slant on the marriage, but the curiosity would still be intense.

"Aunt Diana, do we still call you aunt? Or do we have to call you Mama now?" Vicky's little face was so serious, it broke her heart.

"No, my darling, Aunt Diana is still my name. You have only one mama and one papa."

"We love you," Ned added, swinging Vicky up into his arms, "but we cannot replace your parents. We're just here to look after you."

Vicky stared at him. "Mary says this is *your* house now. That when you have children, it will be *their* house."

Diana winced. She hadn't explained how inheritance worked to the girls yet. She might have to have words with Mary.

Ned hugged Vicky. "It's true that this is my house now, legally. That is, I'm in charge of it. It's my house, but it's *our* home. And even if we had children, it would *still* be your home."

How kind he was! That was exactly the right thing to say. Happy, Vicky scrambled down and the two of them ran off to the nursery, to "tell Mary she was *wrong*."

Left alone, they exchanged glances. "I'll talk to Mary," Diana said, sighing.

"Better you than me."

She laughed sharply. "Which is why you married me, isn't it? To deal with the servants?"

"I cannot lie." He placed his hand theatrically over his heart. "I married you to gain the scullery maid Mrs Keach is so pleased with. Since, naturally, all my efforts are focussed on pleasing Mrs Keach."

This time, she really laughed.

"Idiot."

Pleased with each other, they went down stairs to receive the first of their combined mourning and wedding callers.

CHAPTER 6

The afternoon was tedious but bearable. Inevitably, mourning calls had shifted to become mourning-and-wedding visits.

Ned was surprised that no one questioned the marriage, not by word or tone of voice or sideways glance.

"A shame you couldn't have a proper wedding, my dear," Lady Mundford, setter of standards in Little Foxbury, said, but her tone was commiserating rather than condemning.

"Your nieces will feel the comfort of having you so close," said Lady Yarbury, she of the pointy nose and sharp eyes, and she seemed to be genuinely glad for them both.

"A man needs a wife when he has children to look after," said Sir Hugo Deveny. Since he had married a scandalously young second wife when his motherless daughter was ten, he should know, Ned thought but refrained from saying. His wife Elspeth smiled kindly at Diana, which was all that mattered.

In fact, Little Foxbury was rallying around them with unanimous kindness. He was grateful for it, and he suspected they had Mrs Courtenay to thank. He felt just a little pleased that he'd already organised that shepherding job for Hitchen; at least she would know he appreciated her. A gift to the vestry would be appropriate, too.

After six groups of visitors had come and gone, and the autumn afternoon was closing in with mist and mizzle, they thankfully closed the drawing-room door on the last one and collapsed into chairs on opposite side of the nicely burning fire.

"God help us. How long will this keep up?" he asked.

"A week or so. Those were the high-ranking ones. Except for the new Lord Ashham, and he's still in Italy, last anyone heard."

Lord Ashham had land on the Deveny side of the town. The previous Lord Ashham has been known locally as the Wicked Baron, and was all the better for being dead, according to everything Ned had heard.

"And tomorrow?"

"Tomorrow will be the next level down. Mrs Birch and Mrs Shepherd, most like. If we're lucky they'll come together. The Merryams said a note to say they'd see us next week. "To preserve your sanity", the countess wrote."

He grinned. "I'll be lucky to have any left by then. I think we should go into Norwich tomorrow. We'll tell Mr Haley to say we had probate business to conduct."

"We can't *lie*."

There it was. That straight up-and-down honesty which shone like a flame in her eyes. It was a most attractive trait. This was a woman who would never lie to him. Unlike Petrona, in those final months.

"Don't worry, it's not a lie. There's a solicitor in Norwich Seb occasionally did business with. I was going to get him to come out here to discuss it, but it's just as easy for me to drop in."

"And no doubt any scheduled appointments the solicitor

had would be hustled out of the way of the Earl of Hindmouth."

Her tone was dry and he shrugged. "Do you want me to deny it? Of course they will be. Our business gives them a cachet, not to mention their fees."

Something in that made her face soften, and she smiled at him.

"The girls will be happy you're coming."

"Any you?" he asked lightly. "Shall you swoon with pleasure when I leap into the coach?"

She blinked.

"Of course, my lord. Your company must always be acceptable."

That had put him in his place. Dash it, he deserved it.

The gong sounded; time to change for dinner.

He got up and reached a hand to her and pulled her up. The ring on her finger, hard against his palm, was a reminder that this was his *wife*, and his peace of mind depended on hers. He must ignore the impulse to flirt with her, and the shock that passed through him whenever they touched.

Kissing that hand lightly, he said, "It's an odd wedding day, but I think we've made a good bargain, don't you?"

She regarded him soberly. "Yes, I think we have."

Thank God for that.

He changed so swiftly, from flirting to serious to smiling… but he had said *our* business. Our.

She hadn't expected that.

They dined early and *en famille* in the small dining room, sitting around the table as though they were truly a family.

Dora was particularly happy since she wasn't normally allowed to eat out of the nursery, even when Victoria was.

"I'm a big girl now, aren't I, Aunt Diana?"

"Getting big, certainly."

"Will we eat like this *every* night, Uncle Ned?" Vicky wanted to know.

Diana and Ned exchanged glances. His clearly said, "Your job." Well, that was why he'd married her.

"No, poppet. Sometimes your uncle and I will be out, or have grown-up guests, and the adults will eat together in the big dining room."

"*I* know. Parties!" Dora proclaimed with satisfaction. She put her spoon down and her chin quivered. "Mama always came and said goodnight before parties."

"I need a hug!" Vicky said.

As one, the girls turned to her and she opened her arms. They jumped down and crowded in, crying. Her own eyes filled with tears, her throat hot and tight. The look on Ned's face was sombre and sympathetic. How glad she was that he wasn't one of those "stiff upper lip" men.

It was easy to decide, after that, that the girls should sleep with her that night.

So instead of arraying herself in a negligée and being swept off her feet by her new husband, she snuggled down in a flannel nightgown with two little poppets who talked and talked and then, suddenly, fell asleep.

The room still smelled of Catherine.

Diana lay, one arm around each girl, and prayed: for Catherine and Sebastian, for Dora and Vicky, for Emma, and for her and Ned. For Emma's husband, on some far-off battlefield.

God send them all grace.

CHAPTER 7

The trip to Norwich was put off because the Autumn rains hit, which was just as well because, despite the rains, a multitude of callers came over the next few days.

Diana coped with that, and with Mrs Keach.

The morning after the wedding, she asked the footman (Andrew, was it? She had to learn all their names) to have Mrs Keach meet her in Catherine's office. *Her* office. *Take charge, Diana, that's what you're here for.*

"And have her bring whatever paperwork she thinks I need to see."

"Yes, my lady."

She'd be dead and buried before she became used to being called "my lady".

When Mrs Keach arrived, she was carrying only a couple of thin ledgers. She plopped them on Diana's desk with satisfaction, as one who was off-loading a burden.

"The accounts?" Diana asked, waving the woman to a seat.

"Yes, my lady."

"And your other records?"

Blank-faced, Mrs Keach shrugged. "I don't…there's the stillroom ledger, if that's what you mean. And I suppose Cook has her recipe book."

Odd. Diana picked up the ledgers and flicked through them. Accounts, neatly entered in a couple of hands.

"No, Mrs Keach, I mean your planning records."

Complete bafflement on the older woman's face.

Diana tried again. "For example, your roster of which rooms to clean each month. This is a big house, and most of the rooms are unoccupied most of the year. It's only full for big parties, isn't that right?"

"Oh, yes, miss. I mean, my lady. That's right."

"So you must have a schedule of when to ret up the unused rooms. When to do the chimneys. When to clean the windows. When to go over the linen."

"No, my lady. My lady that was didn't like schedules. She just…told us what she wanted doing each week."

This would make *everything* harder. Damn Catherine and her need to order people around! She'd always resisted letting go of any control; they'd fought over it time and again. Wincing, Diana wondered if that was one of the reasons she'd resisted being married; she'd had enough of someone telling her what to do.

"Well!" she said encouragingly. "We'll spend the next week or so going over the house and making a schedule. I'm sure you'll feel more…more settled when you knew exactly what should be done, week by week and month by month." That was the way her mother had always run things, and it worked.

Mrs Keach's mouth was agape. "Oh, *yes*, my lady, it would help no end to know when I'd need extra help and when to order up the chimney-sweep."

"Let's start with the East Wing," Diana said. "Most of those rooms are empty, I believe."

They set off, both armed with notebooks. *At least I'll be earning my keep*, Diana thought wryly.

He should reorganise that trip to Norwich.

Somehow, they never had time to go. Ned wondered if he should prompt Diana to reschedule. Better to let her control her own actions, though. The one thing she was touchy about was being told what to do, which he perfectly understood.

When the rain stopped, four days later, the girls begged to go riding, and they went out as a family, the girls on their ponies, Diana on Catherine's mare, and Ned on his own familiar bay gelding, Clancy, he'd had brought from his old home in Hampshire.

From then on, they rode together early every morning. She was a fine horsewoman, with a good seat and light hands.

"Do you drive?" he asked impulsively one morning as they rode slowly through chest-high fog, only the girls' heads and their ponies' heads showing.

"I used to drive a gig," she said. "Back in Yorkshire."

"There's a spare curricle in the stables, now I've brought mine from home." Home. He winced. He had to stop thinking of Hampshire as 'home'. It wasn't even entailed. He would put it on the market soon.

"I've never driven tandem." Diana's voice was uncertain. The big difference between a gig and a curricle was that a gig had only one horse, whereas a curricle had a pair.

"I'll teach you!"

"Will you teach *us*?" Vicky demanded, her voice echoing oddly from the foggy trees around them.

"When you're old enough. Next year or so, you can learn to drive a dog-cart. Then a gig, and then, when you're grown up, a curricle."

"But–"

Diana cut in. "Curricles are quite dangerous, Vicky. They often overturn if the driver isn't careful. Which is why *I* have to learn how to drive one very carefully indeed, from your uncle."

Masterful! Containing Vicky's ambitions while reassuring her that Diana would be "very careful", therefore not alarming the children. She was born to be a mother.

In her old blue riding habit, with a shako on her gleaming head, she stood out against the fog as though she were on stage, lit by limelight. So beautiful. Desire surged through him and he forced himself to look away.

They'd made a bargain, and she'd kept her side of it, and more. He had to keep his side, or he'd drive her away, and then what?

He'd rather live with her, wracked with desire, than live without her.

An uncomfortable thought. He put it away to think about later.

They emerged from the fog onto the back lawn, the house windows shining in the morning light. "Come on!" he said, urging his horse to a canter down the bridle trail to the stables.

"Huzzah!" the girls cried, and followed him.

When they all reined in at the stableyard gate, Diana was right behind them, flushed and laughing and delectable.

Dear God, help me to survive this marriage.

After a month of seclusion, Diana was looking forward to choir practice. She had driven the curricle down, behind

Ned's matched chestnuts, with Ned beside her, distractingly large and strong, his competent hand correcting hers whenever necessary. It was clear he could drive to an inch, but she wasn't doing too badly, even on the winding part of the road, near the old ruined abbey. His warmth sent a shiver through her each time their hands met, even through their gloves.

He lifted her down while the groom held the horses, which wasn't really necessary, but she smiled up in thanks. His eyes warmed and her heart picked up its pace…no, no, no.

It was definitely best for her to go inside that church and sing psalms.

Emma was already there, along with the handful of other women and a couple of men.

Mrs Courtenay brought them to order before they could speak to each other. The choir wasn't ambitious. An opening hymn, a psalm, and a closing hymn was all they tried for, in unison. It was quite forward-thinking to have hymns at all; some parishes refused to sing anything other than psalms. But what Mrs Courtenay wanted, she organised until she won.

It was a relief to just stand there and sing. Like a return to her old life which, although occasionally boring, had been beautifully simple. She had so much to *do* these days! So many callers, so many responsibilities, so many demands on her time. She hadn't read more than a few pages of a book in a week. She was beginning to understand why Society ladies scurried off to London each year for the Season. It was as much a holiday as anything else.

Right now, all she had to do was obey each movement of Mrs Courtenay's hands, and sing. It was like a holiday in itself.

Afterwards, she held Emma back as the other left the church. "You're looking pale."

Emma shrugged. "I miss Catherine." Her voice broke on their sister's name, and Diana's eyes filled with tears. Emma had been closer to Catherine that she had been. As the youngest, Catherine had babied her a little; and after Emma's marriage they'd grown even closer. Sharing, perhaps, things she couldn't know about. It hadn't worried Diana. They had still met, all three, for regular meals.

"Perhaps you and I could have luncheon, as we used to?"

"I'd like that. Luncheon on Friday?"

"Lovely." She would have to ask the girls, too, to fill in that empty place at the table.

Ned was waiting for her outside; he'd visited the harness maker to see about getting Vicky a bigger saddle – a side saddle this time, as it was likely to be used for several years. She had had a growth spurt and now looked like a child rather than a little girl. She had changed so quickly! It hurt Diana's heart that Catherine wouldn't see it.

The cross on top of the steeple glinted in the dim light and she flushed as if reprimanded. Perhaps Catherine *did* see. That was a comforting thought.

How nice it was to see Ned standing there waiting! She was growing entirely too fond of him. It was hard to remember to keep her distance, but a bargain was a bargain.

He had said he didn't want an heir, and there was only one way to guarantee that.

Handing her up into the carriage while his groom, Bixton, held the horses, he remarked, "Emma looked a little pale?"

"Don't worry. She's just missing Catherine, I think."

"Ah." He nodded; quick on the uptake. It was so easy to talk with him—when they got the chance to be without the children, which wasn't often. They were allowing the girls more family time than most children of the nobility. They needed to feel secure, and loved, and safe, and that wouldn't happen if they were penned up in the nursery with Mary. Who had been told not to voice any negative opinions to them.

She relaxed back into her seat and sighed as Bixton sprang up onto the footrest behind them.

"Tired?" Ned asked.

"It's nice to have a moment of quiet." He smiled at her with understanding. So different from their first meeting, which had been all scratch and joust.

She watched his hands on the reins as they drove home in the gathering twilight, wanting to say something to start the conversation again but conscious of Bixton. Something anodyne, then.

She was content to sit beside Ned and leave getting them home in his capable hands. It was a quiet, domestic moment; if marriage was like this, she might find some happiness in it.

Against the last of the sunlight, Ned's profile was clear and firm. Handsome. She wished…no, she didn't. She couldn't. That small domestic happiness was all she had been promised, and she would be thankful for it and be satisfied. And if she dreamed of him…well, no one had to know.

Say something.

"I'll need to buy my own horses, I suppose, for the spare curricle."

Catherine hadn't driven herself, so while the curricle had been there, previously driven by Sebastian's father, there had been no horses. Sebastian had kept his in London. Another thing for them to sort out.

"No need. I've bought a pair of matched bays for you. Lord Yarbury's boy wants to graduate to a four-in-hand, and of course they have to be bought together, so his pair was going on the market. I snapped them up."

A cold wave went through her, and she couldn't decide if it were hurt or fury.

"You did *what?*"

Startled, he glanced at her, and then back over his shoulder at Bixton. Of course. Not in front of the servants. She bit her tongue and sat in stony silence until they came back to Swanstead.

Mr Haley let them in. Diana headed straight for the library, where they were least likely to be interrupted.

Ned followed her and closed the door, then stood next to it, his hat still in his hands. She pulled off her gloves and hat and laid them oh so carefully on a table. Time to take a deep breath. Do *not* scream like a fishwife. She couldn't help closing her hands into fists in sheer exasperation and, underneath that, a sense of betrayal.

"They're good horses. A bargain, too," Ned said hastily.

"As far as I'm concerned, they're *your* horses, and you can do what you like with them!"

"I don't see what–"

"*This* is why I didn't want to be married! Someone else making all my decisions for me. I'm perfectly capable of choosing my own horses! And paying for them!"

"But you've never driven a pair before. I just thought–"

"Without asking me. Without finding out if I had the skill to choose my own. You just assumed I didn't. You assumed that *your* judgement would be superior to mine."

She stared at him. The next few moment would set the tone of their marriage. She hoped he realised that.

THAT LOOK ON HER FACE. Stony. Outraged. And underneath that, something else.

He had made a complete mull of this. With the best of intentions, he'd done the very thing which would anger her —hurt her—the most.

The road to Hell.

"I'm sorry." It was all he could say. "I was wrong."

Like a bladder deflating, she sat down suddenly on the desk chair. Had she not expected him to apologise? That took him down a peg or two. Shaming that she had thought him so bumptious, such a Hector, that he wouldn't own a fault.

Diana took a deep breath and let it out.

"Thank you." It was heartfelt. She looked up at him and smiled. *Such* a smile, eyes shining and mouth soft. His heart gave a great thump.

He'd apologise a hundred times over to get that smile.

"I'll tell Yarbury the deal is off," he offered.

"Let me look at them first."

She was so generous. And he *was* pretty sure she'd like them. They were prime pieces of horseflesh, and perfectly matched. From the same dam and sire.

"Tomorrow," he promised.

That smile again.

He was in real trouble.

SHE COULDN'T BELIEVE he had apologised!

They changed for dinner and the meal was so lively and… she wasn't sure what to call it. Friendly? Were they becoming friends?

That would be lovely.

As he smiled at her, the candlelight glinting off his black hair, a flutter started under her breastbone.

Friendly, she scolded herself. *Just friends.*

"Look, Aunty Diana! I can cut my own chicken!" Dora announced proudly.

"Very well done, Dora," she said. "Try to keep your elbows down next time."

Ned flapped his elbows and clucked like a chicken. The girls dissolved into laughter, and so did she.

This silly side was the nicest thing she knew of him. That apology, though…the fact that he could see her side and acknowledge fault meant that their marriage *might* be one of equals. She couldn't be sure, yet it was a good sign.

THE DRIVE TO THE YARBURYS' was a pleasant interlude in an increasingly busy life. Being an earl—and the owner or trustee of three large properties, as well as his own in Hampshire—meant that almost every moment was occupied.

Ned was just tired.

Not too tired to drive Diana to see her horses. He doubted he'd ever be that tired; being in her company was rejuvenating, even when they crossed swords.

Her face and golden-red hair seemed to glow under her straw bonnet. How beautiful she was.

But whenever he thought of reaching out to her, Petrona's face on her deathbed flashed into his mind, her agonising cries ringing in his ears. The pitiful bundle of his son in the midwife's hands haunted him. He suspected it always would.

He was lucky to have a companion like Diana. He would never risk her.

Fortunately, she liked the horses, so he didn't have to back down in front of Yarbury.

They arranged for the two geldings to be brought over to Swanstead, and went home after an excruciatingly boring cup of tea with Lady Yarbury.

Diana was becoming an excellent whip. She took a corner in style and said, "That trip into Norwich never happened. Perhaps we should go tomorrow."

He'd forgotten about that, in the press of work. He'd let her down.

"That's an excellent idea." He half-turned towards his groom. "Bix, what's the weather going to be like tomorrow?" Bix had been Seb's groom, so he was local and knew the weather.

Bix sniffed the air and looked at the horizon. "It's bidding fair, m'lord."

He smiled down at Diana. "Then we shall go to Norwich. Order the carriage for us, Bix."

"Certain sure, m'lord."

He would make sure that Diana found the very best silk for bed hangings and drapes. Perhaps a blue to bring out the blue in her eyes.

They'd have a little holiday with the girls, and enjoy themselves, now that he'd redeemed himself as a good judge of horseflesh who also respected his wife.

CHAPTER 8

Since it was a beautiful day, with the high Norfolk sky a soft blue with streaks of while clouds, her husband (how odd that phrase still was) ordered the landau be brought around instead of the closed chaise.

It was a delightful surprise, given the time of year, but Diana saw that he'd even remembered foot warmers and extra lap rugs. She and her nieces settled in to the forward-facing seat very comfortably.

"I thought it might be more fun for the girls." He smiled at Diana as he climbed in after them and took the opposite seat. Dora immediately scrambled down to sit next to him.

"Vicky can't sit here because she gets *sick* going backwards!" she said triumphantly, takin his hand.

Biting back a smile, Diana took Vicky's hand. "We're very well suited here, aren't we, Vicky?"

"Yes we are!" She wriggled in her seat.

The girls were excited, and Diana realised that she was too. They had dressed in their Sunday best, although they did look rather like a group of crows in their blacks.

"Let 'em go, Johnson!" Ned ordered, and they were off. "I

hope you don't mind, ladies, but I need to drop in on a tenant along the way. I won't be long."

Diana raised her brows in a question. He checked: the girls had their heads back, fascinated by the pattern of leaves above them as they passed under an avenue of elms.

"He's six months behind on his rent. I haven't met him yet, but if he doesn't pay up I'll have to evict him. My estate manager thought a visit from the earl himself might stir him to action."

"Do you know why he hasn't paid?"

Ned shook his head. There wasn't much more to say; there were so many reasons a farming family might fall behind, but six months was a long time. Some farmers paid yearly, after the harvest; Ned's people (*their* people) must pay quarterly.

About a mile down the road, they slowed a little.

"It's coming up, my lord," Johnson called.

The landau turned into a farmyard. The farmhouse looked a little shabby. No one had cleaned the gutters out in a good long while; she wondered if the house was damp because of it. The windows were clean, though the window frames needed paint.

A young lad, perhaps fourteen, was coming out of a pigsty with a bucket in his hand. He stopped and stared at them.

"Mam!" he yelled. "It's his lordship!"

Diana was expecting the woman to come out of the house, but she emerged from another building next to the sty. A dairy? A small barn?

A short, spry woman with black hair pulled hard back into a bun, wearing an enormous apron over a homespun dress and worn boots that were surely too big for her.

She curtseyed, rubbing her hands on her apron, and casting nervous glances back into the house. That wasn't good.

"My lord. What can I do for you?"

"You'll be Mrs Cason, I expect? How d'ye do?" Ned jumped down from the carriage as Diana nodded to Mrs Cason.

"How are you, Mrs Cason? I'm Lady Hindmouth." The first time she'd actually said that out loud. She could feel her cheeks colouring.

Then the door of the house opened roughly and a man staggered out, followed by a stream of small black and white dogs, with their mother ambling along behind.

"Puppies!" the girls squealed together. They shot down to pat the puppies and Diana followed them to make sure they weren't a nuisance.

The man—Mr Cason, presumably—was unsteady on his feet and smelt of alcohol and stale sweat, even from six feet away. His clothes were dishevelled and if he'd shaved, it hadn't been this week. He sniffed loudly and rubbed his nose on his sleeve.

Diana shot a look at Mrs Cason, who was as neat as a pin. Her face was a mixture of embarrassment and fear. Poor woman. It was easy to see where that rent money had gone; the man smelt of liquor, not ale.

"M'lordship?" he slurred. "What brings ye to my house?"

"The matter of six months' back rent, Cason." There was no geniality in Ned's tone. None of the courtesy he'd shown Mrs Cason.

"Girls," she said. "Back in the carriage."

"But Aunt Di*ana*!" Vicky protested. "Look how sweet!" She held up a squirming bundle of pup.

"Can we have a puppy, Aunty?" Dora looked hopeful. Her dress was already muddy from kneeling to pet the pups. Diana sighed. This mothering business was more tricky than it looked, even with nursemaids and laundresses to shoulder the burden.

Cason had fronted up to Ned. He was big man, but so was Ned; Diana hadn't realised quite *how* big until now.

Deliberately ignoring him, Ned turned to the man's wife.

"Mrs Cason, can *you* tell me where my rent is?"

The boy spoke up when she hesitated. "Done his gullet, that's where it's gone. His and his so-called friends, away down at the Bush and Bull."

His father turned on him and the boy cut and ran. Good for him. Diana hoped he had a good hiding place.

"Well." Ned regarded Cason, his face like granite.

"It's not so, my lord! That boy is just lying, as he always does. It's been a hard year—"

"But only for you, apparently. Every other tenant has paid their rent, without excuse or complaint."

Diana moved the girls towards the landau, each of them clutching a puppy. The other three pups gambolled around their feet, yipping. The bitch seemed to be quite pleased to have them removed, so they must be old enough to leave her.

"Into the carriage, girls."

Ned strolled over to the pig sty, and nodded. He looked into the small barn, and nodded again.

"Who's been keeping up with the work?" he asked Mrs Cason. "The place looks like it's being cared for."

"I have!" Cason declared. His red-shot eyes were blinking slowly, as if realising things were going badly.

"Mrs Cason?" Diana came over and stood beside her, and smiled encouragingly. "Is that true?" She wasn't quite sure what Ned was getting at, though it was clear that Mrs Cason and her son had been doing all the work. If Ned planned an eviction, and this poor woman was punished for her husband's debauchery…if Ned would do that, then he felt as the world did, that women were just addendums to their husbands, like an extra finger. Not separate beings, due separate consideration.

Mrs Cason wrung her apron between her hands. "I don't know what to say, your ladyship," she whispered to Diana.

"Tell the truth. My husband is a fair man." She was surprised at how sure she was of that. Perhaps his apology over the horses had convinced her.

Taking a big breath, Mrs Cason spoke rapidly. "I do as much as I can, and my boy Simon does the rest. We have another boy, Edgar, he's out with the sheep. And my niece comes over of a morning to help with the milking."

"And your husband?" Ned asked gently.

She shot a quick, worried look at Cason, then said. "He does *some*. When he's sober."

"How often does that happen?"

As though Ned's calm tone gave her courage, she straightened and let go of the apron. "Not often, my lord, and that's the truth. He hasn't been sober once this se'ennight. Not even on Sunday."

Ned let out a sigh and faced Cason.

"I see. Well, Mr Cason, it seems that you've forfeited your right to this land. You haven't paid rent for two quarters, and you yourself are not keeping it up, in clear contravention of our rental agreement. I hereby terminate that agreement for cause. You have two days to clear everything you yourself own out of the property. That does *not* include the stock. I'll send my estate manager over this afternoon to assess the value of the stock against your debt. I doubt you'll have much left over."

"This was my father's farm, m'lord," Mrs Cason suddenly cut in. "Cason took over his agreement, but it was my family's land for generations past."

What did that matter? It was his now, and if he was evicted, so was she and her sons. Diana's heart broke within her for the woman's plight.

Ned cast her a glance and smiled reassuringly.

"Well, Mrs Cason. Since you are currently the person actually working the land, I'm happy to offer you the same rental agreement I had with your husband."

Diana gasped. Mrs Cason turned pale, and then pink. "M-me? Not him?"

"No, not him. You. Mr Sandiwell will bring the agreement over for you to sign when he comes to assess the stock. Will you sign it?"

"She bloody will!" The son sprang out from behind the small barn. "Say you will, Mam!"

Cason nodded to her, grinning nastily. "Aye, sign it, Ellen."

"So you can come back and lord it over her again?" Ned asked, suspiciously gentle. "No, Mr Cason. There will be a clause in that agreement stipulating that you not set foot on this land without her permission, or the agreement is null and void. And if she does *not* give you permission, you'll be arrested for trespassing."

"I can do that? But he's my husband!"

"Aye, I'm her husband! I have rights!"

"You have rights over your wife, but they don't extend to rights over my land." Ned faced him down. "Or perhaps, Mrs Cason, you could keep the stock and I could have this wastrel hauled off to debtor's prison. Just say the word."

"They're terrible places, I've heard." She sounded thoughtful rather than distressed. How badly had this scoundrel treated her?

"No more than he deserves," the son muttered.

"I-I don't think I could rightly do that," Mrs Cason sounded regretful. "But if I don't, we won't have enough stock to start again next spring. We've already agreed with the butcher on selling our vealers, and if we can't do that, I'm not sure how we can keep going. I *need* that stock. But I can't send the father of my children into one of those places."

Ned's face was full of compassion, but also a little annoyance. Diana's heart felt like a flower opening to the sun. He saw this woman as wholly her own person, and *wanted* her to put her drunkard of a husband into prison. Bedamned to a husband's rights!

It was the clearest possible demonstration that he saw women as *people*, not addendums to men. Elation flowed through her.

No wonder she loved him.

Oh.

This was a *terrible* time to realise that.

Mrs Cason smiled slowly.

"Put him to work!" she said. "Let him work off the debt on your lordship's farm. Then we can keep the stock and we'll just squeak by, I reckon."

Ned laughed and held out his hand for her to shake. Dazedly, she did. "Deal done, Mrs Cason. I'll send the clerk over." He turned to Cason. "Report tomorrow morning to Mr Gurney. Bright and early. I-er-I wouldn't drink any more today, if I were you." He leant in and his voice dropped, low and menacing. "And if I hear you laid a hand on my tenant or her sons, I'll have you up before Lord Merryam and have you transported to Van Diemen's Land!"

"A man's got a right to discipline his wife and children!" Cason objected.

"Not on my land."

How wonderful he was. Turning to her with a satisfied look on his face, he said, "Well. Shall we go to Norwich?"

As they moved back to the landau, Mrs Cason said, "You can take your clothes. That's all. Everything else stays with the farm."

"That's right!" said the boy. "You have to do what Mam says now, because she's a farmer and you're just a labourer." Now *there* was a lad who'd make a fine husband one day.

The girls were ridiculously muddy, and so was the seat of the landau where the puppies had clambered over it. Diana sighed; Johnson tried to stifle a chuckle, but in the end they all laughed.

"Can we have a puppy? *Please*, Uncle Ned!" Vicky begged.

"It might be a way of helping Mrs Cason through the winter," Diana said quietly, leaning on Ned's arm.

He shot her a quick, admiring glance, and called over his shoulder.

"You've bred these, Mrs Cason?"

Cason had sat down heavily on a bench by the door, staring into space as though he couldn't believe what had happened.

After a glance at him, Mrs Cason came over, nodding. "Aye, m'lord. Norfolk Spaniels, they are. We've been breeding them here for a mort o'years."

"*Please*, Uncle Ned, can I have this one?" Vicky asked, holding up a little female.

"No, Uncle Ned, *this* one!" Dora patted the smallest of the litter, which was lying in her lap, fast asleep.

"It's not good for dogs to be raised alone," Diana said to the air. Ned laughed.

"All right. We'll take both of them."

"HUZZAH!" the girls yelled.

Ned turned to Mrs Cason. "In fact, we'll take them all. My brother has been talking about acquiring some spaniels, and it's his birthday next week. They're ready to leave their dam?"

"She'll be glad to see the back of them!" Mrs Cason said. "Are you sure, m'lord? They…they aren't cheap, the purebreds." Then her face turned red. "But of course you won't be worrited about that."

"Talk to Mr Sandiwell and work out a fair price. Fair, mind you, no discounts. You can have it in cash, or some cash and some against next quarter's rent, if you choose. You'll know your own needs best."

She curtseyed deeply. "Thank'ee, m'lord. Thanks from the bottom of my heart." Her eyes had tears in them, and the look on her face was pure hero-worship. Diana knew how she felt.

She'd never hero worshipped anyone before. It was a strange sensation, making her heart thud and her palms sweat.

"You'll known your own needs best." He'd said that. To a woman. An ordinary woman, not a countess or a duchess.

He was *magnificent!*

But she was not getting into that muddy carriage with him. Not in this silk dress.

"Johnson, why don't you take the girls back home?" she asked. "I'll walk."

Regarding the muddy seats, Ned's mouth twitched. "I'll walk with you, I think. Apologies for the mess, Johnson."

"Not to worry, m'lord. Once it's dried, that mud will brush right off."

The landau turned and went back, the girls waving from the back seat, delighted to have their very own carriage ride.

"Shall we walk, wife?"

"Let us, husband."

CHAPTER 9

Walking down the road under the trees, Ned felt a small breeze spring up, which plucked golden-red leaves from the branches and sent them fluttering around their heads.

They were exactly the colour of Diana's hair. He caught one when she wasn't looking, and tucked it into his top pocket. He would keep it on his desk. Foolish, but he *was* foolish about her. Unfortunately.

They climbed over a stile to take the footpath that led towards the back of Swanstead House. Ned lifted her down, momentarily dizzied by her scent. Lemons and vanilla?

Walking in companionable silence, their gloved hands brushed occasionally. He wanted to take her hand and walk like a couple, but…they weren't a couple. Not really. As always, whenever he thought about desiring Diana, images of Petrona's agony flashed into his mind.

One of Swanstead's many streams bisected the sheep pasture, foaming and swirling with the run-off from days of rain. A wooden bridge with handrails stretched across it.

They stopped in the middle and leant on the railing,

looking down the rush-lined stream. It ran through the flat countryside towards the North Sea, a few miles away. Norfolk was growing on him. He was starting to like the sense of freedom these high skies and broad horizons gave.

Diana pushed her bonnet back a little and lifted her face to the wide sky. A pang went through his chest.

She turned and rested her back against the railing, smiling at him, and put a finger out to flick his pocket.

"Why did you keep the leaf?"

He could lie, and say it was for the girls. He didn't want to lie to her.

"It's the same colour as your hair."

That made her colour, pink filling her cheeks. "Oh." She took a breath. "That's very romantic."

The urge to play the fool was strong. He pushed it down and just shrugged.

As though unable to stand still, Diana pushed herself off the bridge and kept walking, briskly. Yes. He'd been foolish to think, even for a moment, that he could care for her and not break his heart.

The path led through the orchard, apple and pear trees full of fruit, the air full of the scent, heady and sharp. The picking had taken all the early varieties, and the pippins were coming on. He'd better tell Sandiwell to get the pickers in next week. He might think about putting in some Ribston Pippins next year. They should go well here.

"A penny for your thoughts," Diana said.

"I was considering whether Ribston Pippins would thrive here." He waved a hand at the orchard.

Diana started laughing. "And I thought you were being romantical!" The deuce she had!

"I know better than to be too romantical with you." No matter how his heart beat faster when she was nearby.

. . .

"Do you?" Slowly, she came towards him and laid her hands on his chest. "I..I've been feeling rather romantical myself." She looked up at him; his clear gaze was locked on hers. Thunder took up residence in her chest, and it was hard to breathe. Fear. That was fear. This conversation would change her life. She almost stopped herself, but she had to *know*. A life with a beloved husband who didn't and would never love her...she wasn't sure she could live that way. If there was even a *chance*, she had to know.

"Oh, my dear." Shamingly, there was pity as well as desire in his eyes. She turned away from him blindly, eyes full of tears, but he caught her hand and brought her back to him.

"My dear," he said again, his hand on her cheek. "If you only knew how much I want to love you."

"Well then–" Hope fluttered against her thundering heart.

"I don't want children. If we can go on as we have been, and add loving each other into that, I'd be the happiest of men."

There was a bench by the orchard gate. She led him over to it and they sat.

"I think you'll have to explain that. Men generally want children."

He sat with his head bowed, breathing deeply. After a moment, he muttered, "My wife died in childbirth."

"Her name was Petrona, wasn't it?"

Nodding, Ned sighed, still avoiding her eyes. "Petrona. She called for me. I was in the next room, you know, waiting. I went to her. It was...appalling. So much blood. So much pain...the child dead, too. I could never risk someone I cared about in that manner again. Who cares if I don't have an heir? Jonathan can be the next earl."

How had she ever thought him unfeeling? "So," she said, trying to understand, "you intend to be celibate your entire life?"

He sat back with a big breath, as though they'd cleared some high hurdle. "Before I met you, I had a…an arrangement with a widow in Hampshire. She was barren, so, so it was safe. Of course, I ended that before I married you."

"And now? Now you're intending for us *both* to be celibate?"

"She died! And the last thing she said to me was "This is your fault"."

Diana jumped to her feet.

"What nonsense!"

He blinked. "It's not nonsense! I was the one–"

"Unless you forced yourself on her, there were two people in that bed who knew a child might be the outcome. Did you rape her?"

"Of course not!" How could she even *think* such a thing! But perhaps she didn't. She was looking at him with a mixture of compassion and annoyance.

"Well, then. She knew what might happen, and she chose to take that risk. As I might choose." No. No, he couldn't bear it if Diana…it had been hard to lose Petrona, but they had been friendly lovers and spouses. He hadn't loved her as he loved Diana.

Looking at her, standing there, arms akimbo, eyes blazing, his whole body yearned towards her, the feeling in his chest so large that he thought he might choke on it. He *couldn't* take such a chance with someone so precious. Surely they could live companionably?

"The risk is too great."

"I see." She jumped to her feet. "This is just like the horses!" She stamped her foot in frustration. "I'm sick of it!"

"What? I mean, I beg your pardon?" He got up, but didn't approach her.

He was looking at her as though she were mad, but she was merely angry. A familiar, almost welcome anger, as the alternative was to burst into sobs and run away.

"Well may you beg my pardon. You're making my decisions again for me, just as with buying the horses. How *dare* you dictate what risks *I* may decide to take? I thought we had an agreement that we would be equals in this marriage? That you wouldn't try to ride roughshod over me?"

"That's different—"

"It is *not*! It's my body, and *I* and only I should decide what risks are appropriate for me to take with it. How *dare* you make that decision for me!"

He was frozen. Obviously he'd never even thought about it from her point of view. As someone who had control over her own life.

Typical. Disappointing.

"I'm not just risking you," he said, forcing the words out. "I'm risking myself. I survived Petrona's death because I merely liked her. But you, Diana…" Moving forwards, he took her hands. Her heart leapt. "If we were lovers, and you died because of it…I don't think I would survive that. Especially knowing it was my fault."

It was clear to Diana that he would never forget her saying that. How could she explain?

"If Petrona was here, I'd box her ears, and I'd like to do the same to you, to knock some sense into you! Ned, women *say* things like that in childbirth. They're angry that men get to have children without all the agony and labour. It's not fair. So they lash out at the man. Catherine did it! When she was having Dorothy, she shouted, "This is all your fault, Sebastian!" into the room where we all waited, and he yelled back, "It was your idea!" We laughed with her about it later. We *laughed*, Ned, because we knew it was normal. And if

Petrona had lived, you and she would have laughed about it later as well."

He shook his head like a bewildered bull before the matador. Clearly, he had wallowed in his guilt until he couldn't see a way out of it. She had to show him a way.

Taking his hands, she pressed them to her chest. "People die, Ned. Women in childbirth, yes. Women, and men, die in shipwrecks. Am I never to be allowed to step on a boat because Catherine and Sebastian died on one?"

"That's different." Oh, the stubbornness of the man! Yet it was rooted in care. Would he fight against this so hard if he didn't love her?

"No, my love, it isn't. What if I said you can't drive a curricle anymore, because curricles have so many accidents? What if I said you couldn't go out in the rain, in case you contracted an ague and died? What if I said that you must never have any more liquor, because it might make you fall down the stairs and break your neck?" He opened his mouth, but she put a finger over his lips. "It's *not* different. When we–we care for someone, we worry all the time." She had to say it. Had to make him understand. "And I do love you, Ned, so I will never stop worrying about you. I love you too much to hedge you in, even if it's to keep you safe."

He was staring at her with such longing and such despair that she couldn't bear it. Was she a modern woman, or wasn't she? She was.

"I need a hug," she said. His arms came around her automatically, but that wasn't enough.

She went up on her toes and kissed him, full on the lips.

He groaned and pulled her close, his mouth warm, his hands strong on her back.

How she had *needed* this! To feel his body against hers, his heart beating against hers.

Melting into his embrace, she slide her hands through his hair and held on tight.

A thought struck her, and she reluctantly pulled her lips free of his. "And if you think you can withhold *this* from me because *you* have self-indulgently decided–"

NED LAUGHED AGAINST HER MOUTH. "I wouldn't dare!" He kissed her again, lighter and happier than he had ever expected to be again. She made a tiny sound of satisfaction, and his blood heated beyond bearing.

He buried his head in her neck and sighed. Had he been self-indulgent? Putting his own guilt above her—above *their* —marriage?

Yes. He had. Thank God for Diana, who had lifted that burden from him.

"My dear." He nibbled on her ear just to feel the tremor that went through her. God, how he wanted her. "I think we'd better go back to the house. This would be an uncomfortable place for our first liaison."

She tilted her head back and laughed at him. "Liaison? How scandalous! Have you forgotten that we're married, my lord?"

"I am glad of it every minute of the day, my love."

That sent her into stillness, a poised readiness to move away…or move closer. "My love?"

"I love you as I've loved no one else. As I could love no one else. And I'm happy to prove it to you, over and over, if necessary."

Her stillness melted into soft warmth. "Then, by all means, let us go back to the house."

They walked back hand in hand, but when they got there, the girls, freshly scrubbed and in clean clothes, raced out to meet them, demanding that they "come and see the puppies!"

Then there were people who needed them: Sandiwell for him, curious about what happened with Cason. Mrs Keach for her, with a question about the number of laundresses they were going to need to refresh all the Holland covers in the unused rooms. Whatever that was about, Diana seemed to know.

Life took over. Married life, as earl and countess, aunt and uncle, and it was good, although frustrating.

After dinner, once the children had gone to bed, they headed for their usual after-dinner spot, the library.

Just inside the library, Diana stopped and glanced sideways at him. "I think I'm quite tired," she said carefully. "I think I will go to bed early."

He moved in front of her and pulled her in for a kiss, which she gave willingly.

"Indeed. I might also retire early. Say, in half an hour?"

She kissed him again, and the kiss deepened. How good she tasted! How richly delicious she smelled!

Sighing, she pulled away. "Half an hour? Oh, I think perhaps ten minutes would be better."

Smiling up at him, she slid out of his arms and went back into the hall. A moment, later, he heard her footsteps, racing up the stairs.

Ten minutes had never been so long!

WELL, she'd done it now. Married, about to be wived, acting (and feeling) like a love-sick mooncalf. Her maid brushed out her hair and helped her into the only lacy nightgown she owned, which she'd bought to go on to a country house party two years ago, just so she wouldn't be shamed in front of strange servants.

She was glad now. It was pale blue, soft and, she hoped,

enticing. Should she get into the bed? That seemed…too brash? Too forward?

What a fool she was, to think too much about it! He loved her. She loved him.

Thank God for Mrs Courtenay and her advice.

The door opened; she turned and there he was. Her Ned. Her nerves were making her feel sick and shaky. He closed the door behind him with equally shaky hands.

He grinned at her. "So, ready to be a true wife? Humble and obedient to her lord and master?"

She picked up a pillow and threw it at him. Ducking, he caught her up in his arms, both of them laughing.

He stopped the laugh with a kiss and, sighing, she knew they were exactly where they needed to be.

Serious now, he turned her palm up and kissed it, then smiled gently at her.

"My lady, will you to bed?"

"My lord, I will."

They went to the bed hand in hand, as though they were in a wedding procession, and sank into each others' arms eagerly.

Forever, she thought. *This is forever.* For the first time, that thought didn't frighten her. No. It made her feel safer than she had ever felt.

Safe and loved.

Forever.

EPILOGUE

The morning Summer sun streamed through the bedroom windows, lighting up the blue bed hangings and drapes.

There she was. His Diana. Sitting up in the big bed, her hair streaming over her shoulders like sunlight itself, holding a small swaddled scrap of humanity. His heart stopped for a moment, but the baby gave a small wail and Diana smiled down on it lovingly.

Alive. Both alive.

Mother Greef, the old midwife who served all of Little Foxbury, grinned toothlessly at him.

"Ye've a son, my lord."

He ventured to the bed and stood looking down at his most precious love. She smiled up at him. She was pale, and her eyes showed red at the edges, but she was *fine*. Just fine.

"Mother Greef," he said, not taking his eyes off Diana, "you rent a cottage from me, don't you?"

"I do, my lord."

"Your rent is paid for the next ten years." He bent and kissed Diana's brow, and then the babe's.

Mother Greef cackled with delight. "Ten years for a boy? What if the next one's a girl? Do I get five for that?"

He touched the baby's cheek. So soft. Facing Mother Greef, he shook his head.

"Ten years for bringing my wife through it safely."

"Hah! That were easy. That one's got the best child-bearing hips I've ever seen! Came out nice and smooth."

He bit his lip to stop a laugh, but Diana was giggling quietly. She would crow about that to him later.

The door opened and two little heads peeked through. "She's awake!" Vicky cried. And there's a baby!"

The two of them ran for the bed. He put his hands out to stop them climbing up but Diana laughed. "Let them. Just not too close, girls."

The bright little heads crowded out his view of the baby, so he feasted on Diana instead. She was fine. He gave a great sigh.

"What's his name?" Dora asked.

Mother Greef looked at him, but he'd learned a great deal about marriage in the last ten months, and he wasn't so foolish as to take *that* decision on his own. "Well, my lady? Have you a preference?"

Her smile widened. "I thought, Sebastian Edward."

He'd thought he couldn't be more happy, but he'd been wrong. Warmth flooded every part of him.

"Seb would have liked that." He liked it too.

"Hmm," Vicky said. "Papa always said, if he and Mama had a boy, they'd name him Edward. So I *suppose* that's all right."

That made him choke up even more. What a sentimental fool he was!

Gently, he sat down on the bed and gathered Diana and the baby into his arms. The girls crowded in for a family hug.

The first of many.

"I think your aunt needs to rest now," he said to the girls, kissing them both on their heads.

"*All* right," Dora said, resigned. She stroked the baby's cheek with one finger, and he turned his head to suck at it. "Erk!"

"I think he's hungry," Diana said.

"Right, off with you all," Mother Greef ordered. "First time mother doesn't need an audience for her first try at suckling."

"What's suckling?" Dora asked as he led them out the door. He looked back. Diana was loosening her gown and Mother Greef was helping her guide the baby to her breast.

His family. Just as these girls were.

"Like when the kittens feed from the cat," Vicky said prosaically.

"Oh." A pause. "Erggh!"

"Come along." Ned closed the door, sneaking one last peek at his beloved. "You can go and tell Mrs Keach and Mr Haley the baby's name."

They ran off instantly, Vicky shouting, "*I* get to! I'm the eldest!"

Opening the door once they had gone, he found Diana gazing fondly at the baby, and Mother Greef packing to go home.

"A natural, that boy is!" she declared. She fixed Ned with a piercing glare. "Ten years, my lord?"

"Ten years, Mother Greef."

She chuckled darkly. "That'll see me out! No rent for the rest of my life! Heh heh. You've got a good husband there, dearie."

Diana's whole face lit up. "I do indeed."

He went to sit by her and their boy, thanking God with deep sincerity.

He hadn't wanted this earldom, but it had brought him deeper happiness than he'd ever thought to see.

"It's funny, isn't it?" Diana said, reading his thoughts as she so often seemed to do. "You didn't want to be the earl, I didn't want to be the countess, but here we are. Happy."

"Happiness and deep contentment." She loosed a hand from the baby's swaddling, and took his.

"I was thinking," she said. "It would be good to have a carriage which was too high for the children to climb up into. Next time we go to London, let's go to Tattersall's and buy me a high-perch phaeton."

He collapsed on the bed, laughing.

"And four horses to drive it? Which you will, of course, choose yourself?"

She clucked her tongue at him, but her eyes were dancing. "Four horses would be far too dangerous to drive around these country lanes. Really, Ned, when will you take life seriously?"

He kissed her hand and went down on his knees by the bed. "Never, my love, while I have you by my side."

Diana leaned towards him, but the movement disturbed the baby, and he began to cry. Ned took him, thankful that he was an experienced uncle, and rocked him to silence.

Looking up at him, Diana's eyes were full of tears, and he could see all their love and steadfast commitment in them.

He was the luckiest of men, and he would never forget it.

The door burst open and the girls came barging in. "Mrs Keach says Aunt Diana should have something to eat!" Mr Haley followed them in with a tray.

"Life goes on, Ned," Diana said.

"Life goes on perfectly," he answered, and they both smiled.

A GENEROUS HEART

CHAPTER 1

*A*nthony, Earl of Merryam, stood at his library table, waiting for his guests to sit before he did so himself.

They'd all come, which was excellent. Sir Hugo Deveny, the local Squire. Thomas Courtenay, the curate, standing in for his father, the parson, who rarely left his study. The doctor, Simons, with his customary air of vague abstraction. Lady Marbury, head of the *grand dames* of Little Foxbury, with her husband. Lord Mundford and his wife. Even the recently brought-to-bed Countess of Hindmouth, Diana Faulkes, and her husband Ned.

"How is the new babe?" Tony asked.

Diana's face lit up. "He's lovely! But he's hardly "new", Tony. He's six months old!"

By deuce, that had gone fast.

He waited until his mother had settled herself, silk rustling around her, before he sat. Around them, servants moved, setting full cups of coffee at each place.

"Welcome," he said. "Welcome to the first planning meeting for our new town school."

Little Foxbury had grown so much since the toll road was put in that the old Dame school just wasn't enough. Especially since the Dame herself was old and getting shaky on her legs, but hadn't been able to find a new Dame to replace her.

"We need a good architect," Sir Hugo said. "And we'll need land for both a school and a schoolmaster's house."

"I'm sure we can find lodgings for the schoolmaster," Lady Marbury said, looking down her nose. "No need to go so *such* expense at first. Just the schoolhouse for now, I think?"

There were murmurs of agreement around the table. His mother, most unusually for her, was keeping silent. Her back was to the tall library windows, which despite the grey Winter morning, gave her a becoming halo around her still-blonde hair. He couldn't see her eyes. What mischief was she planning?

The doctor sat up a little and put his coffee cup down. "I know a fellow. Andrew Grey. Met him at Oxford. He's been working on the last part of the Stratford-Upon-Avon Canal, designing lock-keepers' houses."

"Good!" Ned Faulkes said. "We want someone who does architecture on a small scale, not someone who's only interested in building manor houses that look like Grecian temples."

Tony sat back and let them work it out. He hadn't really wanted to take ownership of this project, given that he had so much to do in London. If Ned and Sir Hugo wanted to take it over, he was more than willing.

But he might get this Andrew Grey's details from the doctor.

An hour later, they had a plan in place. He took on

contacting the architect, two birds with one stone, and the rest committed to fund-raising, sourcing suitable land, and, eventually, finding a schoolmaster. That was his mother's doing: every time a task was mentioned, she slid it off to someone. Belatedly, he realised she was protecting him from too much work.

A good morning's work. As they bade their guests farewell, his mother slid her hand through his arm.

"You did very well not to volunteer for more," she said serenely.

Tony laughed. "You mean I did well to sit there and let you protect me from volunteering."

She twinkled up at him, her eyes as blue as his own. "That's a mother's duty."

"SHALL you come up to London with me next week, Mama?" Tony Merryam regarded his mother over the dinner table with little hope. She hated travelling in winter; which was in direct contradiction to her desire to be in London for the Season.

"Not next week. Isaiah says there'll be a thaw before then and you know how awful it is to try to get the travelling carriage over those muddy roads." Phoebe Merryam, Dowager Countess of Merryam, smiled winningly at her son, her blonde side curls shining in the lamplight. "I may come in a couple of weeks. The Season doesn't start until the end of this month, after all. Must you go up next week?"

The Season was tied to the Parliamentary term, which this year started on 28th January. All the peers came to London at that time, and brought their wives and daughters with them. It was true he didn't need to be in London before then, but he had a lot to manage beforehand.

"It's this Soho business. I've organised with Henry

Gunson to buy that warehouse near Soho Square we were planning to build a school in. My other reason to speak to this architect. I want to get it all settled before the Season really begins."

"Good! This Season is the one for you to find a bride."

Tony put his soup spoon down and groaned, head in hands. "Mama…."

"You know you have to, Tony. You need an heir. You can't seriously be thinking of allowing *Derwent* to inherit after you?"

Derwent Merryam was a young cousin who had all the worst qualities of a rich young buck about town.

"No." Definitely not.

"Didn't you feel odd this morning? All those couples, and you and the doctor sitting there on your own?"

"And Thomas."

She waved that off. "Clergy doesn't count."

"It's not that I *object* to getting married. It's the finding-a-bride process that's so appalling!"

Mama laughed. "Oh, you poor lamb! Having to go to Almack's and, I daresay, spend time with friends you've had for years! You know, Meg Deveny is going up with her step-mama. The Poulteneys are taking John up to see a new doctor."

Meg and John had been engaged almost since the cradle, but this must be a last-ditch effort. He'd been failing for more than a year, a canker eating him away.

"That's why you want me at Almack's," he accused his mother. "To support Meg."

"There are many reasons I want you at Almack's," she said with composure. "That's only one of them. You really need to get out in the world more. Have some fun! You've barely had any fun since your father died." Tears winked in her eyes. For all her frivolity, his mother had been a loving and faithful wife, and his father's loss two years ago had pushed her into sincere grief. And him into a wagon-load of work, taking up management of the estates and investments far earlier than he'd expected.

It was true, he hadn't had much fun lately.

"Diana and Ned are going up. Diana's first Season as countess, since she was in mourning for her sister last year. It would be kind of you to make sure she *takes*."

"How many schemes do you actually have for this Season, Mama?"

She twinkled at him and raised her glass.

"Just enough!"

He was doomed. Once his mother undertook something, it happened. He'd be married by the end of the Season—but he'd make damn sure it was to someone who'd back his cherished school and charitable projects. Someone pretty would also be nice, but less important.

Grinning at himself, he shook his head. Who was he fooling? Like every man, he cared about looks. But not at the expense of a generous heart.

"I'm sorry, Miss Edmonds, but I'm afraid that's impossible." Mr Heiserman blinked at her over the tops of his pince-nez. He didn't *look* sorry. He looked startled.

Adeline took a deep breath. "I understand that it might be *difficult*, Mr Heiserman, but surely not *impossible*." She was rich. *Very* rich, thanks to her grandfather's bequest. Why shouldn't she have some of her own money?

"The trustees will not agree, Miss Edmonds. The terms of the trust are quite clear. The capital is to be preserved for you until you are married, or you turn forty years of age. In the meantime, the trustees will advance such monies as are necessary for the appropriate upkeep of your position. Of course, while you reside under your father's — or, at the moment, your uncle's — roof, those payments are minimal."

Pin money. Just enough for currant buns and wheels of cheese, but nothing more. Adeline stared at him, boiling with frustration but keeping it out of her manner. Nothing made men discount a woman more than visible emotion. "But they do not meet my needs, Mr Heiserman. I find myself embarrassed."

Mr Heiserman—the last in a long line of Heisermans who had acted for her family—was a middle-aged, stout man in an unfortunate waistcoat but a very nicely judged neckcloth. His eyes bulged somewhat at her last statement.

"You have debts of honour?" The implication was clear. He thought she'd been gambling, as many of the *ton* did. It was tempting – tell him she had gambling debts and she'd no doubt the trustees would advance enough to clear them…and then bring her firmly to heel, chaperoned everywhere even more tightly than she was now, to make sure she didn't repeat the mistake. She sighed.

"No. But there is work I wish to do I have not the funds for." Pausing, she assessed him. How open-minded was Mr Heiserman? "Charitable work."

He relaxed immediately. "Ah, you have a generous heart, Miss Edmonds. But you can safely leave charitable donations to your elders."

"My elders don't wish to start a free school in Soho, Mr Heiserman," she said dryly.

"Soho?" Startled, he sat up, disturbing his pince-nez. He fumbled them back on his nose. "Oh, no, my dear Miss Edmonds, that's *most* unsuitable. I do hope you're not intending to examine the site yourself? Soho is really quite, quite…unsuitable for a young lady."

If you only knew...

"There is a great deal of poverty in the area, certainly," she said calmly. "Which is why a school, which can also feed the children a decent noon-time meal, is needed." The mahogany furniture in this office could feed twenty families for a year – more! The rug alone could provide housing for ten families. There was such a discrepancy between the rich and the poor, and the rich were quite comfortable with that.

"Miss Edmonds…" He hesitated. She could almost see the mantle of *Pater Familias* descend upon him as he decided to treat her like one of his own children. "Your parents sent you to London to enjoy the Season, not to concern yourself with the riff-raff of the streets. You should be dancing! Enjoying yourself!"

"Finding a husband." Perhaps her tone that time was too dry, because he puffed up like a peahen.

"Indeed, yes. That *is* the only way you will acquire your capital." He softened. "Perhaps you may find a young man who shares your charitable impulses."

"Do you really think I'm likely to find someone like that at Almack's?"

He tucked a smile away quickly. "It might be difficult. Seriously, Miss Edmonds–"

"What if I never marry?"

"The trust allows that, if you leave your parents' house to set up your own establishment, or they die before you are wed, the trustees are empowered to grant you a greater allowance so that you may continue to live in an appropriate manner."

She pondered that for a moment, and then Mr Heiserman added, "And, of course, at the age of forty…"

"Oh, that's an *age* away! I don't understand why I can't declare now that I'll never marry, and be given my inheritance!"

He was losing patience, she could see. "Miss Edmonds – if you'll permit me to speak frankly, no one who looks at you could imagine for a moment that you will become an old maid."

A shame she wasn't ugly! She fumed even as she smiled at him as though she appreciated the compliment. How hateful it was to be pushed into this dissembling. But she might need his good will later. However…

"It sounds to me as though the trustees have quite a wide discretion over how much to give me as an allowance?"

"Oh yes. Your grandfather was quite clear that they needed to be able to adjust to any circumstance which might arise."

So. Mr Heiserman couldn't help her, but her trustees could. Her course was clear. She rose, giving the solicitor her hand to shake.

"Thank you, Mr Heiserman, you've been most helpful."

Relieved, he shook her hand heartily. "Now you just go and enjoy your Season, my dear."

"I shall."

She left, the clerk opening the door for her and bowing low, her uncle's carriage waiting for her in the street, the footman jumping down to set up the steps for her. Sitting on the richly upholstered seat, leaning back on the satin squabs, she realised, a little tardily, that she was one of those rich who took service from others for granted.

That had to change. She had seen so much poverty on her parent's estate, and had tried her best there, but the poor children in London broke her heart. There were so many going hungry, and cold…Everyone else she knew accepted it as the way of things, but she couldn't help but fight against it. For the children's sake.

No matter how many currant buns she gave out, her

charity in the stableyard of the Soho Club would do nothing longterm. Education was the answer. Education to bring the unlettered classes out of the gutter.

She would get her school by hook or by crook.

CHAPTER 2

Tony lounged gracefully against the wall and assessed the Season's crop of beauties with an expert eye. He'd arrived the day before, delayed by flooding on his estate, so had set off only last week, in the middle of the worst late January weather. It had made him wish he was still snugly ensconced by his fireside in Little Foxbury.

He nodded to Diana and Ned Faulkes as they walked by. Diana was particularly elegant in sapphire silk, but she looked a bit tense. Her first time in Society as Lady Hindmouth. He'd ask her to dance later.

"Tony!"

Henry Gunson, by all that was holy. Henry was on his list of people to see while he was in London Julius' brother, who had agreed to sell him the Soho site. He and Henry had been to Oxford together.

He was with a friend, a curly-headed fellow with apple-rosy cheeks. Tony nodded at him; Henry said goodbye to his friend and came over.

Tony grinned at the nattily dressed young man. Henry's neckcloth was a miracle of snowy expanse, and his small clothes were perfectly moulded to him. But Henry always wore his clothes well. Even the old-fashioned black satin knee-breeches that the Patronesses of Almack's insisted upon suited him.

"Stylish, Henry! I can see London agrees with you."

They shook hands.

"I thought you'd sworn off the Season, man."

Tony sighed theatrically. "M'mother's decided it's time I set up my nursery, so here I am, obediently at Almack's."

Henry cocked a rueful eye at him.

"Marriage has to happen sooner or later, I suppose," he admitted, rather sadly, Tony thought. "But at least you have the choice of the belles of England!"

They turned to survey the room; at just after eleven, when the doors were closed to new entries, it was full to capacity. The cream of England.

Tony knew his duty: to find a girl of good family and good dowry who would do *her* duty and produce a crop of children to continue the name. The chance of him finding someone with whom he could share more than an occasional luke-warm embrace seemed slim. Perhaps if he'd come to London when he was younger, but he'd managed to avoid it. Now, at almost thirty, he was too jaded to be hopeful.

But at least he could be entertained – that was surely Margaret Deveny, standing out in a bevy of young ladies like a heron amongst chickens. Time to follow at least one of his mother's instructions.

"Come along," he said to Henry. "There's someone you should meet."

Henry obligingly followed along; he was a favourite with the ladies, being a kind and solicitous partner for the dance, and the group welcomed the pair with smiles.

"Meg!" Tony said. "Doing the Season at last!"

Meg was not quite as tall as he was, but she didn't have to

tilt her head much to look him in the eye. She was a good looking lass, with rich red hair and hazel eyes, but with that height and beanpole figure, she'd never been popular at balls.

"Anthony Merryam! Good Lord, what's winkled you out of your shell?"

He laughed and kissed her hand. "Duty, m'dear. The House is in session."

"Ah, yes, of course, Ransom's Bill. I might have known you'd be here for that."

He shrugged and nodded, then presented Henry to her.

"Let's not talk politics," Henry said.

"An excellent idea," the blonde standing behind Meg piped up. "Politics is so exasperating!"

She moved out of Meg's shadow and Tony caught his breath. Deep brown eyes stared up at him out of an enchanting heart-shaped face. And the rest of her…no offence to Meg, but he'd always preferred curves to leanness.

He bowed with a flourish. "Your servant, milady."

Meg laughed. "Don't be fooled by that grandeur, Adeline. Tony's the most practical of men. Miss Edmonds, may I present Anthony, Earl of Merryam. Lord Merryam, Miss Edmonds, my dear friend."

The Beauty curtsied and hid her face with a fan in the approved manner, but her eyes peeped out with humour at him.

"Lord Merryam."

"Miss Edmonds—I've always liked Meg, you know, but I never thought I'd be so grateful to her!"

She wasn't falling for that bit of flattery; the girl had a brain in her head.

"You've known each other long, my lord?"

"All our lives," Meg said. "Our families' estates march together in Little Foxbury. Of course, Anthony was always much older and more important than I. It was only because

John insisted that you ever let me come along on your adventures."

"How is he?" Tony asked, suddenly serious. "He's why you're in London?"

She nodded sombrely. "There's a new doctor." The blonde put a hand on her arm in sympathy. "He gets up for a little while in the evenings, so I usually read to him at this time, but Adeline needed a chaperone, since her aunt is otherwise engaged."

"You're not setting yourself up as a chaperone!" Surely they weren't *that* old?

The girls both laughed; Gad, Miss Edmonds had a pretty laugh! "No, no." Meg tapped him reprovingly on the arm with her fan. "My step-mamma is our chaperone." She nodded towards Elspeth. A slight, pretty woman with dark hair, she sat in the chaperone's corner with the older women.

"She's young to be sitting it all out," Henry said disapprovingly.

Meg flicked her fan open. "I doubt she's up to dancing. She's not long been confined. A new sister."

"Let me guess, they've called her Charlotte," Henry said dryly. Every second girl born since the Crown Princess had married last May had been called Charlotte in her honour.

Meg's lips twitched and Miss Edmonds hid a laugh behind her hand. "Alas, no. It's Euphemia." The four of them looked at each other a moment, and then burst out laughing. Far too loudly, Tony realised, as others turned to look at them.

"Shall we dance?" he said, since a new set was forming.

Miss Edmonds danced as prettily as she laughed. And she was no babe – around Meg's age of twenty-three, he surmised; odd that she hadn't been snapped up already. Perhaps there was no dowry. Smugly, he reflected that he could afford to marry a dowerless girl, and then brought himself up short. *A bit early, my lad, to be thinking about marriage! You know nothing about this girl.*

But it would be a pleasure to become better acquainted... although it was a shame she wasn't interested in politics. Gaining a savvy political hostess would be an excellent reason to marry.

This Anthony Merryam was light on his feet, Adeline had to admit. She wasn't sure why she was reluctant to do so. As though admitting any virtue in him would be dangerous.

Ridiculous. As they clasped hands and led down the middle of the set, she assessed him again: handsome, certainly, with that blond hair and deep blue eyes... but the nipped-in waist of his jacket and the rubies flashing in his cravat pin marked him out as a potential dandy.

And therefore no danger to *her*. She was invulnerable to a pretty face; husbands got in the way too much if a woman wanted to *do* anything in the world.

The set moved into the pousette and Merryam took her hands in his to swing them around in a circle and a half. My, his hands were strong! An unaccustomed thrill ran through her. Involuntarily, she smiled up into his eyes, and his grasp on her hands tightened.

No, my girl, none of that! She pasted her most polite smile on her face and concentrated on the figures of the dance.

As he walked her back to their seats afterwards, he asked, "Are you interested in politics, Miss Edmonds?"

"Politics seems to me to be mostly a group of men having silly squabbles."

He gave a shout of laughter which turned heads towards them. "You may be right! Would that it were otherwise. But some of those squabbles have important effects."

And that was true. The Poor Laws, for example, which were well due to be overhauled.

"That's so," she acknowledged, turning to give him her hand. "Thank you for the dance, Lord Merryam."

"May I have another?" He smiled beguilingly at her, just a little too sure of himself.

"Alas, I'm afraid all my dances are spoken for. Perhaps next time."

He sighed theatrically and he bowed over her hand with enormous, overacted panache. "I cannot be surprised. I'm merely grateful to have secured you for even this brief period of time."

Her lips twitched despite herself and he grinned up at her, looking at that moment more like a schoolboy caught in mischief than a sober adult.

"No doubt that will console you in the long, lonely night," she agreed demurely.

Laughing again, he took himself off. Meg's stepmamma watched him with narrowed eyes.

"Don't take him seriously, child," she said. "There must be a reason he's reached nine-and-twenty and never married."

"No need to fret about me, ma'am," Adeline said. "I'm not at all likely to be swept off my feet."

Not at all. No matter how brilliant his eyes or how elegant his hands.

CHAPTER 3

The morning was even greyer than normal, Adeline thought as the carriage jolted over the cobblestones; or perhaps that was just the contrast to the night before, which had been gayer and more lively than any Almack's gathering before it.

"Dreaming over Anthony's deep blue eyes?" Meg teased her. Adeline blushed, just a little. His eyes had been *very* blue, with a thin black line around the irises which made them even more striking.

"I have better things to think about," she retorted. Then she softened. Meg looked drawn, as though she hadn't slept. "You're worried about John."

With a huge sigh, Meg leant back against the side-squabs and closed her eyes. "He's getting worse, Addie. I don't think he'll see out the winter. I'm not sure he'll even make it back to Little Foxbury."

Adeline put her hand over Meg's in silent sympathy. What could she say? The canker which was eating the life out of John wasn't new. He'd been going downhill for years now, and there was nothing doctors or surgeons could do.

"It must be so hard, watching someone die when you're in love with them."

Meg sat up and stared at her hands, frowning. "I wish I *were* in love with him." Her eyes were clouded. "He loves me so much, and I can't seem to give him the same back…I love him, of course I do, but it's a long standing affection, not—not married love. We've been betrothed our whole lives, you know, and I was happy to be marrying him. But it's not the kind of love you read about in novels."

"I'm not sure that kind of love even exists!" Adeline said stoutly. "The kind you're *showing*- staying with him, helping to nurse him—that's *real* love." She believed that; although she was conscious of a barely-acknowledged desire to experience "the kind of love they talked about in novels".

"In that case, you must love the whole world!" Meg laughed. The carriage came to a stop and the footman opened the door and let the step down; chill air surrounded them instantly, and Adeline shivered. The coats of ladies of quality were not designed for this kind of cold. On days like these, the young ladies of the ton were supposed stay indoors, to guard their complexions from chafing.

"How silly of me! I've sat on the wrong side," Meg said. She got down hastily and waited for Adeline to follow her, then climbed back in. "I'll see you back here at one. Or I'll send the carriage for you. You'll need a good nap if you're going to entrance Anthony again at the Sanderton's ball."

Adeline waved and then went up the steps of the large house in front of her; on a discreet brass plaque, it read, *The Soho Club*. She gave a sigh as she passed through the front door. Time to forget this Society silliness and concentrate on something *real*.

. . .

GOOD LORD, that was Meg Deveny! He'd recognise that beanpole figure anywhere, and her brown hair in that terrible plaited bun that she wore. What on earth was she doing in Soho?

Anthony stared from the corner, taking a moment too long to do so – the girls in the brothel on the corner took his hesitation for shyness, and leaned out of the windows to egg him on.

"Come on in, m'lord, we're all friendly here!"

"I'm *very* friendly!" a buxom redhead shouted, jiggling her bosoms at him. He grinned at her.

"Another time, thanks, ladies." Meg had scrambled back into the carriage – that girl was still a hoyden – and the coachman had clicked up the horses. Too late for him to ask her anything. Another woman, decidedly more curvy than Meg, was mounting the steps of a house. Surely that couldn't be…Adeline Edmonds? He didn't want to think so, but he'd studied that figure quite a lot last night, and there was something in the way she moved…

She disappeared inside the house. It couldn't have been Adeline. Perhaps Meg's maid had some business here – dropping her off was just the sort of thing Meg would do. He dismissed it from his mind and walked briskly to his appointment with the architect. He'd looked at drawings of the man's buildings, and he might suit very well.

ADELINE SWIFTLY FINISHED PINNING her hair up inside her Quakerish bonnet, flicked her hands down her even more Quakerish dress and pelisse, and tucked her reticule safely under her clothes. Not that she had any suspicions of the club servants, but some of the members had odd senses of humour.

She went out through the great hall, where, this early in

the morning, there was barely anyone – just a girl curled up on a *chaise longue*, reading as if words were champagne. Lucky her. Adeline couldn't remember the last time she'd had leisure to read. Well, no need to pine over that. There was work to be done.

Out through the servant's corridors, and into the yard. Sure enough, the morning's gaggle of children were at the gates, waiting silently – unnaturally silently. One of the men must have shouted at them. When they saw her, they broke out in chatter, but she merely waved and continued o to the stables, and to the tack room which had been put aside for her use.

The scent of the morning's currant buns filled the small space: delicious. The Club's cook was really *very* good. Adeline filled her basket with them, took her notebook and pencil, and went out. Best not to open the gate – she could pass the buns to the children through its wrought iron bars, being careful not to catch their bare skin on the freezing metal.

"Good morning!"

"Morning, Miss!" they chorused.

"Have you all washed this morning?"

"Bertie hasn't, Miss!"

"Bertie?" Bertie was one of her regulars, a sharp-faced child who looked five years younger than his actual age of twelve. His face was certainly dirty this morning. "Face and hands, Bertie! You know the rules."

He cast a look of loathing at the girl who had informed on him – his sister, who put our her tongue at him. But he ran fast enough to the public pump on the other side of the road, and splashed energetically in the horse trough. Better than nothing, she supposed.

"Very well. Who has a new baby in the house?"

"We do, Miss!"

"I do!"

"We's got a new boy!"

"Up front, then."

The three children moved to the front – after a couple of weeks, she had the others trained to move back and let them in.

"Now, where do you each live, and what's your mother's name, and how many children does she have living with her?"

She took down the details, wincing internally at the number of mouths to feed in each house. Those poor women. Then she handed out a currant bun each. They grabbed and ran, but they needn't have worried; the other children knew by now that there'd be enough for all, and let them pass.

The order was set: the children with new babies, then the crippled and ill, then the youngest, working up to the oldest there, a thirteen-year-old dark-skinned girl who said cheerfully, "This is me last time, Miss. I'm off to the fact'ry tomorrer."

"Which factory, Glynn?"

"The *buckle* fact'ry!" A world of satisfaction was in her voice, and rightly so. The buckle manufactory was a clean and respectable place – it hardly smelt at all. And a very good position for a girl like Glynn, the product of a marriage between a British soldier and an Indian woman he had married when he had been stationed in Bombay.

"Well done, Glynn."

"I got it cos I was clean, Miss!" Glynn grinned at her, sharp as a needle, understanding that saying this would please. Adeline winked at her, and the girl ran off, leaving just one currant bun in the basket. It would do for her own breakfast.

She ate it in the tackroom as she packed up the flour bags

for the new mothers. Flour bags were a new idea of hers – she bought them from the local bakery, who would otherwise send them back to the mill. A bag could be a padding for a baby's bed, or be made over into a dress for the newborn.

Rags for clouts, hard tack biscuits, currants, a wheel of cheese, some salt, a rack of bacon, potatoes. Poor rations, and yet more than these families usually saw in a week. At home on their estate and in the local village, she had had great success in bringing down the death rate of new mothers and their babies, simply by feeding the poor women enough. It was best to start feeding them while the mother was pregnant, but she hadn't had time to do that here.

She put a bar of hard soap in each bag, and then tucked a small pouch of lavender in too. Just something pleasant that had no other purpose than to lift the spirits.

"James!" she called, loading the bags into the handcart kept just outside the door.

James was one of the heavies that Mrs Skarsgard, the club manager, employed to keep order; but he was far less violent than his scarred appearance might suggest. A soft-hearted man, James, he was happy to trundle the cart around for her – and he certainly kept any would-be thieves away.

Walking by his side towards the first address, she at last had time to worry about Lord Merryam. Anthony, Meg had said his name was. She had seen him on the corner, but had he seen her? Surely he couldn't have recognised her under her veil!

She wasn't worried about her reputation; if it all came out, it would scarcely brand her anything but a do-gooder.

But if her aunt and uncle heard…she shook her head. No. She would have to see Lord Merryam's demeanour at the ball tonight, and plan accordingly. If necessary…if necessary, she would have to tell him what she did here. Not that a young man like that would understand. She doubted he ever thought of more than the set of his cravat. He would probably think it a great joke and bandy it all over town.

So why did she find him so memorable? Dancing blue eyes and a charming smile were *not* what one should look for in a husband. His interest in politics did nothing to reassure her…the political class were so focused on power, so harsh to the poor.

He had no proof of anything. She must bluff it out and flat out lie if she had to. After all, she'd been more or less lying for the last two weeks, since she had first come to the Soho Club. Since she and Meg had realised that they could use each other to accomplish their own goals – Meg to sit by John's bedside, where her step-mamma thought it was indelicate of her to be, and she herself, to come here, and do some good. It was an accepted thing now that she and Meg would walk in the mornings together, a country custom they had brought to Town. Odd, but not irregular, her aunt thought.

Lying was a sin; it cheapened you and made you more and more duplicitous. But as she handed over the first bag and saw the mother's eyes grow round as she felt the weight of it, she knew she was doing the right thing. Even though the woman called after as she left, "Doan't think ye I'm going to say thank ye. Ye coulda gi'en us some dosh instead of bloody flowers!"

Adeline laughed, and called back, You keep the cheese for yourself. It'll help your milk come in."

"And what would you know about it, Lady Muck?" But the woman was busy swatting her small children away as they demanded cheese for breakfast, and her retort was half-hearted.

No, this work was too important. She couldn't let Lord Merryam to stop it. She would lie with a clear conscience. And tonight, she would waylay the first of her trustees.

CHAPTER 4

$\mathcal{T}$he Sanderton's ball was a Success—it was crowded, it was hot, it was difficult to find your friends. Adeline listened patiently to her aunt's monologue about who might be there and who might not as they slowly slid through the crowd, perambulating the room.

Meg normally stood out, being so tall, but she was nowhere to be seen. Adeline hoped that John had not taken a turn for the worse.

"Who do you hope to meet tonight, my dear?" Aunt Jane asked.

Without thinking, she blurted out, "Lord Pindar." Her trustee. Seeing her aunt's confusion, she added, "And Meg, of course. And, and…Lord Merryam."

That was the right answer. "Anthony Merryam! Very suitable, very suitable indeed." The small, satisfied smile was infuriating, but she couldn't blame her aunt. Viscount Merryam was a desirable *parti*. Which no doubt explained, she thought, catching sight of him, why he was surrounded by a gaggle of silly girls.

He turned as though he heard her thought, and the most

delightful smile broke across his face, followed by a flicker of an expression of – what was that? Doubt? How odd.

But he gracefully excused himself to his gaggle and came towards them, aiming at her aunt. He kissed her aunt's hand with a flourish which made her laugh.

"My dear Lady Martindale, how delightful to see you again! My mother sends her regards."

"I am sure she did not, you cozening creature!"

"But surely she would have, if she'd known I was to see you! I merely anticipate her inevitable request."

Laughing again, her aunt turned towards her. "I was at school with Lady Merryam, oh, these ages ago! And now... I declare, Anthony, it makes me feel old merely to look at you."

He cocked an eyebrow at her. "You, Lady Martindale? You can never grow old."

She slapped his arm with her fan in the approved manner of a generation ago. "Fribble!"

These pleasantries over, he turned towards Adeline and bowed.

"Miss Edmonds."

She curtseyed. "Lord Merryam." There was no sign of suspicion or curiosity in his look, and she relaxed and gave him a genuine smile, which he returned.

"Ah, you've met, of course. Well, off with you to the dance floor. I'm to the chaperone's corner, to rest my feet and have a glass of ratafia."

So blatant. Adeline blushed at the forwardness of it, but Anthony – Lord Merryam – didn't seem to mind. A dance was beginning, and he offered his hand to her with a smile which lit his whole face.

If only he weren't, as her aunt so justly said, a fribble.

And yet dancing with him – she had danced the waltz many times, and had been approved to waltz by the Almack's Patronesses almost immediately on her first visit, but waltzing with Anthony Merryam was more effervescent than she had previously experienced. The very blood in her veins seemed to be dancing.

He smiled down at her and her heart sped up. Really, she must rein in her emotions! She looked at his shoulder instead of those blue eyes.

"Almack's is not to your taste, Miss Edmonds?"

Did she look so disapproving? Heavens! From one extreme to the other.

"Not at all, Lord Merryam. It is…" Honesty overcame her practised response. "It's not, perhaps, fully to my taste, but then, I'm not a young girl in her first Season, hoping to be swept off my feet by a gallant gentleman."

He laughed. "Surely such hopes are not confined to those in their *first* Season!"

Wryly, she smiled up at him. "I daresay not. But I'm not a green girl, you know."

"Why come to London, then?"

"Because my *parents* have hopes of me being swept off my feet." How could she be so blunt! It was really very indecorous. But he laughed again.

"Mine do too – at least, my mother. She's sent me here to do my duty to my name." He didn't sound enthused.

"So Almack's is not to *your* taste, then." Expecting him to make some flattering remark, she was intrigued when he merely sighed.

"I admit, I have other concerns I would prefer to be pursuing." Then he looked down and seemed to collect himself. "At least, I would prefer them if *you* were not present. Since you are, Almack's delights me!"

They were back to inanities. Just as well she hadn't had to confide in this man. She smiled perfunctorily. 'At least you have the choice of whether to be here or not, Lord Merryam. Young ladies have no such control over their lives."

As the music ended, he offered her his arm to walk back to Aunt Jane. She was conscious of the gazes of the younger girls, who stared admiringly at him. He cut, in truth, an admirable figure; tall, handsome, titled – and, according to her aunt, rich. If she had wanted a husband, no doubt she would have been as admiring as they.

"Don't tell me that you're an advocate of Mrs Wollstonecraft's ideas?" he said.

Disappointed, she flicked a glance up at him as they rounded the end of the dance floor and headed for the gallery. "Why should I not be?"

"She scarcely set a proper example to young women."

"She had a lover. Men do that every day, and no one raises an eyebrow. She was a brilliant mind who propounded, simply, that women should have the same rights as men."

"It would be a true revolution were it so."

Now that was an enigmatic statement, and his face gave nothing away. She fell silent. She didn't dare show her own cards too clearly. It would be disastrous if she became known as a do-gooder, a new thinker. Aunt Jane was suspicious already of her intentions.

In fact…why not put Lord Merryam to good use? If her aunt thought she was encouraging his attentions, all her fears would be allayed.

Adeline smiled up at Lord Merryam with all the brilliance she could command. He blinked, but then his expression warmed and he smiled back. Her heart stuttered in its beat. Good Lord, he was handsome! And that would serve her purposes well. He would be an excellent decoy.

"Lady Martindale, you see, I deliver your niece back to you, safe and sound!" He bowed, hand on heart, eyes dancing.

"Anthony, you mock me!"

"Never! Do not misjudge me. You can't be so cruel as to deny me the pleasure of seeing you—and Miss Edmonds—

again. I shall call on you tomorrow." He bowed to each of them in turn, as they dipped in curtseys, and left. Her aunt's face was full of delight.

"Oh, Addie! I–"

She had no time to say more, as Henry Gunson came up to request Adeline's hand for the next set. Smiling, Adeline went into the dance.

Afterwards, she asked Henry to escort her to pay her respects to Lord Pindar.

"A very old friend of my grandfather's," she explained airily.

Old and fat. Pindar sat in the corner, chatting with animation to a middle-aged man with blond hair which was surely artificial. Her trustee's bulk overflowed the chair seat, but he sprang to his feet as they approached with alacrity.

"My dear Adeline!" he said. "Come to lighten the heart of an old man?"

"Why, an I would, my lord, but I see no old men here."

He pinched her cheek and laughed. "You have a cozening tongue, my dear, I'm delighted to see." He turned to his companion. "Off you go, Blandish, give my ward your seat. Gunson, you can take yourself off, too. She's quite safe with me. Dandled her on my knee."

The blond man bowed and smiled and obediently left, taking Henry with him.

"Now, my dear." Lord Pindar sat as soon as she had, and regarded her with a tolerant eye. "You're looking as fine as fivepence. But what have you come to talk to me about?"

Startled, she met his eyes, and found them strangely knowing.

"Ah, you're surprised. But I'm awake on all points, m'dear, and a gel doesn't leave off dancing at Almack's just to pay her duties to an old man. Did you think your grandfather picked me as trustee because I was his bosom bow? On the contrary!

We were at odds more often than not, but we both preferred straight dealing, and so I still do. What's the matter?"

This "old man" saw too much. What should she say? The truth? All the signs of indolence and self-indulgence were there in his bloodshot eyes and heavy mouth. Would such a man understand the impulse to help the poor? But his eyes… those were the eyes of a shrewd man of the world, and she doubted she'd put anything past him. So she spoke baldly.

"I want to open a charity school in Soho, and my pin money isn't enough to do it."

He reared back in his chair in surprise, and laughed. "And here was I thinking you had a *tendre* for someone quite unsuitable! Well, well." He pulled on his bottom lip, and considered. "I can't see it, m'dear, I'm sorry. The terms of the trust are quite binding."

"Would you if you could?" There was a knot in her chest, and she didn't know what emotion was causing her breath to come short. So many lives depended on this. Could she convince him?

He assessed her. "I'd set safeguards. A man of business to oversee the funds. A sensible schoolmaster to keep the children in line. But yes, given the right supervision, a charity school is entirely appropriate for an Edmonds. Your grandmother was a very charitable woman. No doubt you get it from her."

"Well, then–" she said, her heart leaping with hope.

"No." He shook his head, decisively. "I'm sorry, child, but there is no legal way I can release that much money to you while your parents are alive. The law is the law. And neither of the other trustees would consider it for a moment. To get the trust set aside, you'd have to take us to court – and you'd lose."

She opened her mouth to argue, but Lord Pindar's sister, Lady Penelope, came up just then. A flighty woman, with a reputation for forgetfulness coupled with a tendency to gossip, but Adeline had always found her kind.

"Lady Penelope," she said, and presented her cheek for the inevitable kiss.

"My dear, how nice to see you!"

After a few minutes' conversation, they walked her back to her aunt, and they all exchanged pleasantries until another young man came to ask her to dance. Before she was led onto the dance floor, she thanked Lord Pindar. At least he hadn't laughed at her.

"I'm glad to have become better acquainted," he said, and kissed her hand with a flourish.

"You always did have nice manners, Claude," her aunt said.

Adeline missed her steps several times in the dance, and the young man – what *was* his name? – handed her off to the next prospective beau with no apparent regrets. She went through the motions of polite conversation with a heart as heavy as one of her flour bags. It was hard to blink back the tears which threatened to overcome her. She'd had such hopes that Mr Heiserman had been wrong.

In the carriage on the way home, her aunt tolled through each of her partners and their prospects.

"Now, Henry Gunson – no title, but very well off. However, he danced twice with the Carstairs chit and the on dit is that they will be betrothed. But Lord Merryam! The most distinguished attention, my dear! And he will come to call."

"Well, we'll see if he does," Adeline said practically.

CHAPTER 5

$\mathcal{A}$nthony's business had come to a satisfactory conclusion. He shook hands with Grey, smiling.

"I think you're exactly what we need," he said. A solid, down-to-earth architect was hard to find. So many of them wanted to make their name building huge, ornate edifices.

They walked out together into the streets of Soho. A few urchins, snacking happily on currant buns, watched them walk by, making loud comments about the richness of his and Grey's attire. He couldn't help grinning. These children were full of vigour—he hoped that the hard life they led wouldn't wear them down to the nub, as happened with so many of their parents.

He handed a sixpence to the youngest of them, a tow-headed boy of about five. "That should buy a pie each," he said, and looked sternly at the rest. "If you menace him, he's under no obligation to give you anything."

"We're no hectors, mate," the oldest said, affronted. "As if we'd cloy off our own!"

"Glad to hear that," Anthony replied, having no idea what

the boy meant, but understanding the tone. He laughed. "Enjoy your lunch!"

"Now every time you show your face here, they'll be onto you for more," Grey said.

"I can afford it."

They parted at the corner of Soho Square. A hackney passed them as they said goodbye, and stopped at the house where Anthony thought he had seen Meg. He halted, wondering yet again if he'd been right.

A veiled woman alighted from the hackney. The way she walked…it *couldn't* be Adeline Edmonds; he must have been wrong to suspect it before. But the rounded, compact figure ascended the steps with a familiar grace. It surprised him that he recognised her walk, but he did.

Curiosity fired up, he went down the street towards the building and regarded the discreet brass sign: The Soho Club. That was all. What the hell was Miss Edmonds doing in Soho? At a *club*? A women's club? Was there such a thing? And, if so, why in *Soho*, of all places?

The neighbourhood had once been fashionable, but it was now home to more brothels than private homes, more illegal drinking and gaming than families – and the families which did live here were only one step away from the gutter.

The only private clubs in this neighbourhood were thinly disguised whorehouses.

He had to find out what she was doing here. It wasn't *safe* for a woman of her class to walk these streets. She'd be cudgelled and robbed – if not worse – before she'd gone a block.

Outside the sturdy wooden door, he hesitated. Should he knock? One didn't, normally, at a club.

The door opened easily, its hinges well-oiled. He was in a mood to find that suspicious – even more suspicious was the entryway, a small, closed-off space with doors leading in three directions. As he moved towards the one straight in front of him, which led to the interior of the club, the left-hand door opened and two burly men came out fast, sliding themselves between him and the door in a practised manoeuvre.

"Naow, naow, sir. This club is for members only," the taller of the two said in a Cockney accent.

He could take them both on, but the state of their knuckles showed that they fought regularly, and he doubted he'd come out on top, despite his regular sessions in Gentleman Jackson's Boxing Saloon. Holding up his hands, palms out, he grinned. "No need for violence, gentlemen. I want to enquire about joining the club."

"Do you now?" He spun around. A woman had come quietly out of the right hand door and was regarding him with amused speculation. It jolted him; she had been entirely silent. She indicated the open door behind her and went back through it, so he followed.

He'd never seen anyone quite like her. Her skin was dark against her pale blue silk gown, and her hair was piled up and fixed with combs adorned with sapphires – the combination, of African blood and expensive accoutrements, should have made her look like a rich man's mistress, but something in the way she regarded him told him she answered to no one.

"You'd best come and discuss it, then." She ushered him into the room, a beautifully appointed office, complete with a rich Turkey carpet on the floor.

From behind a solid mahogany desk, she looked him over coolly. "So, Mr…?"

Should he give his real name? Oh, why not! He wasn't a woman, to have to worry about his reputation.

"Lord Merryam." He waited for her to introduce herself, but she didn't.

"How may I help you?" Since she didn't sit down, he couldn't, but he took off his hat and laid it on the desk.

"I'd like to join your club."

"Why?"

He blinked. "Why? It, er…it was recommended to me by a friend."

"Who?" Her cool wasn't the slightest bit ruffled.

If Adeline's name wasn't known here, he would be doing her the worst of turns to reveal it.

"The lady who entered your club immediately before me."

A smile flashed across her face, and she suddenly looked ten years younger, barely older than he. "If you do not know the lady's name, sir, I'm afraid that it's unlikely she recommended you. And our members' identities are, of course, confidential. If you want to meet this young lady, Lord Merryam, you must do it elsewhere."

"Membership, though…?"

Smiling ruefully at him, she shook her head. "I'm afraid our books are full, Lord Merryam. Perhaps next year."

He blinked. He was the Earl of Merryam. There were no doors closed to him.

She was quite calm about it. She gestured to him to leave, and sat at the desk, opening a ledger. Ignoring him.

Well. There was no point in taking a stand. He bowed slightly and left. For a moment, he considered making a dash for the inside door, but the two heavies were still there, grinning at him.

He bounded down the steps, anger giving him energy. How dare she? Then, at the bottom of the flight, he laughed at himself. He was being very high and mighty – more like his stiff-rumped grandfather than himself. It had probably done him good, being treated as though he was a nobody instead of a peer. It should happen to every lord at least once a year!

But it got him no further towards finding out what Adeline was doing here.

He turned towards home, and found Henry Gunson and the man he'd seen at Almack's walking along as if they owned the street.

"Are you going to this club?" Anthony demanded. Henry blinked and cast a swift, curious look towards his companion. Ohoh! The man was one of Henry's *affaires*.

"The Soho Club?" Henry asked. "What if we were? This is Felix Trengrouse. Felix, Anthony Merryam." Trengrouse—he must be one of Earl Trengrouse's sons; the man had a whole clutch of them. Anthony nodded to him. But he didn't have time to be polite.

"What kind of place is it?"

Henry and the young man laughed. "Not a place you need to concern yourself with," Felix said. "It's not for the likes of you."

It was a molly house? Why on earth would Adeline visit a place where men like Henry and Felix could…indulge themselves? He was more confused than ever.

"No," Henry agreed. "You're yourself everywhere you go."

What the hell did that mean? That he didn't have to pretend to be something he wasn't, like these two did, he supposed.

"Is something the matter, Tony?" Henry peered at him, concerned.

He laughed it off. "No, no. Just curious." Clapping him on the shoulder, Henry grinned at him.

"Well then, Felix and I have an appointment to keep." He exchanged a glance full of promise with Felix, and they went on towards the club, talking quietly. No doubt Henry was reassuring his friend that they wouldn't be betrayed; his and Henry's friendship went back to school days, and had suffered not at all when he'd discovered Henry's proclivities.

It takes all kinds to make a world, his mother had always said, and that seemed fair enough to him.

It was ridiculous, foolish, to feel empty. God knows he didn't want to have to skulk around like those two. But that look – he'd give a lot to have a woman he cared about look at him as Trengrouse had looked at Henry.

And he had no right to knock those doors down and demand to see Adeline. Miss Edmonds. Why did he wish he did?

*A*deline was changing into her working clothes when Mrs Skarsgard put her head around the door.

"My dear, do you know a Lord Merryam? I'm afraid that he saw you coming in and tried to gain entrance to the club."

Cold seemed to drench her. Lord Merryam! Of all the people it could have been!

"What did you tell him?"

"That our books were full. But he seemed like a very determined young man. Perhaps you should tell him what you do here?"

"I barely know him." This feeling that he was, perhaps, someone she could trust was just an illusion. Nothing he had said at Almack's had suggested anything other than a young sprig of nobility, as light-minded and selfish as all the rest. "I was veiled. He can't be *sure* it was me."

"Then brazen it out, my dear. And could you make sure the children don't come into the yard?"

"Yes, of course." Mrs Skarsgard nodded and went out.

. . .

ALL THROUGH THE morning she worried; first about Lord Merryam discovering what she was about here; and then about Meg and John. She had hired a hackney this morning because Meg had been called to John's bedside the night before; he was failing and had asked for her.

Meg didn't have to hide this last visit from her parents, as she'd hidden all the others, which was something to be grateful for, but how heart-breaking, to say goodbye forever to the man you'd hoped to spend your life with.

And she was guilty that, along with that sympathetic thought, came a question about what she herself would do, now that she couldn't excuse her absences to her aunt as keeping Meg company. Meg would be in mourning, and no doubt would go back to Little Foxbury.

How she would miss her!

But these children, and the mothers…if she couldn't come herself, perhaps she could hire a woman to do the charitable rounds for her. Another expense, when she had only just enough to keep the new mothers fed and the babies clothed! If only Lord Pindar hadn't been so *certain* about the trust, she would have approached the other trustees. But the other two were far more straitlaced and disapproving than he was. There'd be no help in that quarter.

She went home dispirited.

ANTHONY MERRYAM WAS as good as his word. He paid his call that very afternoon.

His manner was—odd. Perfectly polished, but with a look in his eyes, a kind of hesitance. Her stomach clenched with nerves.

When he invited her to go for a drive with him to Hyde Park, since the early February sun was shining, she went out of fear that he'd blurt something out in front of Aunt Jane, but she wished she were anywhere but perched in this smart curricle, threading through the streets of London. She prayed that the cold would take the tell-tale flush out of her cheeks.

He didn't speak as he navigated the traffic, but once they were in Hyde Park, he turned to her and said, seriously, "Miss Edmonds, I am concerned for your safety."

She didn't have to feign her look of astonishment. She was speechless. Concerned for her *safety*! That wasn't what she had imagined him saying.

He went on, with an annoying air of knowing what was best for her, "Soho is not the kind of area a young lady should frequent. It is far too dangerous."

At that, anger gave her courage. "I have no idea what you're talking about, Lord Merryam."

He blinked at the firmness in her tone, his blue eyes narrowing. "I saw you yesterday, going into the Soho Club."

"I *beg* your pardon? You think I went into a *club*? How dare you!" She wasn't *quite* lying. "In *Soho*? My aunt would never allow me to go to such a place!" All true. Every word.

His face was aghast, and he pulled his team over to the side of the carriageway. "Miss Edmonds–"

"I think you had best take me home, my lord."

Letting out a big breath, he turned more fully towards her. "I'm so relieved. I've been worried sick about you."

Guilt struck her just under her heart. She could barely look at him; he took it for anger.

"Please, Miss Edmonds, forgive me. I spoke only out of concern—I saw a woman yesterday in Soho Square and-and I was sure it was you."

"*Why?* Why on Earth would you think so?"

He regarded her helplessly, his colour rising. "She walked like you."

He could recognise her by her *walk*? Good Lord. "That seems a very thin basis for identification." Her tone was dry, and he relaxed and brought his hands up again to take the horses out into the light flow of carriages which wound through the park.

"It was…silly of me. Please accept my apologies."

"Perhaps a little more than silly. If it *had* been I, what would give you the right to chastise me over it?" That was risky, but she did so want to know. Was he just a busybody?

"I have no right, obviously." His eyes were on the horses' heads. They picked up pace, and he brought them back to a walk. "It was merely… merely my great admiration for you, and my concern for your welfare."

One part of her was impressed with his kindness, and desire to protect her; the other was furious with him for his high-handedness. She could show neither reaction.

"I see. Your imagination appears to have run away with you."

He gave a chuckle of relief. "And I'm very glad indeed it was only imagination. Now I may rest easy."

She had no idea how to respond to that. She felt a dreadful urge to confess it all to him, to throw herself on his mercy and ask him to keep her secret. It would be so good to share this burden. For a moment, she imagined the two of them tackling the problem together. But, given his "concern", he would no doubt go straight to Aunt Jane, and then where would she be? Worse, where would her new mothers be?

"Do you go to the Carmichael's ball tonight, Miss Edmonds?"

And they were back to inanities. Safely back. She drew a breath in, and smiled.

"Why yes, of course. Uncle Thaddeus is an old friend of Lord Carstairs."

The rest of the drive was spent waving and nodding to

their acquaintances, and discussing only the most insipid of *on dits*. She was a perfect lady; a model of decorous womanhood.

She only hoped it convinced him that she would not, *could* not, have been that woman in Soho Square.

CHAPTER 7

"I have to go, Aunt. Meg needs me."

Aunt Jane looked her up and down. "I don't know why you girls are so close – you have nothing in common. Meg is a *blue-stocking*." She sighed. "Very well, but you can't go in that. It's too light-coloured. Wear your brown merino."

So she sat in her sombre brown merino, holding Meg's hands, waiting for Meg's father to come back from John's burial. Was there ever a more dispiriting occupation? And why could women not attend the graveside? Surely they needed to say goodbye too?

Meg's step-mamma was in the nursery with the new baby; all the other brothers and sisters, of which Meg seemed to have a surprising number, were back in Little Foxbury. The house seemed to echo.

She'd expected Meg to be red-eyed and weeping, but she seemed to be stunned into a daze. Perhaps that was just exhaustion. She'd spent so many hours by John's sickbed; it must be discombobulating to be free of that responsibility.

"What will you do now?" Adeline asked her.

"Go home." Meg gave a big sigh. "I know I'm leaving you in the lurch–"

"Don't be silly! Our arrangement was only ever going to work temporarily. I'll just hire someone to do the work."

"That will be expensive. Can you sustain it?" An excellent question. But there was only one answer.

"I'll have to. I can't let those women down."

"Why not ask Anthony for help?"

What on Earth? "*Anthony Merryam?*"

Meg laughed. "You're misjudging him. He's the kindest creature. I'm sure, if you asked…"

"It would be most improper, Meg!" *Appallingly* improper, for a young lady to ask a man for money.

"Not if you were betrothed."

"I–" Adeline had no idea what to say. Betrothed. "But–"

"Adeline, every time you walk into the room his whole face comes alight. And the same with you!"

"Oh, that's…" Nonsense. Surely. Unbidden, the memory arose of his arm around her, her hand in his, those blue eyes…if she came alight, it was with pure desire. Which she was ashamed of, as she ought to be. No young woman should think like that. Or dream, as she had been dreaming, of his touch, his kiss, his body.

Meg smiled and shook her head. "I don't know why you're so against the idea."

"Because if I marry, my entire fortune will become the property of my husband. And any hope I have of doing good in the world goes up in smoke!"

"Don't discount Anthony. I've known him a long time and he's a good man."

"He's a fribble."

Meg regarded her with shrewd eyes. "I think you need to get to know him better than you do before you make that judgement."

. . .

ADELINE SENT a note to Mrs Skarsgard, asking her to get James to dispense the currant buns, and to look for a reliable woman to continue her work with the new mothers. She'd included a banknote with the message, but it was risky. She had to find a better way of transferring the money.

It was so *frustrating!* Instead of helping others, she was spending her mornings either shopping with her aunt or sitting and doing *needlework!* Not even useful sewing, but embroidery, done in the cold grey light from the big windows in the drawing room. At least there was a fire, but the weather made her fret for her new mothers, few of whom would have such a luxury.

Her uncle was approving. "I'm glad to see you have given gadding about with Margaret Delaney," he said. "Time you started keeping your aunt company. Learn from her what a wife and mother should be, and you will not go wrong."

"Yes, Uncle Thaddeus." She bent her head over her embroidery frame so he wouldn't see the anger in her eyes.

After he had walked ponderously back to his study, Aunt Jane said soothingly, "He means well. He wants to see you happily established."

"And if I do not wish to marry?"

Her aunt laughed heartily. "My dear! Tell me that when you do not dance two dances every night with Anthony Merryam, and then allow him to take you into supper!"

She couldn't help a blush, and Aunt Jane gave a satisfied chuckle. Adeline frowned over her stitching. She had been too friendly to Lord Merryam, too obvious in her enjoyment of his company. Perhaps he, too, thought her to be partial to him – if Aunt Jane believed he was courting her, others would too, and that might include him.

That was unfair. She must draw back; to use him as a

decoy with a little light-hearted flirting was one thing, but to mislead him into thinking she was serious…no, a woman of conscience could not do such a thing.

"I assure you, Aunt, I have no intention of marrying Lord Merryam."

"Best to wait until he asks you before you make up your mind." Aunt Jane twinkled at her. "It would take a strong-minded woman to reject that one!"

True. Adeline tried hard to banish the memory of warm blue eyes smiling down at her. It would take a *very* strong-minded woman to not find him attractive. It was just as well she was strong-minded enough.

Of course she was.

The weather had been too bad for drives in the park, or even for many morning calls. Anthony wouldn't trust his prize horses on the frozen cobblestones. So he walked to the Carstairs' ball, the Cholmondeleys' recital, another dance at Almack's…and he went about his nightly activities with only one goal: to get Adeline Edmonds to trust him.

Something had changed lately. She'd been reluctant to grant him more than one dance on any occasion. She was never without partners, of course – such a beautiful and, he was told, well-dowried girl was a magnet for both fortune hunters and moonstruck swains. She had been graceful and tactful about refusing him, but refuse him she had.

It made him think.

He had been relieved when she'd so unequivocally denied being in Soho. Later, he'd run the conversation through his mind more than once, and had realised that she had not, in fact, denied it. Saying that her aunt would not permit it was *not* the same as saying she had not been there.

Perhaps she had not. But perhaps she had. And the more

time he spent in her company, the more he became convinced that, if it *had* been her, she must have been coerced in some way. He could imagine no reason a gently-bred girl would frequent such a place unless she was forced to.

Why someone would coerce her, and what they would coerce her into…that was unpleasant to think about. He clung to the idea that it was Mrs Skarsgard, rather than some member of the club, who had a hold on her. Because this girl, surely, was still without taint.

As they danced the one waltz she would grant him at Almack's, and she smiled up at him from guiltless brown eyes, he could not believe any calumny of her. She was *good*, all the way through.

He only wished she were more interested in the wider sphere of politics. But perhaps he could educate her.

"Do you follow the doings of the House at all, Miss Edmonds?"

Her bright eyes blinked, and she looked at him with astonishment. He *had* spoken out of the blue, he supposed.

"Women are not supposed to be interested in politics, according to my uncle," she said. "I have little opportunity to learn about such things."

"You could read the newspaper," he said, amused.

"Could I? The newspaper is delivered to my uncle's study each morning. I am not allowed in my uncle's study."

Her voice was sharp. For a moment they revolved in silence, and then he said, hesitantly, "Your family puts strict limits on you?"

"My aunt and uncle believe that girls should concern themselves with frills and furbelows, and catching a husband." The bitterness in her tone was unmistakeable. He sighed.

"My father believed that the aristocracy should concern

itself only with their own estates, and have no further interest in the welfare of the country."

They exchanged glances full of understanding, and she seemed to relax further into his embrace.

One step further into her good graces. But when he invited her to take his arm for supper, she smiled kindly and turned to a scapegrace young lad barely out of leading strings.

"I'm afraid Mr Danvers is before you, my lord." She sailed off on the boy's arm as if leaving him standing like a fool meant nothing.

He *couldn't* have mistaken their rapport. He wasn't a green boy, to imagine a woman's interest. Which meant she was keeping him at a distance for a reason. And that twisted something in his guts, hard.

She was trying to keep her secret.

Time to find out what it was.

REALLY, it was ridiculous to feel so bored. Mr Danvers was a pleasant young man, and very eager to please. Adeline forced herself not to look over his shoulder to where Anthony Merryam was directing a smouldering gaze at her.

He had no right to expect her companionship at supper. But that look…a frisson ran through her. He was so *very* handsome. Warmth pooled in her abdomen. No. To marry was to put leading reins on herself. No independence. No independent income. No ability to do what she *knew* she was called to do.

For the first time, though, the idea of proud, solitary independence seemed rather cold and lonely.

CHAPTER 8

Three mornings in a row, Anthony Merryam had waited, impatiently, at the window of a whorehouse which overlooked Soho Square.

He'd paid handsomely for the privilege, but it was worth it to not be out in the freezing rain.

He had seen the woman in the hackney at this hour twice—he'd come here every day for a month if he had to. But perhaps today was his lucky day.

A hackney turned into the Square and pulled up outside the Soho Club.

Anthony was on his feet and out the door before the horses' hooves had stopped.

Someone—yes, it was a woman—got out as he ran down the slippery steps and across the Square. A veiled woman. Good. Now he'd have the truth.

"Miss Edmonds!" he called breathlessly. "Miss Edmonds!"

The woman turned as the hackney pulled away. He slid on the treacherous pavement and almost fell. She put out a hand to steady him—a large hand, in knitted woollen gloves.

"Watch yerself, young'un," she said, in a strong Cockney

accent. He found his feet and stared at her. She was the same height as Miss Edmonds, and she had curves, but…

The woman put back her veil and smiled at him broadly, showing two missing teeth. She was a good ten years older than Adeline Edmonds, ruddy-cheeked and dark-haired. "Now why's a rum swell like you runnin' after an old mort like me?"

He stammered in shock. "For-forgive me, madam. I mistook you for another."

"A sweetheart, eh? May't be you need a serve of cold pudding to settle that fire in yr eyes. But good luck to ye." She nodded kindly and went up the steps with a firm tread.

Good Lord. Had he been on a fool's errand this whole time?

"Madam!" he called. The woman turned at the top of the stairs with an enquiring look. "Have you – have you been attending this club for some time?"

She laughed. "Aye, you might say that. I strap here regular."

"Thank you, ma'am."

He stood there for a moment as she went inside. What a damned fool he'd been!

Imagining things, mooning after a girl, hanging out in *whorehouses*, for God's sake. He'd made a cod's-head of himself for nothing.

And worse. He made his way back to the whorehouse slowly, despite the icy drizzle soaking into his coat. If she was hiding nothing, then there had been no reason for Miss Edmonds to draw back from him.

No reason except that she had tired of him; had seen his growing infatuation and moved to squash it.

He stood there at the bottom of the brothel steps, head bowed, and accepted that all his excuses for her recent behaviour were nonsense. She just didn't care for him.

. . .

THE THOUGHT STRUCK at someplace deep inside him; heart and gut together felt as though he'd been punched. His hands fisted and he shook his head. Was this pain the result of caring too much? Was this pain what poets called love?

If he hadn't accused her of impropriety, would she have drawn back from him?

He'd wrecked everything.

CHAPTER 9

"Goddam it!" Anthony threw the papers in his hand onto his desk just as his man showed Henry Gunson into the room.

"That's a fine welcome!"

Anthony grinned. "Sorry."

Henry nodded towards the papers. "A problem?"

"Oh, those damned Whigs. Dead against the Catholic Emancipation Bill, and now they're digging their heels in over the Poor Employment Act! It will be months before we get it sorted out."

Henry was a political ally—they both knew how desperately the poor needed relief after the disastrous year they'd all had. "The Year Without a Summer" the newspapers were calling 1816, the year just past. That a nation like Britain could be brought so close to famine by one year of bad weather was a judgement on his class, and he was determined to do something about it.

He poured Henry a tankard of ale and took a drink from his own.

"I'm behind you, as you know," Henry said, "but I'm neither an MP nor a peer. There's a limit to–"

Anthony waved him silent. "That's not what I wanted to talk to you about." He hesitated. Was he a fool? Very probably. "It's about Miss Edmonds."

"Ohoh!"

"Yes, yes." Henry was grinning, damn him. "I need your help. And Lady Sophia's."

Henry lost his smile. "Sophia Carstairs and I have our own problems." Anthony raised an eyebrow. "Her parents have found out that I'm Catholic, and there's the devil to pay."

"Ah." Anthony paused, the said delicately, "I'm rather surprised that you are seeking marriage at all." He wouldn't have thought Henry would cozen a young girl into marriage when he couldn't be a proper husband to her.

With a roll of his eyes, Henry took a swig of his ale. "Don't you worry about that, Anthony. Lady Sophia knows exactly what she's getting into."

That was all right then. It wasn't his job to protect every young damsel in the *ton*.

"So," Henry prodded, "what's this about Miss Edmonds?"

"I'm afraid I've given her a distaste for me–"

"How?"

So it all came out – the Soho Club, seeing the veiled woman, everything.

At first, Henry was suitably attentive, but when Anthony reached the description of the woman he'd accosted, Henry outright laughed.

"That's Madge. You were lucky she didn't give you the sharp side of her tongue. She does various bits of work for the Club."

"What the hell is that place, anyway?"

Henry regarded him sardonically. "It's a place where like

minded people can congregate in the knowledge they can be themselves. Felix and I use it."

"A molly club."

"Not quite," Henry said. "The persons who frequent it are…more varied than that, and visit for more than one reason."

Good Lord! A specialist place for debauchery. Like that club Alderson established – Phoenix Society or something like that. The successor to the Hellfire Club. He was ashamed he'd ever imagined Adeline anywhere near it. Thank God she didn't know the worst of which he'd accused her.

"I fear Miss Edmonds has withdrawn her friendship, and who can blame her? I was damnably heavy-handed."

"I'm sorry to hear it, old chap, but I can't see where I come in."

"She's refused to go out driving with me twice. I thought if Lady Sophia asked her for a picnic or some such, I would have a chance to apologise in private."

"A *picnic*? In this weather?"

They both looked out the window. It was grey again, a miserable day, half rain-half sleet hitting the glass in gusts.

"A musical evening or something. *I* don't know. I can't invite her myself, obviously."

Henry considered it. "The Carmichaels are having a soirée next Tuesday. You've probably got a card for it already. I'll speak to Sophia about finding you somewhere private to talk."

"She'll be a ministering angel if she does."

"I have to say, it does me good to see the great care-for-nothing Anthony Merryam brought so low by a chit of a girl." Henry's eyes were brimful of amusement.

"Not so funny as seeing you trying to put your head in parson's mouse-trap!" Anthony retorted.

"Love brings us to strange places," Henry agreed, but

Anthony didn't think he was talking about loving Sophia Carstairs. Felix Trengrouse? Well, it was none of his business, but he hoped they were headed for a happy ending.

He hoped he was too.

That night, he wrote to his mother, replying at last to her almost daily missives.

My dear Mama,

You'll be pleased to know that your loving son has obeyed your directive and found a young lady he intends to ask to wife.

She is not a child – she's three and twenty, but new come to Town. Miss Edmonds, Thaddeus Edmonds' niece. Well dowered, and all that could be desired in Lady Merryam, as I'm sure you will agree.

Do you have any good advice as to how to go about the business? I blush to admit it, but I'm not at all sure she will accept me.

Wish me luck.

The other business is advancing slowly but surely. We shall be ready before the Spring,

Your dutiful son, as always,

With love,

Tony

IF HE KNEW HIS MOTHER, that would bring her hot-foot to Town. Bringing in the big guns. He needed all the artillery he could muster if he was going to get over this heavy ground to safe haven.

Safe haven in Adeline Edmonds' arms.

PHOEBE, Countess of Merryam, put down her son's letter and laughed until she cried.

Reading between the lines, Tony was love-struck and completely at sea.

This she had to behold with her own two eyes.

"Rufford!" she called to her butler. "Order my carriage for tomorrow morning, and arrange a post chaise for the servants! We're all going to London."

Tony had left everyone but his valet and gone to rooms in Albany rather than open the town house for just himself.

Time for her to join the Season.

Perhaps she'd give a ball. Or talk Diana Faulkes into holding one in Hindmouth House. That would be fun.

And the first name on the invitation list would be Adeline Edmonds.

CHAPTER 10

What on Earth?

Adeline stood at the door of the tack room and stared.

Madge was sitting on the knee of Collie, the stableman, laughing and, and—*carousing*! Her breasts were half-out of her dress, and his hand was—Adeline looked away. At a time when Madge should be out and about, seeing to the new mothers!

"Is this what I have been paying for?" Adeline said grimly.

The two scrambled to their feet and hastily put their clothing in order. Adeline had to glance sharply downwards to avoid seeing much more of Collie than she should. How *dare* they?

But Madge didn't seem to feel any shame.

"No harm in a bit of fun, miss. I've done my job, right enough."

That gave Adeline pause. She was not someone who held others to her moral standards. But it was so early! It had taken her *hours* to do her rounds.

"How many mothers today?" She tried to ask calmly, but

Madge gave her a quick look and grabbed a notebook off the bench. Madge had got the job in the first place because she could read and write, an unusual skill in a woman of her class. Adeline wanted records kept, in case she could follow up with the mothers herself in the future.

Madge showed her the list, fully filled out.

Three mothers, bags delivered. Currant buns, twenty-one. Two children sick who usually got their buns – visited and given barley for barley-water and some small ale. Keeping them drinking was the main thing with fevers. Missus Bragg's baby had a rash; Madge thought it was a reaction to the hard soap.

"I start a good bit earlier than you do, miss," Madge said. Was that an edge to her voice?

This was the Soho Club. It was established for those who wanted to be themselves...and, deep down, Adeline had always known that included those who wanted to express the more earthy side of their natures. It would be hypocritical of her to object now; although the sight of this couple in an embrace had stirred up feelings she was sure an unmarried woman should not have.

"My apologies, Madge," she said. "This looks as though you are doing very well."

Madge blinked in astonishment. "Thank'ee, miss."

"Carry on," Adeline said, and walked out of the stable. In the yard, she stopped, trying to regulate her breathing more. She waited by the iron gates for a moment, regaining her poise, before she went in to discuss finance with Mrs Skarsgard. Perhaps she could send money directly to Mrs Skarsgard's bank? That might be simplest. Lord Pindar would help her with that, surely.

"Mis Edmonds? Adeline?"

She froze. No no no no.

"It *is* you! What in God's name are you doing in that place?"

Slowly, she turned. Anthony Merryam stood outside the gate, his whole face full of astonishment and…yes, disgust.

Time to explain. It might not be socially acceptable, but she'd done nothing to be ashamed of.

"Good morning, Lord Merryam."

"Is that all you have to say?" He was furious. "You *lied* to me!"

"No. I did not. Allow me to explain."

"Yes, you'd better! Do your aunt and uncle know you're here? How could you?" He grasped the bars of the gate with gloved hands and shook it a little. "Let me in."

Anger rose up in her. He had no authority over her. Why *should* she explain?

"Are you a member of the club, my lord? I'm afraid only members can be admitted."

Perhaps that was deliberately provocative, but Lud! he was overstepping his mark.

"Adeline, what's going on? Why are you at this—this *place*? How can you lower yourself to this?"

His face betrayed a kind of hurt fury. Well, he wasn't the only one who'd been hurt. Or who was angry.

"*Lower* myself? I'm doing the best I can while being constantly watched, constantly told "No", constantly being stopped from living my life just because I'm a woman!"

"But to play the doxy at a place like this! To sully yourself as a wanton!"

She stopped, aghast that he thought she was – that she *could*… her heart was squeezed as though it were in a press.

In the sudden silence, tittupping footsteps came closer. She turned aside, pulling her veil down. But it was only a couple of the girls from the brothel on the corner, back from their morning visit to the soldiers' barracks.

"Ooh, if it isn't Lord Merryboy!" one said. Adeline turned to watch. The two women were pasting themselves against Anthony, and they were not holding back.

"You haven't been to see us for a while, m'lordship," the red-headed one added, with an inviting grin. "Don't want to leave it too long. It ain't healthy for a man to go without."

"No," Adeline said coldly. "It's not healthy for anyone."

She turned on her heel and walked away.

"Adeline!"

Adeline ignored him, torn between fury and shame and a wild, ridiculous heartbreak.

SHE COULDN'T GO BACK to her aunt's like this. By instinct, Adeline turned towards the safety of the stable tack room. But Madge and Collie were there. She stood, bereft, unmoving, for a moment until James came up behind her and guided her—like a dog with a sheep—into the warmth of the Club, ignoring Anthony Merryam's pleas behind her.

Mrs Skarsgard came to meet her. "My dear, James has told me. Are you all right?"

Adeline stared blankly at her. "No. No, I don't think I am."

"Come, then." Mrs Skarsgard led her up the stairs to one of the bedrooms. She halted on the threshold—who knew *what* kind of behaviour had taken place in there? But there was a fire in the hearth, and the room smelt of lavender and cinnamon. "Come," Mrs Skarsgard said.

Adeline sat in an armchair next to the fire, and stared into the flames. She had behaved badly. Yes, she had. But *he*! To think so poorly of her, with so little evidence—while *she* had good evidence! The way those girls had spoken to him. She was no fool; if he knew wenches like those, it wasn't through polite conversation. They even knew his name!

He was a—a rake. A man of fashion, with no morals and

very few manners, once you got him out of the ballroom. She was better off without him.

"I'm better off without him," she said to Mrs Skarsgard.

"Of course you are." Mrs Skarsgard handed her a big handkerchief just as she burst into tears. "Of course you are."

Patting her on the shoulder, Mrs Skarsgard let her cry herself out. She was kind. Kind to everyone. Perhaps that's what she should do – move out of her parents' house and set up for herself, as Mrs Skarsgard had done.

But the law would be on her parents' side, even though she was an adult. Women had no rights. Dully, she let the handkerchief drop. All she could do was wait until her parents died, or she turned forty, whichever came first.

Seventeen years of, of *nothing*. She got to her feet, impelled to movement.

Mrs Skarsgard had gone, closing the door silently behind her.

He thought she was a doxy.

Adeline flung herself on the bed and wept.

CHAPTER 11

There had to be a way to join that club.

If she had to play the doxy, by God, she could play it with *him*. Anthony lay awake, fists gripping the sheets, eyes fixed on the dark ceiling. Image after image presented itself to him. Adeline smiling up at him from a rumpled bed. Adeline naked.

He flung the coverings back and lay in his nightshirt, but even the sharpness of the February night did nothing to cool his desire for her.

He should have taken that red-head up on her invitation. It was unmanly to lust so after a woman who didn't want you.

But perhaps she did—or could. If she was so driven by her passions to use a place like the Soho Club to sate them, perhaps she *would* want him. They didn't need the club. He could hire a house, a set of rooms…somewhere discreet. If she was determined to set morals and respectability aside, he would enter into an arrangement enthusiastically. Wouldn't he just!

What had she said? It wasn't healthy to go without. Of

course, many people believed that about men—could it be that she believed it applied to women, too? If so…any man would do, surely, as long as he was clean and considerate?

Fury overtook him at the thought that anyone but he had touched her. If he knew who they were—oh, God, had they been watching his courtship of her and laughing at him?

That cured his lust as nothing else could. She had made a fool of him.

But if anyone could have her…he would.

There had to be a way to get into that club.

"No, Lord Merryam," Mrs Skarsgard said. "There is no way."

"If it's money–"

"It is *not* money. You are not suitable as a member."

Her voice was as serene as her face. She sat at her desk, back straight, dark eyes assessing him with too much insight. Damn her. All right. If he couldn't get in, could he get Adeline out?

"I'm concerned about Miss Edmonds." Better to be blunt. Mrs Skarsgard jerked her chin a little, as if she were surprised at his honesty.

"There is no need. Miss Edmonds is perfectly safe here."

"How *can* she be safe, at a place like this?"

That lovely mouth thinned. "I assure you, Lord Merryam, that nothing happens to Miss Edmonds here that she has not organised herself—except mannerless people insulting her in the stableyard."

Organised herself.

"What if she gets pregnant?"

Laughter lit Mrs Skarsgard's face. "That is *most* unlikely."

A possibility struck him. No. It couldn't be that Adeline was a Sapphic. He would have known, surely? When they danced, she clung to him as though she were surrendering herself to him. Surely no Sapphic would do so?

Unless she spends her entire life playing a part—as Henry does. It would certainly explain why she came here; for the same reason as Henry and Felix did. Because there was no other place where she could be herself.

He rubbed a hand over his face. Impossible. "Mrs Skarsgard, I am motivated entirely by concern for Miss Edmonds."

"I think not *entirely.*" The dry note in her voice scratched at his conscience; reminded him of the fantasies he'd spent the night fighting. This woman knew too much. He scowled at her.

"Whatever you think of my motives, please—please contact me if Miss Edmonds is ever in any need. Of any kind whatsoever."

Mrs Skarsgard hid a laugh behind her hand. Damn her.

"I will let her know that she can call upon you to satisfy her every desire…but you might be quite surprised by what her desires centre around."

He left without any formalities, although he felt quite rude doing so. But be polite he could not.

"You should tell him the truth, Miss Edmonds."

Adeline sighed. "Yes. I suppose I should."

"It might be worth it to see him eat humble pie."

Laughing, Adeline shrugged. "As long as he doesn't report the whole matter to my aunt and uncle."

"He hasn't done so yet."

"No, he hasn't, has he…"

She had come to the club to organise the payments with Mrs Skarsgard, only to have to hide behind a cart so he would not see her as he strode down the steps with a thundercloud upon his brow.

"He said he'd be happy to fulfill your every desire…" Mrs Skarsgard was teasing, but Adeline could feel a blush creep up her face anyway. Her stomach clenched at the thought of Anthony satisfying her. But what he really meant was that he'd be happy to use her as a mistress.

The arrogance!

She finished her business with Mrs Skarsgard and left after getting James to have a quick look around for her.

"All's clear, miss," he announced.

"Good. I'll just slip around to Missus Bragg's place to make sure she has everything she needs for the baby. I've brought her some soap without sheet's fat in it – it should help with that rash that Madge noted." She had found that "Missus" was a courtesy title given to any woman who had children and a man in the house. That was quite respectable for Soho.

"Yes'm. I'll come with you."

No sense in objecting—James was quite right to protect her.

They walked around to the Bragg's house and found the baby's rash even worse.

"It's all this washing, miss," the mother said. "I don't hold with washing."

"Try this soap instead." Adeline gave it to her. "It's specially for babies."

Missus Braggs looked dubiously at the sweet-scented bar, and sniffed. "Well, I dunno. Might make the little bastard smell better. Got any dosh, miss?"

"You know I don't give money, Missus Braggs'" It would have been madness to walk around Soho if people knew she had money on her. "But Madge'll be around as usual with the bag of food."

Missus Braggs, a skinny, pock-marked woman who

couldn't be more than twenty-five but who looked forty, sighed with disappointment. "Can't drink food, miss."

Adeline laughed. "That's the idea. But I'll send some small ale around as well."

You couldn't blame the people here for preferring ale to water; the water from the pumphouse was disgusting – almost *brown*.

They left the Braggs with relief; the mother had been right, the whole place had smelled of baby faeces – and perhaps worse. Five doors down, the big building on the corner was showing signs of being worked upon.

Corner buildings in Soho were much prized as brothels, because it gave the girls twice the number of windows to hang out invitingly. No doubt another was springing up, exploiting the young women and spreading disease.

Perhaps 'Lord Merryboy' would patronise this one, too, she thought viciously.

There were men on the other side of the street, even at this time of day, eyeing the women in the "house" next door to the worksite. They eyed her closely, but at least they didn't call out obscenities, as often happened.

As she and James reached the corner and turned, he ran ahead to get her a hackney from the stand in nearby Carnaby Street.

She waited on the corner, as she had many times before. But this time, a party of workmen came out of the building. With Anthony Merryam in their midst. And she had forgotten to pull down her veil!

They both stopped dead. Then she curled her lip at him, and began walking towards Carnaby Street after James.

The dissembler! Building a brothel. How *dare* he judge her, when he was involved in this disgusting trade himself.

She couldn't abide a hypocrite!

Adeline walked past with her nose in the air, and ignored his low voiced, "Please, may I speak with you?"

No, you may not.

Footsteps behind her. A hand on her arm, pulling her to face him.

"Miss Edmonds, I must speak to you. These streets are not safe for a lady!"

"Let me go!" She glared up into his ridiculously blue eyes and tried to pull her arm away, but he held fast.

"Oi! You! Get orf Miss!"

"Let 'er go!"

Two men ran across the street and barrelled into Anthony, tearing his hand off her arm, hitting him, throwing him to the ground. One of them kicked him in the stomach. It happened in a second, leaving her breathless.

Adeline gasped. "Oh, no!"

"S'all right, Miss, he won't hurt ye." There was satisfaction in the voice, and she recognised the face.

"Mister Bragg!"

The other man, she realised, was the father of Glynn, the girl who had gone to work at the buckle factory; he was the ex-soldier who had brought a wife home from India. He nodded to her.

"All's well, miss. Won't let the likes of this one get a hold on you." He kicked Anthony again. "You're a sight too good to be mucked around by a lordling."

"Oh, pray, don't hurt him any further!"

Anthony was curled around his stomach. She felt a stab of concern, but also, unworthily, a certain satisfaction.

"'e's just winded, miss."

Excellent. She prodded him with her foot. "It appears, Lord Merryam, that I am considerably safer on the streets of Soho than you are. Thank you, gentlemen."

The workmen who had been with Anthony gathered, but

none of them intervened. She recognised a few of them from her home visits, and nodded to them.

"His lordship meant no harm, I'm sure," she said.

"Just needs to learn a little respect," Mr Bragg said.

The other men murmured agreement.

A clatter of hooves and harness announced the arrival of the hackney. Anthony had begun to clamber to his feet, his face white. Oh, if he had taken some serious hurt, she'd never forgive herself! But that look on his face was rage, not pain.

"Thank you so much, Mr Bragg," she said briskly. "Sergeant. I'll be seeing more of you, no doubt. I'm in your debt."

They pulled their hats off and grinned.

"Nah, miss. 'Tis our pleasure—ye've been that kind to our good women."

In a positive fog of reciprocal admiration, she climbed into the hackney. She forced herself not to look back at Anthony Merryam.

"Thank you, James."

"Right you are, Miss!"

The hackney pulled away, and then the driver opened the hatch in the roof. "Where to, Miss?" he asked in a strong Scottish accent.

"Gloucester Square," she replied, still a little breathless. What a moment! She would be less than human if she hadn't enjoyed the irony, but poor Anthony. Still, he *had* seemed no worse than winded…

The hackney driver had left the hatch open and seemed keen for a chat.

"Ye'll be working with the orphanage lord, then?" he asked.

"The orphanage lord?"

"Aye. Him what's payin' for that old whorehouse to be turned into an orphanage. Merryboy, they call him."

"An *orphanage*?"

"That's it. D'ye know if mayhap they'll take bairns with one parent? My wife's gone and I'm finding it gey hard to take care of the littlest."

"I-I don't know, I'm sorry."

"Hmphf." The hatch clacked shut.

An orphanage. Not a brothel. She had misjudged him so badly. Shame swept over her, a hot blush of embarrassment and regret.

He had been trying to help her, as apparently he helped others, and she had repulsed him—worse, caused him to be set upon!

Any chance that they might have talked over their differences and shared the truth was gone.

All she wanted to do was throw her veil back and cry unimpeded, but a lady never showed unbridled emotion in public. She deliberately breathed in, feeling the hard ache of misery under her breastbone, and sat up straighter.

He would never forgive her.

She would have to scrape and save to pay Maggie's wages, but her children and mothers would get what they needed. That would have to be enough, even if it felt—literally felt— as though her heart was breaking in two. He was lost to her.

*H*is mother looked at him with astonishment, and plumped herself down on his sofa. She'd arrived from Little Foxbury an hour ago, and had waited impatiently for him to come home.

"What do you mean, you've changed your mind?"

He cursed his own impulsiveness—if he hadn't written to her, he wouldn't have to deal with this now. She had, just as he'd expected, set out immediately upon receiving his letter, and her maid was even now unpacking in the countess's suite while Mamma had come down to have a glass of ratafia. He had chosen brandy. He needed it.

"We've decided we will not suit," he said stiffly.

"She's rejected you?"

"We—had a disagreement." He could still feel the bruises on his solar plexus. Those boots had been hard.

She waved a hand as if brushing away a fly.

"Then make up with her! You're not cheating me of grandchildren because of a silly argument."

How much should he tell her? How much did he *know?* Not much for certain, still, despite his fears. Perhaps his mother could give him wise counsel. Because despite seeing Adeline again, in broad daylight, parading through the streets of Soho with the man he must assume to be her body-guard—if not worse—he still wanted her.

Even as his wife. It was madness. True madness, deuce take it.

What the hell.

He told his mother everything. But, astonishingly, she did not react at all badly.

"Ah…the Soho Club…" A faint blush pinked her cheeks. "Yes." His mother was only fifty, and still showed the beauty which had swept many a man off his feet in her youth. Or so his father had always said. An "original" in her day, Anthony was aware that she'd caused more than one scandal. But marrying the Earl of Merryam had put paid to the gossip. Still, she knew every *on dit* in Society. What did she know about the Soho Club?

"Mamma?"

Her still-blonde hair gleamed in the candlelight as she bent her head over her glass. Then she looked up, hazel eyes full of thought. "It…may not be exactly what it might appear, Tony. Don't judge your Adeline too harshly just yet."

"It's a place for, for—it's debauched!"

His mother—his own *mother*—pursed her lips and considered that. "Do you have proof of that?"

"I know what kind of person goes there!" He had never had a serious argument with his mother, but today was the day.

"Really, Tony, how can a son of mine be so *bourgeois*! So quick to judge."

Infuriated, he flung out of the salon and thundered down the stairs. By God, it would serve them all right if he ran straight to that red-headed doxy and went to the devil with her. *Bourgeois*! How dare she. As if he were some damn Cit who proselytised over dinner.

Where was he promised to tonight? He'd intended to stay in with his mother, but now…oh, yes, Sophie Carstairs' bloody musical evening.

Women were intolerable.

Halfway down the front steps, he halted. Carstairs' musical evening…he'd organised, back when he had honourable designs on her, to be alone with her. Henry had put a word in Lady Sophia's ear. No doubt they were expecting him to propose…

But Adeline and he needed to have a different conversation.

CHAPTER 13

The last thing Adeline wanted to do was to go to a musical evening. But Sophia Carstairs had been so welcoming when she first came to Town—it would be a poor repayment of friendship to ignore the invitation.

Besides, her aunt was looking forward to it and so, surprisingly, was her uncle, who rarely came to evening entertainments.

"It's not often you get the chance to hear Mrs Dussek play her own sonatas," he said.

"It's Mrs Moralt now, Humphrey," Aunt Jane said. "She remarried."

Mrs Moralt was a harpist, Adeline realised as they walked into the Carstairs' ballroom and found a small stage set up with a standing harp.

Normally she liked harp music, but she found herself on edge. What if Anthony Merryam had bruited about her visits to Soho? It would be fair turnabout, after being so harshly handled by her friends. Her reputation would be in tatters, given what he thought she was doing there.

She had dressed in her best finery—a white silk dress

with a cerulean overskirt and a flounce of Brussels lace—the better to face down criticism, but it wasn't needed. Around her, the cream of Society nodded and smiled at her. Slowly, a knot she hadn't realised was beneath her breastbone loosened.

He hadn't betrayed her. And she had misjudged him so badly. The first chance she got, she would confess everything to him, and repair his misjudgement of her character. He deserved that, and perhaps he would understand why she'd had to lie to him.

It made her a little light-headed. A glass of lemonade from a passing waiter helped calm her down, and so did fielding enquiries for Meg from Sophia Carstairs.

"She writes that she is well settled by her own fireside, Lady Sophia, and happy to be there," she reported. "But of course…"

"Of course," Sophia nodded. "She must be feeling the lack of Mr Poulteney. They were childhood sweethearts, were they not?"

Was that the right term?

"They had known each other their whole lives," she agreed. Despite herself, she remembered Meg saying that she would like to know the kind of love they had in novels…she sent a prayer up that her friend would know that love, soon. And herself?

She'd just have to do without it. It had been easier to commit herself to a spinster's life before Anthony—no! before *this Season*. It had nothing to do with Anthony Merryam at all.

He walked in and her heart did a double stutter at the sight of him. A blush, part shame and part…something else, swept over her. It wasn't fair. It wasn't fair of God to send her Anthony Merryam as a test of her resolve. Why did it have to be *him*? She'd never even *liked* blonds before!

The way he moved through the crowds…it wasn't the polished manners or the gleaming smile…it was the assurance and the grace, the strong legs and upright carriage. He'd clearly taken no harm from Mr Bragg's kicks.

He had thought her given over to vice, and looking at him made that possibility more than attractive. Which was a shocking thought for a young gentlewoman.

Smiling internally, she continued to discuss current fashions with Sophia and her friend, Miss Maddox, a striking redhead.

A woman came onto the stage: Mrs Dussek, no doubt, a buxom woman with sandy-blonde hair in ringlets. As she settled into her chair, the guests likewise found seats on the sofas and chairs set around the room.

"This will be a lovely place for you, Miss Edmonds," Lady Sophia said, and placed Adeline on a sofa near the door. She smiled and sat, looking around for her aunt who had lingered in the foyer. But instead, Anthony Merryam sat next to her.

She froze, looking straight ahead.

"Miss Edmonds, we must talk," he said.

An elderly couple tottered past, and he rose smoothly and offered them the sofa. She had to do likewise. The couple sat with grateful smiles, and Anthony took her hand—actually took her hand in his, as though they were married!—and drew her back.

She might be ashamed of her misjudgement of him, but he had, after all, misjudged her first, and badly. Anger came bubbling up through the regret, and made her stand tall.

"Let go of me!"

He regarded her with troubled eyes.

"Come," he said. "Lady Sophia says there is a small drawing room we can talk in."

"You involved *her*?"

"Through Henry." He caught her look of fury and dismay and shrugged. "Don't worry—he's a member of that damn club of yours, too."

The room was elegant; a small room for writing and reading in, with a secretaire and bookcases either side of the fireplace.

Adeline faced him down. Going on the offensive was the only way to keep her dignity.

"I'm glad to see you suffered no lasting injury, Lord Merryam."

His mouth firmed in anger, and then he shook his head. "I'm not here to discuss that."

"Then what?"

He hesitated, and took a step towards her. "I acknowledge that I was wrong. That you are, indeed, safe on the streets of Soho."

That took the wind out of her sails. She should definitely explain *why* she wasn't in danger…but as she opened her mouth to speak, he stepped forward, took her by the shoulders, and kissed her.

Hands, mouth, his firm chest under her fingers…his lips were hotter than she'd thought possible, moving on hers. Vaguely, she thought *How dare he*, but all thought vanished as his arm came around her, pulling her closer, until she could feel the length of his body against hers. One hand cradled her head as he kissed her again, and again; his tongue – good Lord, his *tongue!* – touched her lips and teased its way inside.

He tasted of wine and coffee, of maleness and, and, impropriety. Her body was on fire; it ached, and something writhed inside her that needed to be closer to him. She kissed him back with all her passion, surprise at her own desire swamping her as strongly as the need itself.

She wanted *more*. His neck under her hand was tense, the skin hot and smooth.

"Adeline!" he gasped, pulling back.

Dumbly, she stared up at him. Her mind had stopped working.

"Adeline," he said again, more softly. He stroked her hair back from her forehead. "My dear, this is what I came tonight to say—if you must slake your desires like this, do so with me. I can arrange a house–"

Words like an ice bath. She hauled her arm back and slapped him full across his damnable mouth.

"I'd rather join a *brothel*," she hissed, and turned to the door. A moment, there, to make sure she was respectable, and then she walked out, head high, cool as a cucumber.

ANTHONY WAITED. He *had* to. A gentleman's unmentionables were a damned sight too tight and revealing—perhaps that's why Petersham was always parading around in his bloody trousers.

A few moments forcing himself to think about Beau Petersham and his ridiculous clothes was enough to cool his blood; but not his exasperation with both himself and Adeline.

What did the woman *want*, for God's sake? Those kisses—Lord, those kisses! He shook himself. Not the right time to remember the feel of her in his arms. Better to remember the roundhouse she'd given him.

He felt his jaw. Her slap had hit right where one of her heavies had punched him yesterday. Her face had been completely outraged. Had she been expecting a *marriage* proposal?

That set him back for a moment. *Could* she have expected that?

Well, why not? No one knew about her visits to the Soho Club; or, at least, no one who was in a position to reveal her. There was no obvious reason they couldn't be married.

But *he* knew.

He was prepared to bed her, despite it all. Was he prepared to *marry* her?

A part of him revolted at the idea of the mother of his children being a...a stale. And yet, and yet...the idea of having her by him, every day, every *night*...

But she had been so outraged. Was it possible that he had been mistaken about her?

A leaden weight landed in his stomach. He'd been in no state to hear what her heavies had said to her, but he knew what they'd said to him. "Get orf Miss!" *Miss.* Hardly what one called a—a lady of doubtful virtue.

Was it?

Henry's amused reassurances. Adeline's own character; seemingly so open, so fresh. Even Mrs Skarsgard, laughing behind her hand, "What her desires centre around may surprise you." Had he completely misunderstood that?

If he had, she would never want to speak to him again. He might never see her again, except at a polite distance at Almack's. He steadied himself with a hand on the high back of an armchair, and realised something. Even if she *were* the stale he'd thought her, he would still marry her. This yearning was unlike anything he'd ever felt. Irrational, all-encompassing, *insane.*

He *still* didn't know what the truth was. Did that matter? Was this feeling that he'd damn the world for her—was this love? He was very much afraid that it was.

CHAPTER 14

$\mathcal{M}$eg Deveny looked at the letter again, and laughed. The first time she'd laughed since John's death. It made her feel a little hollow inside. At least this letter gave her something other than grief to think about.

Phoebe, Lady Merryam, wanted to know what Adeline got up to at the Soho Club.

Meg would never tell Adeline's relations, but Lady Merryam was another matter. Meg would trust her to take a secret to the grave. Lady Merryam was Little Foxbury's chief secret keeper, her blithe manner concealing a shrewd and compassionate nature.

If she were matchmaking…how lovely it would be, to have Adeline living as her neighbour! Yes, it was definitely a good idea to tell Lady Merryam the truth.

She looked out the window at bare oak branches under grey February skies, to collect her thoughts. London seemed so far away; her evenings in Adeline's company like a dream.

. . .

My dear Lady Merryam,

I can assure you that Miss Edmonds' visits to the Soho Club are quite respectable...

An invitation to dinner with Lord Pindar and his sister.

Adeline let out a heavy breath. She couldn't say no, but she would have preferred to stay at home and…and do what? Cry? Rage around the room trying to find the right insults for Anthony Merryam? Nonsense!

At least she'd have the relief of an evening without *him* anywhere in sight. Without having to remember how warmly he had held her.

So here she was, in her best winter cloak, trudging carefully up the icy steps of the Pindar house in Grosvenor Square. Not even any need for a chaperone; Lady Penelope was all that could be required.

The house was warm and rich with the smell of roasting meat. Lady Penelope rushed forward as the butler announced her to give her a hug. Adeline clung for a moment; it had been so long since she'd had any real affection shown her. She put aside the memory of that kiss…that wasn't *affection*.

"Come in, come in, my dear, how brave of you to venture out in this weather! Come and have a glass of egg-nog."

They sat on an old-fashioned settee near the fire, and the butler poured her egg-nog. It was delicious, full of cinnamon and sugar, with the bite of brandy underneath.

Lord Pindar was enthroned in what was clearly his customary chair, smiling genially. He really was much nicer than her own grandfather had been.

"Well now, I daresay you're wondering why I've brought you out on this beast of a night?"

She *hadn't* wondered, in fact. Why should she?

"No, sir. I was just pleased to have the opportunity to see you both."

"Lovely manners," Penelope said. "Just lovely."

Lord Pindar's mouth twitched and they met each other's eyes with suppressed humour.

"Even so," he agreed with his sister. "But there was another reason. I've been thinking about your charity school."

Adeline sat up, instantly alert. "Yes, sir?"

"I'm too old to start something like that. You want a young benefactor, someone who'll see it through until it's well established and bringing in regular donations. A patron."

She blinked. It had never occurred to her to ask anyone *else* for the money, not when she had so much herself. Besides, who would give it to her?

"So I've asked a young fellow here tonight to have dinner with us. He's got his fingers in half the charitable works in the city, and more in his home county. Very strong on the Poor Employment Act. Well, you wouldn't know about that, but take my word for it–"

The bell interrupted him.

"Ah, this'll be him now." Adeline waited with held breath. This could be the answer – a shame she wouldn't be able to organise it all herself, but it was the children who mattered. If she could find someone to do it *for* her, she'd be grateful indeed.

This young man sounded like a paragon. Not the kind of person she'd have danced with at Almack's. Not like Anthony, whose charity was outdone by his, his *stupidity*.

She turned to the drawing room door with a small smile on her lips, as decisive footsteps came up the stairs. Her heart beat faster. Someone to *help*, at last!

The butler entered, and announced the guest. "Lord Merryam, my lord."

Time stopped. Her heart froze, gave a huge single beat, and then raced madly.

"Anthony!" Lord Pindar said. "Come in, come in, my boy."

Tony was looking at her as if he hadn't heard anything. Pole-axed, just as she was.

"Anthony!" Lady Penelope bustled forwards and kissed his cheek. "How nice to see you again. It was *such* a good idea of your mother's, to bring us all together tonight."

He shook himself out of his daze and came forward to shake Pindar's hand. "How are you, sir?"

"Not so bad, not so bad. Now, I think you've met Miss Edmonds?"

She rose and dropped a curtsey. "Yes, indeed we have met, my lord."

He bowed, but his eyes never left her face. She couldn't read his expression at all, and that put her on her guard.

"Sit down, Anthony," Penelope said. He sat on a sofa next to Pindar's chair, and Penelope sat next to him, chatting happily about the dinner to come.

"Enough of that, Pen!" Lord Pindar ordered. "Time to come to business."

"Ah, yes," Penelope said. Her air of flightiness fell away as if she'd put off a shawl, and she picked up a notebook. "I've been doing some figures. We will need a considerable endowment to begin."

"Begin what?" Tony asked. Pindar looked at Adeline, and gestured encouragingly.

"A free school. In Soho."

She willed him to say nothing of their meetings there. The Pindars might be charitably inclined, but they would never countenance her being directly involved.

He seemed to understand, because he turned to Lord

Pindar. "Are you thinking it might be part of the orphanage, sir?"

"Hah! I'd forgotten you were planning that. That might do very well."

She had almost forgotten how badly she'd misjudged him. She burned again with shame at the things she'd said to him; the assumptions she'd made. But his offer to her had been real, and reprehensible.

She should have explained weeks ago. A few words would have cleared all this up. She had been so worried about being thought *odd* by Society, about her activities being curtailed by her aunt, that she had allowed him to go for weeks in suspicion of her. And the longer it had gone on...yes, she could see how all the pieces would have fitted together in his mind.

She didn't like being fair to him, not when her heart beat so hard and fast at the sound of his voice, but it *was* only fair. But how could she have known she could trust him? Even a whisper of her activities would have been disastrous. Knowing she *should* have told him the truth, and wanting to have done so, were two different things, it seemed. She was more stubborn than she'd realised.

She had to speak. "It would be better to have the school separate. The local children won't go into an orphanage in case they're kept there. But the orphanage children could go to the school."

Tony nodded. There was nothing heated about his tone or his face now. His tone was dispassionate. She had given him a disgust of her which was adamantine, and she could not blame him for it. "Yes, and that would give us more accommodation space for the orphans—we've already received more applications than we can handle. What would we require as an initial investment, Lady Penelope?"

Lady Penelope, it transpired, had a turn for figures, and

kept her brother's complex accounts. Another instance of the surface being an illusion—or, at least, not sufficient to understand the person beneath.

She had prejudged both of them; and she realised, listening to them talk about endowments and bursaries, that they had done far more than she in alleviating the lot of the poor. Adeline felt a long blush begin in her abdomen.

"Once we get the Poor Employment Act through, there'll be much less hardship," Penelope said.

"But only for those who can work," Adeline said timidly. "Is that not so?"

"It's true," Anthony acknowledged, finally meeting her eyes again, "But getting work for many will mean the measures which are in place for the truly needy won't be overrun. There will be more for everyone."

Over dinner, they continued their plans, and Adeline lost her timidity—she had thought long and hard about what was needed at the school, and this was her chance. The more she talked, the more thoughtful Tony became; she couldn't tell if he were repulsed by her unwomanliness or merely considering how to implement her schemes.

Well, it didn't matter. The children were far more important than her feelings.

"I'm afraid we may have to start in a small way," Tony said as the dessert was brought in. "I have most of my funds committed to the orphanage."

Lady Penelope looked archly at him.

"You two should marry," she said. "Then darling Adeline's inheritance could pay for the school."

The two of them froze. "Penelope!" Lord Pindar chided, and they managed to laugh.

"It would be better, my dear, than handing out currant buns from the back of the Soho Club," Penelope added. So they had known all along. She shouldn't be surprised. Lord Pindar had a reputation for knowing everything.

She couldn't help a quick glance at Anthony. His face was granite, suddenly, but there was a wounded look in his eyes. Good. He *should* feel bad for misjudging her. Drat him. Just because he shared her vision for the poor, that didn't mean he'd had the right to criticise her, let alone offer her a *carte blanche*.

"Well, we've sorted out the main things," Penelope said with satisfaction. "I'll tell our man of business to put it all in hand."

The school was going to happen. Without her, yes, but it was going to be a reality. She felt hollow inside; as though the need to make the school happen had been all that was keeping her upright. She should feel happy. No doubt she would, once it had all sunk in.

The elderly siblings kept early hours when at home, so she had ordered her coach for nine, and the butler announced its arrival right on time.

"May I see you home, Miss Edmonds?" Tony asked. He was *bound* to ask, in the circumstances, but there was something in his voice…

"Thank you, Lord Merryam."

In the darkness of the coach, with the sidelight the only illumination, Tony caught only flashes of her face. Her hands, clasped tightly on the top of her reticule. Her shoulder. The sapphires in her ears gleaming.

He had to break this awkward silence.

"This was what you were doing in the Soho Club?" He had misjudged her with spectacular stupidity. Shame had been eating at him all through that dinner; how could she ever forgive him for the things he had suggested? The way he had *touched* her!

When he'd realised the truth, he'd almost vomited. And he'd have a strong word with Mama when he got home; she'd clearly known the truth and not told him. Otherwise she wouldn't have organised this dinner with the Pindars.

Adeline cleared her throat. Nervous? "I was operating a kind of…a kind of food service from the stables. The local children got currant buns every day, and the new mothers were given bags of food and cloth. I—I've had some success in reducing the deaths of mothers and babies by proper feeding. In…at home, in Derbyshire."

No wonder she was safe in Soho—she'd helped the people there in far more practical ways than he had.

"And when you came to London–" He was beginning to understand.

She turned to him suddenly. "Oh, Tony, I'd never seen so much poverty! The *children*…" A shudder ran through her. "I *had* to do something! I couldn't just go to balls and enjoy myself when they were suffering so."

He took her hands in his. "No. Nor I. I had to do something too. That's why I started the orphanage project. And, of course, supported the Poor Employment Act, which will do more than either you or I can."

"Yes," she said. She seemed almost unaware he was holding her hands. Almost dazed. "I've never thought much of politics; so often it's just the rich making themselves richer. But you're right—it can make the changes we need."

Enough of politics and the poor. They were important, but not more important than her face, turned up to his. He kissed her hands, one by one. His blood was running hot; the softness of her skin, the scent of roses on her fingers… The memory of her kisses overwhelmed him.

"We could do much more if we pooled our resources."

She laughed. "Tony, are you actually asking me to marry you so I can continue my charitable work?"

His finger traced the soft contours of her mouth, and she shivered. "If that's what it takes to get you to say yes." He paused. He had to get this right. He had to get this *perfect*. "I wanted to marry you when I knew nothing about you except how beautiful and intelligent you are. I wanted to marry you after that, even when I thought you were…not respectable. I couldn't help it. I was in love with you. But now I know your generous heart, Miss Adeline Edmonds, and it's as big as the ocean. How can I not love you even more?"

He loved her; but did that make any difference? Her whole body thrilled to the thought, but was it enough, to give up all her plans for her inheritance? So he was charitable—but the most charitable of men had the habit of treating their wife's money as their own, and the law backed them to the hilt. To marry was to give up hope that she could order her own life. And the school would happen, no matter what she said. She was free of that pressure.

The carriage drew to a halt, and the light of one of the new gas-lanterns fell on his face. He was so earnest, so solemn. She wanted to cry, and she didn't understand why.

"My lawyer can draw up the marriage settlements so that your inheritance is fully within your control."

She gasped. She couldn't stop it; it was as though she had been kicked in the stomach, as he had been. She'd never *heard* of such a thing! For a man to give up so much power…it was a different world, if that could be true.

"Is that *possible?*"

"I daresay it may be."

His voice was amused, and that was infuriating. She slapped him on the arm.

"Don't talk to me as though I'm a child! All my life I've been told I will lose control of my inheritance when I marry, so be sure to marry someone worthy. *All my life.*"

"Yes. I see. I didn't understand that. No doubt they wanted to warn you off fortune hunters. But I'm sure it's possible. Ned Faulkes, the Earl of Hindmouth, did so with his wife's money, so I know it can be done."

The footman, with immense tact, lowered the steps but then walked away. Cold air curled around them. Tony leant forward until his head touched hers, their mouths only inches apart, the cloud of their breath enveloping them like a mask.

Her heart raced, and warmth exploded through her, as though a dam had burst. She shivered with delicious excitement.

"I am sorry that I didn't look beneath that act you put on to see your true quality," he whispered. "I am sorry that I misjudged you. But I do love you so very much, Adeline. And I promise, your money shall remain your own."

Tears pricked her eyes. "No need," she whispered. "I trust you."

He moved forward, just a little, and his mouth hovered next to hers. Waiting for her. Smiling, she tilted her head, and their lips met.

His mouth was hot, his lips soft, but the body he pressed to hers was hard…she clung to him, moving closer, pressing against him, kissing him wildly. After a good while, the footman cleared his throat.

"Oh dear! The poor man must be frozen. We're coming, Jenkins."

"I see what my life is going to be like," Tony teased her as he handed her down the steps. "The servants' needs put above my own, barely a pillow to rest my head upon that you haven't given away."

She smiled sunnily up at him. "Yes. Isn't it *wonderful*!"

The Dowager Countess of Merryam stood in the hall of Merryam Hall with her son, his new fiancée and her parents, greeting their guests for a ball celebrating the betrothal.

She smiled encouragingly at Adeline. Really, she hadn't thought Tony had this much sense. The girl had perfect manners, was beautiful, and apparently was as hip-deep in charitable works as her son.

An excellent addition to Little Foxbury. She'd been instantly approved by the Ladies of the district; even Lady Yarbury had found nothing to criticise. More importantly, she was someone Phoebe could live with quite easily.

Their friends arrived, full of smiles and congratulations: the Devenys, minus Meg who was still in strict mourning, Diana and Ned, Lord and Lady Mundford, Thomas Courtenay, the Trengrouses from Kirwich Manor, and more, including Adeline's aunt and uncle.

During a lull in the arrivals, Phoebe whispered to Adeline, "An early marriage, don't you think? Honestly, why wait to go back to Derbyshire, since your parents are already in

Little Foxbury? Then you could have the reception here at the Hall."

"Why not?" Adeline agreed. "Could we, Mama? Papa?"

"The church here is very ancient and beautiful," Phoebe put in.

Adeline's mother, a dreadfully mousy woman, smiled deprecatingly at Phoebe, God alone knew why, and her father huffed a bit, but nodded, looking a little self-satisfied. Probably realised he wouldn't have to pay for anything, if they held it here.

"We'll need a special licence," he pronounced. "I'll arrange it." He visibly swelled at the idea of his daughter marrying an earl in such a prestigious location.

"A shame we can't have the reception at the Soho Club," Phoebe whispered to Adeline, and they both dissolved into laughter.

Yes, this daughter-in-law would do very nicely.

LONG MEG AND THE WICKED BARON

ACKNOWLEDGMENTS

Many thanks to Nicola Robinson, and to Ebony Oaten, who first got me writing about my Long Meg.

CHAPTER 1

*L*ittle Foxbury shone in the morning sunshine, the cream and brown of its Tudor buildings crisp and pleasing, their diamond windows sparkling. Meg Deveny kept a firm hold on Michael's hand – he was still inclined to run across roads at unexpected times, which was fine on their estate or out in the country, but here in the county seat there were far too many carts, hackneys and coaches for it to be safe.

And noisy! Good Lord, cobblestones might make travel cleaner in the towns, but a dirt track was a lot quieter.

She pulled Michael away from a cobbler's window where Mr Davies was repairing a brown boot. The two older children stayed for a moment longer, watching the neat stitching with honest admiration.

"Toby, Violet, come along. We must get to the stationer's before it closes."

Violet responded immediately, dragging her younger brother after Meg with brutal efficiency.

"Can we really get better paints?" she asked Meg as they came up level.

Meg nodded and smiled at Lord and Lady Mundford, who were passing on the other side of the high street. Lady Mundford was a fading blonde with shrewd green eyes. She returned the nod, and the smile, but frowned a little at the gaggle of children. The Mundford children were rarely seen, let alone heard. Lord Mundford, a stately man of middle age, smiled at her with nicely-judged condescension.

"Yes, we'll get better paints. It's my birthday present to you. And some India ink so you can practice your drawing skills with a little more precision."

Violet snorted. "It's all very well to *say* I should be more precise, but *how*?"

"That was a very unladylike noise, Violet. Please don't make it in front of your mother or Papa." But Violet had a point. There was no drawing master in Little Foxbury – or, indeed, in any surrounding village – who could tutor Violet at the level she deserved.

Her talent was unmistakeable, as was her total devotion to drawing and painting. At only ten years of age, it was quite remarkable, if not always convenient; Meg had had to threaten removal of all drawing materials in order to get her to do her sums. Perhaps the new governess would have better luck, and more knowledge about drawing than Meg did.

But the new governess wasn't coming until September, when Toby went off to school for the first time.

As they went into the stationer's, a well-dressed young man came out. He held the door for them, raised his hat to Meg, and smiled at her.

She'd never met him before, so it was rather forward of him. She knew she shouldn't even acknowledge him, but the man's hazel eyes had such humour in them she couldn't bear to give him the cut direct. That smile was irresistible.

Pushing down an unladylike desire to grin back, she gave the smallest possible nod in return; depressing the pretensions of a mushroom was always hard for her.

"Who was that?" Toby asked sternly. Although only eight, he was the eldest boy, her father's heir, and he took his duties seriously.

"Never mind," Meg said. "Let's see what we can find."

They spent a lovely half hour in the stationer's, choosing watercolours, sketching pencils, India ink and a good thick sketch pad which should last Violet at least a month. It had deckled edges so the drawings could be easily mounted and framed, which sent Violet into raptures.

Even the boys enjoyed it; Toby found colouring pencils and Michael a book with drawings of guardsmen and cavalry officers which could be cut out and played with.

And Meg's own order of the first volume of Gibbon's *Decline and Fall of the Roman Empire* had arrived. She had had to order it in her father's name, as when she had last been in London, the bookseller had assured her that it was "quite unsuitable" for a young lady to read.

With any luck, it would have some information on Roman Britain – if she couldn't go to Italy, as men did, perhaps she could find some ruins more locally to visit. They had Roman ruins in Bath, didn't they? The more she understood about the Romans, the more those places would make sense to her.

She and the children walked back to the church with great satisfaction on all sides.

Her stepMama's barouche was waiting for them, with Bill

Coachman loading some bags of groceries into the luggage space underneath. Polly would have given him a list, no doubt.

"Here we are, Bill. On time, as promised."

"Up you go, Miss Meg." He pulled down the steps, she went up first, and the children scrambled in after. She would have to give Violet some lessons in how to enter a carriage gracefully … actually, that was a lesson Violet's Mama would be better placed to give – Meg herself was too tall to be really graceful, and her stepmama Elspeth was a wisp of a thing; Violet bid fair to be her twin.

The journey home in the afternoon glow was beautiful. After 1816, when the sun had hardly shone, unable to pierce the grey drifts of cloud, and a very wet summer last year, it was uplifting to see a glowing sun. And reassuring to see the crops ripen in the fields after such hardship in the countryside. The hay would be ready for harvest soon.

Halfway home, they were passed by a horseman – that same young man they had met. He had a very good seat, she couldn't help but notice, and that was a fine mare he was riding. Again, he tipped his hat to her and she nodded very slightly, but Bill was watching, and he frowned at her as the man cantered ahead of them and turned off the road.

"Now, Miss, don't you be nodding to that one. That's the Wicked Baron, that is. You'll lose your reputation in two shakes of a lamb's tail!"

"The Wicked Baron!" Michael's eyes were huge. "But he's *dead*!"

"We do *not* call Lord Ashham "the wicked baron"," Meg said sternly. "It's most uncouth." She paused. She'd better tell them, or they'd get it all wrong and then blurt it out at the worst possible time. "The person who was *called* the wicked baron was the fifth Lord Ashham. The man who just rode past must be the *sixth* Lord Ashham. The son. His father *is* dead, Michael. So we should be sorry for him."

"If *my* father was the Wicked Baron," Violet declared, "I'd be happy he was dead!"

Toby shook his head at her. "That's a very bad thing to say, Violet. You should never be happy that someone is dead."

The word sent a blade of sorrow through her; every so often she would be reminded that John was dead, and grief would hit her. They had been affianced almost their whole lives—*John's* whole life. He had been ill of a canker for years of that life. He had died almost seventeen months ago, holding her hand, and she was still in mourning for him, still in her blacks.

While she had been distracted, Toby and Violet had started a long argument about death and whether you could be glad that really evil people were gone from the world because then they wouldn't hurt anyone else. It lasted all the way home, so Meg leaned back on the squabs and watched the flat green fields go past, the malt houses, the sheep grazing … she did so love the high skies and distances of Norfolk.

But there was a niggle in the back of her mind; how hard it must be for this new baron, burdened with his father's reputation, which could hardly be worse. There hadn't been a family in Norfolk which had received the old baron when he was alive, and for good reason. Meg herself, since she was a young woman, had not been made privy to the full details, but words like

"orgy" and "debauched" and "blatant immorality" had been whispered.

Certainly it was true that his wife had abandoned him and gone to live in Bath, taking her son with her – and, although such an act would normally have attracted blame and disapproval, the county had united in saying, "She had no choice."

Poor little boy.

Of course, this new baron might be his father's spit and image, so she would reserve her pity until she knew more— no matter how appealing his smile was. A rake would *need* an appealing smile, after all.

The image of a tall vision with startling blue eyes accompanied Nick de Courtenay all the way home.

The barouche had had the Deveny family crest on it—although a mere Sir, rather than a Lord, Deveny was a baronet, so he was entitled to the crest.

Nick's mother had taken Nick away from the district when he was nine, but she'd made sure he knew all about his neighbours. Once he went to Italy, she had written often, and just as often included "news" about Little Foxbury and its inhabitants. No doubt she had various correspondents in the area, because she was determined he should stay up to date. "For the future," she had said, over and over again. And now the future was here, and she was dead.

He wrenched his thoughts away from that grief. Best to think about the here and now …

The girl must be the eldest, Margaret. And the others, her step-brothers and sister.

What a face! Strong bones, astonishing eyes…he longed

to paint it, but the chance of that! Hah. No young lady would allow him anywhere near her.

For the first time, he regretted that his father's behaviour had made him *persona non grata* to the county. Up until now it had been convenient. No boring dinner parties, no Assemblies, no matchmaking mamas. He had always known he would be shunned. He'd been planning on spending most of his time in London, where his rank and money would make him acceptable, even with a rake and dastard as a father.

His mother had wanted him to marry, and recommended London for his search for a bride. *What kind of husband and father could I make?* he thought darkly. He'd had no example he'd be prepared to follow, that was certain. The very idea made him nervous.

He turned into the stableyard of Foxchester Hall, dismounted, and threw the reins to his stableboy.

The light would be good for a few hours more. He could get a session in, sketching that ripening barley field, with the river beyond. No more than sketching and watercolours – he had used so much cerulean blue and flake white trying to paint the changing skies of Norfolk that he had to wait until replacements arrived from Rowney's in London.

"M'lord!" His reeve, Moffat. Nick forced his face into a smile, although the urge to ignore the man and just run made him shift his feet.

"M'lord, about that tenant farmer …" And he was plunged back into the business of the estate, which took up a damnably large amount of his time. *Merda!*

"Yes, Moffat," he said wearily, giving his parcel of brushes to the stableboy, who would dutifully pass it to the scullery maid, who would give it to the chamber maid, who would give it to the valet, who would place it, not in his studio, where he needed it, but in his bedchamber, on the table by his bed.

Oh, for his simple lodgings in Firenze, where no one looked after him!

He followed Moffat back to the library, where he was conducting business while his father's office was being refurbished. It hadn't been used as an office for some time – in fact, according to Moffat, his father had refused to either listen to business matters or expend any cash on the estate.

Which was why, although he himself was now notionally a rich man, any monies which came in went straight back out again, mostly, it seemed, on drainage, ditches and stone fences. And on something called mangelwurzles.

Part of his substantial education, planned by his mother, had been the care and nurturing of an estate. He knew what he should do, so he did it. He knew his duty to his shamefully neglected tenants, and he did it. He poured out every penny he had, and he begrudged not a farthing.

But his *time*. Oh, he begrudged spending that on these tiresome affairs. When the high Norfolk sky, the broads, the wide barley fields and, above all, the elusive, beckoning light were calling to be caught on canvas … he sighed and sat behind his desk and waved Moffat to the other chair.

"So then, about this tenant…"

TWO HOURS later he had a chance to grab his watercolour box and set off to catch the last of the light. The days were lengthening, but it was still a long way off Midsummer's Eve.

The light lay over the fields like a blessing, far beyond his competence to catch. But he could try.

He sat beneath a tree and brought out his sketch book, but put his pencils aside to grab his paint box. There was no time to lose; the light changed with the moment.

Moment by moment, he raced the lowering sun. Madder lake on the bottom of the clouds, gamboge and Oxford ochre along the edges where the last rays struck, a hint of cinnabar, then azurite deepening to lapis behind … he laid the strokes in delicately but quickly. It was the most exhilarating of pursuits—far more exciting than fox hunting. Finally, as the sun hid behind carmine hills on the horizon, he sighed and put down his brush, massaging his hand.

The picture wasn't *terrible*—his eye was used to the sharper, warmer light of Italy, and he had some way to go before he became attuned to this more subtle sky. But this was good enough as a study for an oil painting, once his paints arrived.

Nick packed up and turned towards home. A rustling in some bushes nearby startled him and he stopped, his first thought, *Banditti?* Then he laughed at himself. Bandits in an English countryside?

Highwaymen, or footpads, perhaps, but he was a long way off any road. Probably just a rabbit or fox.

He whistled a Rossini aria as he strode homewards. It was more than the Italian light he missed; opera and ballet and even that astonishing Florentine game of football. It was certainly quieter in the country.

The face of the Deveny girl flashed across his mind. So clear, he stopped, propped his sketchbook against the stile, and did a quick sketch. He looked at it, astonished. That was definitely the best portrait sketch he'd ever done. He was a landscape man.

But there was something about that face … no milk-and-water miss, Margaret Deveny was a woman; her face in the sketch full of life and laughter. Something tugged at him. Call it a muse. Dangerous to call it anything else, when that road was definitely barred to him.

Besides, he and the estate had a long way to go before he could afford a wife.

'Pshaw!' he said aloud. One sketch, and he was building castles in the air. He didn't *want* to get married.

He began to climb over the stile, but there was a piece of paper on the step on the other side and he picked it up before getting down.

A note. The light was dimming, but he could still read it.

I think you are a good painter.

Your sekrit admirrer

It was finished with a small flower – a four-petalled rose, perhaps? Or a violet?

He smiled. A child's writing. One of his tenants' children. Well, that was a nice compliment, and probably explained the rustling in the bushes. As he headed home, his heart was lighter than it had been in weeks. Perhaps he was making a place for himself here after all.

CHAPTER 3

"Now, Mr Chiltstone," Meg said.

She smiled at the not-quite-young, not-quite-well-dressed man. Her stepMama was supposed to conduct this interview, but Elspeth, bless her, had a shy and retiring disposition, and found talking to strangers quite a chore, so Meg had volunteered to help.

"We are looking for a drawing master for my young sister, Violet." She opened the folder which lay on the small table between them and spread some of Violet's sketches and watercolours in front of him. He sat up straighter and leaned forward.

"She is how old?" His voice, high and precise, held a note of disbelief. Did the foolish man think they would pass someone else's work off as Violet's? What possible good would that do?

"Ten," Elspeth ventured. "I have taught her myself so far, but I have reached the limit of my knowledge."

He nodded, leafing through the sketches. "The young lady certainly has talent," he acknowledged. "I would be delighted to take her as a pupil."

Meg relaxed. Mr Chiltstone was the drawing master for a number of highly born young women in the next parish, and she had been uncertain if he'd be willing to travel this far.

The door burst open and Violet ran in; her apron, as usual, stained with India ink.

"Mama!" She skidded to a stop when she saw Mr Chiltstone, and gave a hurried curtsey. "I beg your pardon, Mama, but I had to make sure that you were asking Mr … Mr …"

"Mr Chiltstone, Violet," Elspeth said, gently chiding, as she drew Violet to her and arranged her collar to lie flat.

"I just wanted to make sure that Mr Chiltstone could teach me oil painting!"

Violet fixed earnest eyes on their visitor, who had sat up in astonishment.

"Oil painting! A young lady! My dear Lady Deveny, I am sure you do not want me to do that!"

"Do I not?" Elspeth's brow furrowed.

"Why not?" Meg asked. She eyed him coolly.

"It's most unsuitable! The materials, the smell, the – the – the *physical* nature of the work! Oh, no, Lady Deveny, I cannot recommend it. I will not do it!"

"But I *have* to learn oils!" Violet's eyes filled with tears. "I can't be a proper painter will just *watercolours*." Her tone was so full of disgust, as though watercolours were slime and mud, that Meg had to bite back a smile.

"My dear young lady," Mr Chiltstone said, "there is no point in equipping you for a life you will be unable to lead. Ladies do not become "proper painters". It is impossible. Drawing and watercolour, yes, naturally, a lovely accomplishment for a lady of quality. But oils … you do not know what you are asking, but I am sure your Mama is far too sensible of her duty to allow you such an – an exploit!"

"Are you?" Meg said. "So sure of my step-mama's mind. I see." Elspeth put a hand on her arm, which stopped her saying something she might regret. This was the same attitude which had stopped her buying Gibbon; the same which had prevented her aunt and uncle taking her to the Museum of Natural History to see the Roman Gallery last year.

"Thank you, Mr Chiltstone. I believe we must trouble you no longer," Elspeth said.

He looked startled.

Meg rang the bell, and the butler appeared. "Veitch, show Mr Chiltstone out, please."

The man went out in high dudgeon. He was probably a gossip and would try to ruin Violet's reputation in retaliation, but bedamned to him!

"You should not run into a room so violently, my dearest," Elspeth said, drawing Violet to sit next to her on the sofa.

"But Mama, I *must* learn how to paint in oils. I was afraid you'd forget."

"Forget what?" Her father's voice came from the door. He came in, holding the baby of the family, Euphemia, a cherub of nineteen months, who was pulling on her father's side-whiskers and gurgling. Elspeth held up her arms and Euphemia launched herself into them for a cuddle.

"Oil painting, Papa!" Violet looked at him reproachfully. "That man said I couldn't learn."

"Why not?"

"Mr Chiltstone appeared to think it, er, unladylike." Elspeth put her arms up to take the little girl, clucking and cooing over it in a way which caught at Meg's heart.

"Nonsense!" Papa said. "Who is that upstart to tell me what a daughter of mine should or shouldn't do?"

"Oh, *thank you*, Papa!"

"The trouble is," Meg said, "we may not be able to find someone who *can* teach you. If you hadn't come crashing in here, we might have been able to persuade Mr Chiltstone to at least try it."

"Oh. Sorry." Violet didn't look at all sorry.

How wonderful it must be to want something so desperately! To know who you were meant to be, and strive for it daily. Even her own interest in the past was merely a *hobby*. Nothing could ever come of it. Abruptly, Meg got up and went to the door, saying over her shoulder, "I just have to pin up this hem."

She ran up the stairs to her bedroom and closed the door behind her, leaning back on it as tears filled her eyes.

It wasn't just John she was crying for: it was everything, the life she had planned and waited for since she was no older than Violet. She would have been Mrs Poulteney, mistress of Cursten House, mother to John's children, stalwart of the parish. Travelling to London for the Season, caring for the people on John's estate. A busy, productive, happy life.

Now, it seemed entirely too possible that she would dwindle into an old maid, looking after her father, living as Elspeth's companion when he died. Becoming an aunt. Stuck in this village for the rest of her life.

She loved Little Foxbury, and yet… There had to be something more, but she didn't know what. She was so tall and scrawny that she never received more than the most common politenesses from men. She was a bluestocking, too, which made it worse. A Long Meg with blue stockings, spending her free time reading about ancient cities and long-abandoned ruins. Hopeless. The memory of Elspeth cooing to her baby pierced her heart.

A sob wracked her. She pushed a closed fist against her chest, under her bosom, as if to keep the misery in, but it escaped her and she sank to the floor, crying bitterly.

Oh, to be like Violet, with a great passion and no remorse about following it!

CHAPTER 4

There was rustling in the bushes again. Nick bit back a smile and kept painting. Watercolours, of course, since he was outdoors. How he wished there was some way to bring oil paints into the fields! He'd tried, but the small pig bladders in which the paints kept fresh dried out too quickly once taken from their air-tight containers.

One day he must give that some more thought. But for now, he'd finished his sketch of the ruined abbey, and behind it, the Hindmouth Maltings, their long low roofs red against a greying sky. Back to the studio to work it up into an oil sketch.

As he climbed the stile, there was another note, this time scrawled in charcoal.

The rooffs were redder. But it's still a good painting.
Your sekrit admirrer

He laughed out loud, and spoke to the copse a few yards away. 'It's true the roofs were redder. But it's quite hard to get a full red in watercolour, and this is just a sketch, so that I can get the proportions and composition right in the oil painting.'

A scuffle and a small voice hissed, "See? I *told* you I need oils!"

"All *right*!" another voice said, not so quietly.

Chuckling, Nick tucked the note away and climbed the stile. "You should show me some of your drawings," he said to the copse. "We can compare techniques."

The encounter cheered him greatly, although he wasn't sure why. He walked home jauntily, and almost didn't mind when Moffat pounced on him to sign some lease documents.

THE NEXT DAY, he had Johnson, the footman, take his big easel out to the copse. There was an oak sapling there, alive with the brightness of spring leaves, before a background of dark green holly. It would make a good study – he planned to sketch directly onto the canvas, and then complete the painting in oils in the studio.

After he'd set up his canvas, he went down to the nearby stream to get a cup of water – just in case he decided to make colour notes in his sketchbook.

When he got back, there was a sketch propped up on his canvas. Hindmouth Maltings, from almost the same position as he had used yesterday. But a lower view. A child's view, but surely this wasn't a child's sketch? It was rough, yes, but it had a sureness of line…

"This is very good," he said. "Your perspective isn't quite right: you've overemphasised the foreground and not given us a sense of the ground continuing on behind the buildings, but overall, it's a good sketch."

The rustling in the copse intensified, and then stopped.

Had he insulted the young artist? A movement down the field caught his eye—a young girl, running full tilt towards the Deveny lands, which marched with his own.

A girl? *Dio mio*, she must be one of the Deveny crop. The

beautiful one's stepsister. Her hair flew behind her as she leapt up onto the stile at the bottom of the field and scrambled down. Had he insulted her so badly? But she didn't look insulted. She ran around the barley in the lower field as though she were happy.

Foreboding hit him. There was no chance at *all* that Hugo Deveny would allow the Wicked Baron's son to discuss art with his daughter. Not a chance in hell.

That *bambina* was heading for disappointment, he feared.

"ABSOLUTELY NOT," Meg said.

"But *Meg*—"

"No." With fine campaign strategy, Violet had tried to enlist her support before broaching the subject to her mother, but she was getting no support. Definitely not.

"But he is a *magnificent* painter! He took one look at my sketch and he knew *exactly* what was wrong with it! He can teach me *everything*!"

Violet's whole body vibrated with need. Meg sighed, putting Gibbon down reluctantly. His dry, precise style was proving a balm for her recent unpredictable emotions. And the trials and tribulations of Rome put her own little problems into perspective.

"Look, dearest, there are two problems. The first is that Baron de Courtenay may not wish to teach you—"

"But he *said* I should show him my sketches! And he told me where I went wrong. So he must *want* to teach me!"

"Yes…" How to explain this to her in a way which wouldn't crush her? She should never have been on de Courtenay land in the first place, but the baron had been absent in Italy so long that the local children had taken the gardens as their own to play in, and Moffat hadn't minded. "Even if he does, dearest, he probably thought you were a boy. A gentleman wouldn't have offered to teach a girl—not without getting permission first from her parents."

Violet sat on the end of the settle and pulled a face.

"That's not *fair*!"

"No," Meg agreed. "It's not. But that's the way of the world. It's no good pretending you will have the same freedoms as Toby will. You won't."

Violet's face was a mixture of anger and sadness. "I'll *never* be able to paint!"

"Never say never, Vi."

Violet never let go of anything.

"You said there were two problems."

Meg hesitated. Violet was old enough to know, surely? "The baron does not have a … a gentleman's reputation. So even if he wished to instruct you, Papa would never allow it."

"But he's *nice*!"

Was he? Violet had a shrewd eye for an upstart, but she was only ten. Meg doubted she could spot a rake.

"His father—"

"His father is dead! He's *different*! It's not fair if people judge him by his father!"

That was true. That was certainly true. However …

"He has spent the last ten years in Italy, making no attempt to come home when Napoleon's defeat allowed him to. And his manner of life there …" How to tell Violet about the lives artists led, especially in *Italy*? The *affaires* with models, the drinking, the low company … she had read a life of Caravaggio only recently, and she rather wished she had not.

"Oh, pooh!"

"Violet!"

"You are all being mean to him for no reason at all! He's *lovely*!" She ran from the room, her footsteps clattering down the hall. Meg sighed. It did seem hard to condemn a man sight unseen, but what could *she* do about it?

Restlessly, she set *The Decline and Fall* back on the bookshelf and decided to walk over to the Merryam's, to see Adeline.

Unburdening herself to a friend would do her good.

CHAPTER 5

After a morning spent with Moffat, Nick made himself scarce, taking just a sketchbook and some charcoal in a snuff box.

He headed for the Maltings again but was soon conscious of being followed. By not one, but two little blond heads. He grinned to himself and picked up the pace. Stalk the Baron was apparently a game more than one child played. He'd done it himself as a child, although his target had been Anthony Merryam's father, who so inexplicably (it seemed to him then) had stopped coming to call and no longer invited his father to the hunt.

Looking back, Nick realised that being cut by Merryam had stranded his father with only his own company, and he'd never been able to stomach that. His less reputable friends had begun to visit—and, after a particularly rowdy party, Mama had packed them both up and set off for Bath.

Quite a reputation to live down—and did he want to? He'd promised his Mama to marry an English girl, when he finally married, but he didn't have to do that *here*. The Dowager Lady Merryam, though, had been his mother's faithful correspondent, and had written him a letter of condolence on her death. The only one he had received from Little Foxbury, although there had been many from his mother's acquaintance in Bath.

He would like to visit her, but he had left his card and had heard nothing from them… shrugging, he cut through a stand of hazel which Moffat had earmarked for coppicing—it had been left too long, but they had hopes of bringing it back to usefulness. Rustling behind him made him smile again.

Stopping in a clearing, he turned to face in their direction. "You might as well come out. I can hear you."

Sure enough, the girl he had glimpsed the other day slipped out from behind a hazel trunk, and was followed by a boy a year or two younger. The girl was a little thing, and both she and her brother had the same extraordinary blue eyes as Margaret Deveny.

"Deveny brats, eh?" he said, mock threatening, then straightened and held his hand out as they flinched back. "No, no, it's all right. No need to be scared of me."

A third head peeped around the willow; a much younger boy, no more than four or five.

"You're wicked!"

"Shh, Michael!" the girl said.

He laughed. "That's my father you're thinking of. He was the Wicked Baron. I'm the Good Baron."

"Oh."

The boy came out and joined hands with his brother and sister.

"You've been following me for days. Surely I'm not that interesting?"

'You're the most interesting person we've ever *seen*!' the girl said.

"You appear to know who I am—what are your names?"

"Violet, Toby, and Michael," the older boy—Toby—said.

Children always introduced themselves in order of age, he'd noticed that many times. The inescapable hierarchy.

"Well, Violet, Toby, and Michael, what can I do for you?" He bit his lip as soon as he said it, because he knew what she'd answer.

"You can teach me!" Violet blushed red and twisted her hand in her apron, but stood tall. "I *need* to learn."

Oh, how he remembered that feeling! That *yearning*. His father had refused to pay for drawing lessons. "Namby-pamby nonsense!" he'd called it. Only fit for women. He remembered the despair. And, later, the joy when Mama had found him a teacher in Bath.

There were some rocks nearby. He gestured to the children to sit on them, and took a seat himself.

"Miss Violet, I'd be happy to teach you—" She started forward in excitement, but he put up a restraining hand. "*If* you can get your parents to agree. And I'm very much afraid that they will not."

Violet jumped up, grabbed his hand and dragged him off, back down through the wood and towards her home. "We'll go ask now!"

He laughed and let himself be taken. It was good to be treated like a normal human being, instead of either a master or a devil.

As they turned into the road which led to the Deveny house, Toby yelled, "Meg! Meg!" A tall girl, crossing the field in front of them, turned, and his heart leapt. It was the Amazon. Good Lord, she was beautiful! Seeing her standing there, he realised she had perfect proportions. The grace of a Botticelli. The firm mouth and clear jaw of a Michaelangelo. And those eyes!

He smiled and took off his hat. Bowed. She stood in a very dark grey muslin gown, astonished and unsure.

"You shouldn't speak to me, I know," he reassured her.

"But Miss Violet wants me to ask her father if I may teach her drawing."

She drew in a breath and he watched, raptly. Even her collarbones were lovely. A sudden determination to achieve teacherhood hit him. If he taught Violet, he could be around this bewitching creature often. Perhaps they could make sketching her a class project …

"I'm afraid Papa will not allow it."

"My terrible reputation." He grimaced. "Truly, I'm an innocent and harmless creature. As mild as a lamb."

A dimple flashed in her cheek and was gone. "Indeed? I wonder if the ladies of Italy would agree?"

He put a hand to his heart and staggered back as if struck. "You wound me, gracious lady! Such cynicism in one so young!"

She was laughing openly now. "Not so young. But seriously, Lord Ashham … my father will not allow it. It would be ruinous to Violet's reputation."

"She's a child!"

"I'm afraid your father …" She trailed off, clearly embarrassed, but he knew what she meant.

Disgustingly, his father had had a taste for young girls – some of them no more than thirteen or fourteen. It was the main reason he'd been universally hated amongst his tenants.

It had been a shock, when Moffat had warned him after he first arrived. Stomach-turning, and explaining so much about the black looks he'd received from tenant and neighbour alike. Nick had made careful enquiries, in case there were half-brothers or sisters to provide for. But there were no by-blows of his father's on the estate. He'd been careful about that, if nothing else. It revolted Nick to even think of it.

Perhaps his face gave his feelings away.

"I'm sorry," she said. "But if we are not on visiting terms, there is no chance that Papa would allow it."

"*Meg!*" Violet protested. "That's not fair. I'll ask—"

"You're not to speak of it to Papa," Miss Deveny said firmly. "Give Lord Ashham some time to reestablish himself in the parish, and then we may consider it, but you know, Violet, that once Papa has said no, he will never change his mind."

Violet apparently knew this *was* true, because she fell silent.

"Do you think I may reestablish myself?" he asked humbly. And, by God, he *felt* humble before her! The old anger against his father surged through him. The bastard was reaching out from his grave to blight his own hopes.

Her mouth opened as if to speak, and she gave a helpless shrug. He nodded his understanding.

"Now, you shouldn't waste any more of Lord Ashham's time," she said to the children. "Off with you to the kitchen and have some afternoon tea."

The boys raced away, but Violet lingered. "Did you really think my drawing was good?"

"For an adult, it was good," he said honestly. "For your age, it was remarkable. I have no doubt of your talent."

She beamed at him, rushed forward and jumped up to kiss him on the cheek, then ran after the boys.

Miss Deveny sighed. "She *is* talented, isn't she?"

"Very much so. She needs good instruction."

They fell into step together, away from the Devenys', towards Merryams'.

"The best of the local drawing masters refuses to teach her oils. He says it's not suitable for a girl."

"Oh, what a lot of damned nonsense!" He stopped in mortification. "I'm sorry. It's been rather a long time since I've been in company, and I've forgotten my manners."

But Miss Deveny was smiling at him. "I've heard worse," she said dryly. "I must leave you here. If we go any further together, we will be in sight of the road and of the Merryams' windows."

That hit home. She couldn't risk being seen with him.

He bowed his understanding, and stood watching as she went over the fields towards the Merryam house.

Madre di Dio! There had to be a way to get back in the good graces of the local gossips. He had to draw that girl. He *had* to.

Meg. Margaret. Margherita. A pearl, the name meant. A pearl indeed.

Meg entered from the terrace, through the library doors. She had been in and out of this house her whole childhood, when she and John and Anthony would race around the countryside together. Anthony was a couple of years older than John, but he had tolerated them both, and he was a good friend.

It had been wonderful when he married her best friend from school, Adeline Edmonds.

Since John's death, Adeline had been a comfort and a blessing, despite her insatiable appetite for good works.

Meg found Adeline sewing in the morning room, a yellow-papered chamber decorated with Delft plates. Addie didn't bother to get up – there was no ceremony between them. They kissed cheeks.

"Pull the bell, Meg, and we'll have tea," Adeline said, so she did so, and sat beside her friend on the sofa.

She touched the filmy white garment Addie was working on. It was fine lawn; the smocking for a baby's dress.

"Oh, Adeline!"

"No," Adeline sighed. "It's for my cousin. I have no good news. Again."

"I'm so sorry, my dear."

Tears stood in Adeline's eyes. She had been married fifteen months, and it *was* odd that she hadn't conceived. If Tony had been a different kind of man, Meg might have suspected a pox had prevented him being fruitful. But as it was…

"I'm sure there's no need for concern …" she ventured.

Adeline shrugged. "There's nothing to be done, apparently, except, well …"

Meg laughed at her. "Except keep on trying?"

Adeline slapped her hand in remonstrance.

The butler came and Addie ordered tea, "And some of that pound cake we had yesterday, thank you, Baxter."

While they waited, as if lancing a boil, Adeline deliberately began to discuss her cousin, swaddling clothes, and lyings-in. Admiring her courage, Meg joined in enthusiastically, until Adeline laughed and put her hand over her mouth. "Oh, I'm not supposed to be talking of such things to you!"

"Because I'm not married?" Meg stood and walked to the window, staring out blindly. "Another whole sphere of life I'm barred from?" If John had married her, instead of saying he didn't want to "burden" her, she might have had a child of her own by now. They might have managed it … he had had some good days. She was surprised at how bitter she felt towards him.

Addie sprang up and followed her, placing a hand on her arm.

"My dear! You will find the right man."

"I'm twenty-four next month. And even when I was a girl, I didn't *take*. I'm too tall, too scrawny, and too well-read." Something about that young man bowing to her, smiling at her, had brought back all the awkwardness she used to feel when she went into company; although at the time, she hadn't felt at all awkward.

"The right man won't care about any of that."

Easy for Adeline to say, with her big brown eyes, her womanly curves and her curly blonde head which reached only to Meg's shoulders. She sighed and went back to sit down as the butler brought in the tea tray, complete with pound cake.

"Have you seen anything of the new baron?" she asked, trying for airiness and sounding like a pigeon-brain instead.

"Oh, no! He left his card, but of course Anthony didn't return his call."

"Why not?"

"The de Courtenays and the Merryams have been at odds for decades—ever since the old baron said something quite crude about Lady Merryam to her husband. There's no possibility of Anthony establishing friendly relations."

"The sins of the father…"

"Yes…" Adeline looked troubled. "It does seem hard on the young man, but really, could any of us trust him? The stories I've heard about the old baron! I can hardly credit some of them."

"Credit them," Meg said dryly. The half-formed idea that she could promote a rehabilitation of Nicholas de Courtenay so that he could teach Violet stuttered. Her father was a high stickler. He'd never allow it.

But Adeline was a champion of good works, possessor of the most generous heart…

"It does seem hard on the young man, though," Meg suggested. "He was raised away from his father, after all. And his mother was a lady of good character."

"Oh, yes! Anthony's mother was a correspondent of her all these years. She speaks very highly of her."

"Well, there you are! For his mother's sake, I do think we should make a push to bring him back into society."

"We?" Adeline twinkled at her.

"You," Meg acknowledged. "You know I can't act in this in any way."

Adeline shuddered. "Lud, no! The gossip mills would grind fast and long." She paused, her needle poised over a stitch. "I think we should ask the vicar."

CHAPTER 6

Sunday church. Nick knew he had to go, and he'd suffered through a month of it now, but it was a bit awkward, sitting up in the front right pew with the vicar's stern eye on him, and the rest of the congregation pretending he wasn't there at all.

He was pretty sure the vicar would have liked to throw him out, but since Nick owned the living, that wasn't going to happen. In fact, the vicar was some kind of second cousin, his mother had said. So he could jolly well be polite.

Today, though, something was different. The vicar's eye was assessing rather than stern, and he got a definite half-smile from Lady Merryam, although she didn't nod.

The Devenys were there, but they'd gone to their pew before he arrived, so all he saw of the beauty was the back of her head in a black bonnet as he walked past. She'd been wearing dark colours before – was she in mourning? It was bad of him to hope it was for an intended, but he did.

The vicar preached about forgiveness and the Good Samaritan, looking meaningfully at him a couple of times, which was deuced odd. He wasn't sure what message he was supposed to take from that.

As he followed the vicar down the aisle after the concluding hymn, he managed to get a glance at Margaret Deveny. In the soft light from the stained-glass windows, she looked even more beautiful. Violet grinned at him, and he sent her a tiny smile, shielding it from her father with his hand. What could he do to reestablish himself—perhaps he could enlist his mother's cronies in Bath somehow?

At the door, the vicar smiled and shook his hand, saying, "I shall see you at luncheon, Lord Ashham."

Nick blinked and smiled. He had sent a general letter of invitation to the vicar on his arrival, saying something like, "and you will always be welcome to lunch with me after church on Sunday", but so far had seen neither hide nor hair of him.

So it was with some curiosity that he rose to welcome the Reverend Thomas Courtenay into the drawing room. The vicar was a tall man with grey eyes, only a few years older than Nick himself. He'd inherited the living from his own father, so he'd grown up here; Nick vaguely remembered him as a quiet boy who avoided the other children. Probably teased too much for being a parson's son.

"A glass of claret before lunch, Reverend?"

"Why thank you, my lord, yes, thank you." Flustered, definitely. But why? The man took the glass and smiled perfunctorily.

"I'm glad to see you, Vicar, obviously, but I can't help but wonder what brings you here ... *today?*"

A flush rose on the man's face. Nick bit back a smile. And then the vicar flashed an extraordinary grin, which changed his face entirely.

"Touché!" he said. "A fair touch." He half-lifted his glass in a toast.

"Well?"

'It's time you were rehabilitated.'

Nick gave a shout of laughter. "*I* don't need rehabilitation. I'm just fine."

"Your reputation, then."

The butler came in to announce luncheon and they went through together. Nick had ordered the table have its leaves taken out so they could sit close enough to talk—the vicar on his right hand. The cook had moral objections to cooking on Sunday, and she was the only one willing to stay there after dark, so he had to put up with it. It was a cold collation, but a fine one, with ham and roast beef, cold potatoes, mustard, a digestive salad and a gooseberry pie for dessert.

"My reputation, Vicar?" Nick prompted him around a mouthful of roast beef. English cooking was dull compared to Italian, but a good roast beef couldn't be beaten.

"For Heaven's sake, call me Thomas! We've known each other all our lives."

"So we have. All right then, Thomas—my reputation."

"Say rather, your father's reputation."

"Yes, yes, I know. The Wicked Baron. But what's to be done?"

"Lady Merryam thinks we can rehabilitate you."

"Lady *Merryam?*" He sat back in astonishment.

"Lady Merryam is a very fine person; a lady of enormous charity and good will."

That hurt, somehow. Nick covered it with another mouthful of beef. Thomas cast him a shrewd look and stayed silent

"So I'm a charity case?" Nick said at last.

"Would that be so bad? You need the parish's goodwill – or, at least, your tenants need it, and any children you may have eventually. Why not do something to earn it?"

Nick grinned. "The church roof need repairing?"

"Yes, as it happens. When doesn't it? But I was thinking of something more substantial."

The butler cut the pie and brought it from the sideboard. Nick was pretty sure he'd deigned to do this himself out of sheer curiosity. Good butlers were awake on all suits.

"Such as?"

"Lord and Lady Merryam are in the process of setting up a free village school, with the assistance of other gentry in the parish."

"So I become a benefactor?" Where would he find the money? It was a good cause, but so were the half-dozen other projects he had in hand. Draining the Lower Forty, for a start. But Meg Deveny's face flashed into his mind. Goddammit, it was ridiculous for a grown man to moon over a girl like this.

But if throwing in for this school would get him access to That Face …

His mouth twisted in a wry smile. "Do you remember that ruby ring my father always wore?"

"His signet? Yes, of course. He was never without it."

"It's about the only piece of unentailed property he left me. Given how much pain he caused this village, it's only fitting that it pay for a school."

"Are you sure?"

"I'll never wear it, Thomas. I'd sooner choke on it." He busied himself with his pie; he'd revealed enough. His hatred of his father—hatred wasn't too strong a word—was his own business.

'Well then …" Thomas tapped his fork against the table in thought, and nodded. "It's a good symbolic gesture, too. But money isn't enough. You need to be involved in the planning, then the local people can see you're nothing like the old baron."

· · ·

MONDAY MORNING SAW him in the vicarage dining room, awkwardly greeting Lord and Lady Merryam.

The lady, at least, was warm. Anthony Merryam, whom he had gone to school with (Anthony had been several years older), was stiff at first but, on receiving a *look* from his wife, had laughed and held out his hand.

"I suppose old schoolmates should be on good terms, Ashham?"

"I'd be glad to be," he responded, and found it was true. It *had* been a tad lonely, having no one of his own kind to talk with. In Italy, it hadn't mattered, but here … lunch with Thomas had reminded him of what it was like to chat with a like-minded friend. He would welcome more of that.

They shook heartily. Lord and Lady Hindmouth arrived. He'd seen them at church but not been introduced until now. They were relative newcomers to the parish, and hadn't lived here when he was a child.

"Ned, please," Lord Hindmouth said as they shook hands. "We're neighbours on your eastern side."

Lady Hindmouth smiled kindly at him and even curtsied, which was quite a piece of condescension. Her hair was a richer red than Meg Deveny's and she was beautiful, but... she didn't wake his muse in the slightest. Was that bad?

Her husband laughed. "Diana's the free-thinker among us. She'd probably love to run off to Italy to paint."

"Not to paint," his wife said.

"No—" A voice came from behind them. "Diana shares my interest in antiquities."

Margaret. She came through the door, helping the vicar's maid to bring in the tea.

She had the light behind her, giving her a halo around her rich brown hair in its strict crown of plaits. Her slender, lissome body was outlined against the light. Oh, she was lovely!

"Miss Deveny," he stammered.

She smiled at him with a natural friendliness. "Lord Ashham."

"Meg has been very interested in this project, so we brought her along to look at the plans." Was Lady Merryam's voice just a little too casual? Nick smiled at her and she positively grinned back.

A knock at the door heralded the architect, who was introduced to Nick as Andrew Grey. He seemed a nice enough chap, but he smiled at Meg Deveny too much.

Tea was served at the dining table, where the school plans were laid out.

Nick realised, when he looked at them, that inviting him to join the project really was a charitable act; planning was well advanced and they could clearly have completed it without him.

But he did have something he could offer, because the one thing they had not settled was where, exactly, it should be built.

"The old gatehouse," he said. "That would make a good schoolmaster's cottage, and we could build the school next to it."

When the toll road had come through Little Foxbury, his father had had their gate moved so his friends could drive straight off it up to the house. The old gatehouse had housed a couple of superannuated servants when he was a child; now it was empty—but it was much nearer the village than the current gate, and it was a good piece of land.

The vicar and the Merryams exchanged quick glances, and then nodded.

"That would save on lodging for the schoolmaster, certainly," Ned said.

"It would be just the thing," Lady Merryam said. "As long as …"

Nick grinned. "As long as there's a good stout fence between the school and the Wicked Baron's lands?"

His tone reassured them. "I am glad that we don't have to beat around the bush," Lady Merryam said. "We need to bring you back into Society, Lord Ashham. For the good of the parish." She gave him a speculative look. "And for the good of Violet Deveny."

"Ohoh! Now I understand."

"You can thank Meg," Anthony said. "She's determined to get that sister of hers proper instruction, and apparently you're it."

Margaret looked at him warily, but gave him a little, hesitant smile.

He wasn't sure how he felt about that. He'd like to be more interesting to her than a few drawing lessons. But this was a test—Adeline Merryam's brown eyes were assessing, and Margaret had her hands twisted together. This was important to her. Step by step, and this was an important one.

"I'd be happy to teach Miss Violet," he said soberly. "She's very talented. It would be a shame to see a gift like that left to lie fallow. Use the talents you're given rather than burying them, eh, Thomas?"

Adeline Merryam and Margaret both smiled and nodded, and Lady Hindmouth gave a small laugh. Yes, he'd passed the test. They relaxed into discussing the details of the school and who should be got to build it.

He took a pencil and showed Andrew Grey the shape of the windows on the gatehouse. They were larger than normal.

Matching them on the schoolhouse would improve the quality of light.

"More expensive," Mr Grey said.

"I daresay I can bear that cost," Nick offered. He laughed

when Thomas complimented his drawing skill. Then they all had tea and discussed what the Norfolk Chronicle called "His Majesty's disorder" and the much more worrying spasmodic attack the Queen had suffered at the Duke of York's party.

He watched Margaret; as she spoke, her face was alive with every fleeting emotion. Perfect honesty reflected in the contours of her face. A man living with her would always know exactly what she was thinking and feeling.

He pulled himself up. All he wanted to do was paint her, not *live* with her!

As the conversation went on, he couldn't help but notice the particular blue of her eyes, the way the light gleamed over her hair, the long, elegant hands. And her comments about the school showed her intelligence and insight.

Over the discussion, the others seemed to lose their constraint with him; he was no longer the Wicked Baron, but just another benefactor.

In fact, it was a thoroughly successful morning, if all he'd been after was rehabilitation in the eyes of the county.

But that was just the first step.

The next was to meet Margaret Deveny in a more social setting.

As they all left the vicarage, he contrived to be beside her.

"Do you attend the Assemblies in Norwich, Miss Deveny?"

She looked startled. "Oh no! I'm in mourning. I was engaged to John Poulteney, you know."

"John died last January twelvemonth," Adeline Merryam put in. Sixteen months was a long time to stay in blacks for a mere fiancé. She must really have loved him.

He was filled with a quick dislike of John Poulteney, who had been a perfectly nice boy of about his own age, though they hadn't known each other well. Now he came to think of it, Poulteney had gone to Harrow instead of Eton, which would explain it. He was ashamed of his immediate antipathy —the poor soul was dead, after all. And Margaret was mourning him, which was a definite barrier to social meetings. He should have realised. Her black silk dress was a visible reminder.

His artist's brain immediately imagined her as Mary Magdalene, mourning Christ outside his tomb. She would be perfect—that long hair of hers loose, the elegant hands disposed just *so*.

It was a favourite subject of Italian painters, who were all Catholic, but would go down very badly in Protestant England. He forced himself to put it aside. Better to paint her as herself; she needed no elaboration.

He would have to meet her at the lessons.

"Perhaps..." he said slowly, "perhaps I could teach Miss Violet here, in the vicarage? I perfectly understand that your step-mama is not currently able to invite me to her home, but surely if you were to chaperone her and come here to the vicarage, the proprieties could be maintained?"

"Better yet, have the lessons at our house!" Adeline Merryam said brightly. "I can chaperone!"

"I will ask my father," Margaret said. Her voice was quiet. "But ..." She hesitated. "I would suggest waiting until he has heard about the school and, and so forth. Once he's made up his mind, it's quite hard to change it."

Stubborn old fool.

Bowing to the ladies, he took his leave, wishing he could walk Margaret home. The key to all of this was clearly to become friends with her father.

He might have a way to do that.

CHAPTER 7

"You have a partiality for him! Admit it!" Adeline tucked her hand in Meg's arm as they walked to the Merryam barouche.

Meg honestly didn't know what to say. Nicholas de Courtenay was *not* the kind of man she had previously admired. She'd always liked tall, slender men—men like John.

By contrast, de Courtenay was her own height, solid and strong, with curly hair which was just a little too long. She supposed you could call that haircut windswept, but it was definitely not The Windswept which Anthony sported. The baron's clothes were unexceptional, but his neckcloth was merely adequate, and his boots utilitarian.

And yet … those eyes! Hazel tending to green, warm and responsive and admiring. And his hands, sketching the gatehouse windows, had been quick and competent, his manner changing utterly to show the real man beneath the cheery exterior. He was intense, Nicholas de Courtenay. She was not at all sure she wanted to be around someone *so* intense. It brought up feelings in her that she didn't quite recognise.

"Well?" Adeline prompted.

"He'll be a wonderful teacher for Violet." Meg shrugged. "I would need to know more of him before I formed a partiality."

"Mm-hmm. If *that's* going to happen, we need to rehabilitate the man in the eyes of the parish. An afternoon tea is in order."

"Addie, you can't invite him to tea! No one would come."

"No, silly, not *him*. All the strictest ladies. Time to start some counter-gossip."

Oh, Lord. Adeline was right, but that was the kind of social occasion Meg most hated.

"Since I'm in mourning …" But Addie was having none of that.

"Nonsense! In fact, it's a perfect occasion to put off your mourning. You've been in blacks and greys far too long."

"I …" She knew it had been too long. But moving out of mourning would just underline how pedestrian the rest of her life was going to be.

"You know only the highest sticklers would keep an affianced woman to even a year in blacks," Adeline prompted.

"These *are* the highest sticklers. I'll wear … I'll wear half-mourning."

Adeline had smiled at her, a dimple peeping out.

"And I'll send the invitations out for Friday."

THAT AFTERNOON, Meg went through her clothes to find something appropriate to wear to Adeline's tea party.

She hadn't bothered to get anything new made except one good black wool skirt; her muslins and silks had been dyed instead, and she had already had a dark grey pelisse. Half-mourning was lavender and white and pale grey—she was too old now to wear her white muslins, which were more suitable for a girl just out.

Besides, her clothes were already out of fashion.

The best of the bunch was the black dress she'd worn this morning; for some silly reason she'd wanted to look good.

"Primping for the vicar, eh?" her father had said as she went out. "Good idea. He'd make a fine husband."

She had grimaced and shaken her head. Thomas Courtenay was a fine man, but she was very sure he did not admire her.

"No need to be too high and mighty, my girl! You're almost an ape-leader now."

Oddly, she knew he had meant it out of concern; he wanted to see her established with a family of her own. But the term had sent a shaft of sheer terror through her. No woman wanted to be called *that*. The single women who lead the apes in hell, a punishment for not obeying the "increase and multiply" dictat from the Bible.

Utterly unfair, and of course she didn't believe in such a thing, but the *idea* of being such a woman was chilling.

She would *not* think of that now.

She would take one of her old white muslins, and add a lavender frill and sash and fichu. Which she would have to borrow from Elspeth.

But not a matching cap, although Elspeth had one. She wasn't that old *yet*.

Perhaps she should go back to London for the next Season. It was no good sitting around waiting for an acceptable gentleman to present himself.

Was it?

He couldn't see her in company. He couldn't invite her anywhere.

But he *could* invite her father …

He hadn't bothered to leave a card at the Devenys'. Hugo

Deveny's contempt for his father was well known, and well deserved. But he had been kind to Nick's mother when she left—lent her his own carriage and horses to get her to Bath, all those years ago.

That should be acknowledged.

So he wrote a letter.

My dear Sir,

Having now gone some of the way to restoring Foxchester Hall to make it fit for respectable guests, I make so bold as to invite you to dinner on Thursday inst.

My intention, if you are so kind as to accept, is to thank you for the support you provided to my late mother on the occasion of her quitting this locale. She held you in great esteem and I continue in that esteem, both in her memory and on my own account, as my life may have been very different without that night's work.

Hoping you will honour me in this way,

Deepest regards,

Nicholas de Courtenay.

Either the man would throw it in the fire, or he'd come.

Step by step. Step by step, he'd get closer to Margaret Deveny. He didn't want to examine too closely why he wanted it so badly. Call it artistic instinct.

Best to leave it at that.

CHAPTER 8

*A*deline's tea party was on Friday.

Meg duly arrayed herself in her white dress, with the new lavender details, did her hair in her most modest style, and took herself off in the barouche, instead of walking over the fields.

Lady Mundford was already there, and her bosom-bow, Mrs Birchleigh, with her. Also Phoebe, the Dowager Lady Merryam, visiting from the Dower House, and Lady Shilsbury, Countess of Northholm, and of course Lady Yarbury, the most censorious of them all. The cream of the area's Society and all, apart from Phoebe Merryam, tight-lipped moralists.

Meg curtsied to them and took her seat demurely, answering routine questions about her father and step-mama's health, and asking her routine questions in return while Adeline's servants served tea, and Addie poured it.

Talk soon turned to the school project.

"I couldn't believe my ears when I heard that the Wicked Baron was donating his gatehouse and land!" the dowager said, eyes sparkling.

"He's been all that is generous." Adeline sipped her tea as though not caring a jot. She was such a good actress! "Really, I think he is nothing like his father."

"Blood tells," Lady Yarbury said darkly. "Blood *always* tells."

"But his mother was a woman of strong moral fibre." Lady Mundford was a contemporary of Nicholas's mama. "And she did just as she ought, removing the boy from his father's influence. It's possible he has grown up into a proper young man."

"Proper!" Mrs Birchleigh almost snorted her tea. "Running off to Italy, living there even after he could have come home, living Lord knows *what* kind of life …"

"Now, Susan, that's not fair. The war in France kept him there for many years." The dowager seemed bent on defending Nick. Had Adeline primed her? Or was Phoebe Merryam just defending a kindred free spirit?

"And after? He could have been home this twelvemonth since!"

"Well …" Adeline leaned in, as if to impart a secret, and the ladies all leaned forward, as one. "I *have* heard—via the servants, you understand—" They all nodded. "I have heard that the reason he didn't come home earlier was so he wouldn't be forced to wear black for his father. He didn't want to be a hypocrite, his butler told my chambermaid, who is his niece, you know."

"Hmmmm." Mrs Birchleigh put a buttered scone on her plate and sat back. "I'm not sure that's any better. Not mourning your father—"

"Oh, be honest, Susan!" the dowager said. "The man was improved by death, and so would anyone say who knew him." As one, the ladies looked at her and then at each other, and burst out laughing.

Meg had never seen them so relaxed.

"True, true, Phoebe, but only you would say it aloud!" Lady Shilsbury said, wiping a tear of laughter away.

"I do think that Lord Ashham deserves the benefit of the doubt, at least," Adeline added.

"Yes," the dowager agreed. "We don't want him taking his title and his wealth off to London to bring some incomer to the county, just because we're giving him the cold shoulder."

Lady Yarbury had two daughters who were out, and another two—twins—waiting on their elder sisters' betrothals before they could be launched. She took in a thoughtful breath, and nodded agreement. "Perhaps we could send him a card for the Assemblies? That is public enough. And then we can assess for ourselves if he's up to snuff."

"Penelope! Such slang!" The dowager wasn't above teasing her friends, it seemed, because Lady Mundford simply shook her finger at her. But then she turned to Meg.

"And you, Miss Deveny? What is your opinion of Lord Ashham? I believe you have met him?"

The room seemed to quieten, waiting for her answer.

"Yes, I met him when he came to the vicarage to discuss the plans for the school." She must keep it simple and not too enthusiastic. "He seemed … well, rather ordinary. I was a little disappointed." She smiled. "I was expecting someone much more outré." She paused as though considering. "His linen was impeccable."

That caused an exchange of glances, and nods. Impeccable linen was very respectable. Meg bit back a smile. Violet's future was at stake, so she had to play her part perfectly. Violet's future as a painter.

At once Meg was struck by an idea so extraordinary that she lost track of the conversation for a moment. *She* could liberate Violet! Once she turned thirty, she would be in possession of her mother's bequest, which would be enough to take Violet to Italy herself! She could pretend to be a widow, and chaperone Violet to all her lessons. Even if she had to wait until Violet was of age. And then she could see Rome! The Forum, the Colosseum…

"Miss Deveny?" Adeline's mama-in-law was offering her more tea.

"I'm so sorry, Lady Merryam. Yes, thank you."

An English country house drawing room was a surprising place for a revelation, but here she was. She *wasn't* doomed to an ordinary life and dwindling into a spinster. All it would take was some resolution. And she could find that, for Violet's sake.

"THAT WENT WELL, I THINK." Adeline sat back down on the sofa and stretched out her legs, yawning. "You were magnificent, Mama-in-law!"

"Oh, for Heaven's sake, Addie, call me Phoebe! I've told you a hundred times! You too, Meg."

"Sorry. Every time I do it, Anthony looks at us strangely."

Phoebe gurgled with laughter. "It's because it reminds him I have a life other than being his mother! But you're right, it went well. At least we have poor Lord Ashham invited to the first Assembly in September, if he's not gone to London." She turned an assessing gaze on Meg. "And by September, Meg, I hope you'll have put off your mourning altogether, and you'll be able to dance with him. I am glad to see you out of blacks, at least."

Meg sat up straight. "It's not about me dancing! This is about getting him accepted so that he can teach Violet."

"Mm-hmm. Of course it is. But if *I* were your age, I'd be dropping my handkerchief in front of that young man. I saw him in church. He may not be the Wicked Baron, but he has the eyes of an angel and the hands of a devil! Don't let him go to waste, Margaret Deveny!"

She waved gaily and let herself out, leaving Adeline and Meg speechless.

"Your mother-in-law…" Meg said eventually.

"I know! She's wonderful." Addie grinned at her. "But although I respect her opinion, I think she's wrong about this."

That brought Meg up short. It was one thing to object herself, but to have Adeline criticise Nicholas was somehow *wrong*.

"Why?"

"Because you should have some adventure in your life, not settle down in the estate next to where you grew up! A couple of London seasons is hardly enough to satisfy your interest in the world, is it?"

Addie knew her so well. "No, it's not." Should she confide her new plan? Well, why not? Briefly, she outlined the idea of travelling to Italy with Violet.

Mouth agape, Adeline stared at her. "Meg, you're so *brave*! Could you do it? Yes, of course you could! You've always been braver than I—oh, what a plan! Could we come, do you think? Anthony and I? I would love us to travel together!"

"Let's not get ahead of ourselves!" Meg laughed, and got up to hug her friend. "It's years away."

"I suppose it is," Addie sighed. "But it's a *magnificent* idea, Meg!"

Meg rather thought it was. She had sent Bill Coachman home when she arrived, so she walked back over the fields. It was a grey day, and the wind was coming off the sea, setting the new hay to dancing. She wished she could run as she had when she was Toby's age, letting her bonnet fall back and her hair loose.

She was a lady now, worse luck. But the sense of being enclosed and confined had lifted. She had a plan, and the means to execute it. Even if it *did* take years, it was there, a way out, a way forward, with no one to please but herself.

She put aside an image of Nicholas de Courtenay and herself strolling through the Forum. Ridiculous. He was becoming a staid country squire, and she ... she suddenly had much broader horizons.

CHAPTER 9

$\mathcal{N}$ick had gone further afield today, to a small copse of aspens which acted as a windbreak for his sheep. The trees were alight with their spring yellow-green leaves—a hard colour to capture, but he was determined to do it.

He plucked a couple and laid them on his drawing pad, across his knees, and opened his watercolour box. It was getting depleted—he'd put in an order with Ackermann's and was expecting its arrival daily.

His water bottle was full; there were advantages to having servants, he supposed. He began doing colour mixing on the little built-in ceramic palette, trying different ratios of yellow, green, red, brown and white.

"What are you doing?" a young voice asked.

Not a surprise. He'd been expecting Miss Violet, sooner rather than later, but he was very glad he'd kept to two glasses of claret last night. He was about to give his first lesson, it seemed. He might never be any closer with her sister, but he could help her. He glanced up and smiled.

"I'm trying to match the exact colour of the leaves."

There was a pause, as Violet inspected the leaves on his pad, the leaves on the trees, and his colours, while Toby ran around, weaving in between the trees.

"But why are you putting red in when there's no red!"

He grinned. "Oh, yes, there's red there—look, on the curl of the leaf. You can't get that colour without a tinge of red." He got her to sit down and explained how to make a colour wheel, then gave her a small brush and a page from his sketchbook and let her get on with it.

The first lesson on colour was always to make a colour wheel. It took him back to his own lessons, in Bath, and how happy they had made him. It might be his duty to patch walls and drain fields, but it was *also* his duty, as an artist, to share his craft with this young lady, who so needed his help.

Violet looked up at him and grinned, a streak of crimson madder across her cheek. He grinned back, and they settled companionably to their tasks.

"Violet! Toby!" He knew that voice. He scrambled to his feet—there, coming through the aspens, her grey dress sharply contrasting with the light filtering through the bright leaves.

"Miss Deveny!" He bowed.

"Lord Ashham." She curtsied, then hesitated. In the trees, no one could see her. But if she emerged from them to stand by him, she might be noticed … and the gossip would begin flying. No one paid much attention to two children running around, but a young lady being seen with the Wicked Baron would be talked about.

He smiled wryly and held up his hand to stop her coming forward.

"Don't risk yourself," he said. "I quite understand."

"Oh, it's ridiculous!" She looked beautifully annoyed; he memorised the line between her brows, the fresh rose in her cheeks.

"Ridiculous but true, I'm afraid."

Sighing, she nodded. "Violet?"

"In a minute, Meg. I'm almost finished."

"Finished what?"

Nick began to pack up his things, leaving the watercolour box until last to give Violet more time.

"She's making a colour wheel. Our first lesson, I suppose you could call it."

That lovely mouth made an O. "It's very good of you … but you shouldn't allow her to impose …"

She couldn't come out to him, but he could go to her. Nick went to her side and bowed again, just to show he was being respectful.

"She's very talented. It's a pleasure to help her."

Up close, her skin was delightful, the rose blending into a pale pink to a very pale cream next to her ears. And her eyes – not just blue, they had flecks of grey and navy, with a slighter darker rim around the iris...he could use marine blue mixed with black for that...

"Lord Ashham?" Damn, he'd been staring.

"Oh, sorry, sorry...the painter in me, you know—you'd make such a fine subject for a portrait."

"Me?" Her astonishment was genuine. Why was she surprised? She had to know how beautiful she was.

"You're perfect. So beautiful, the finest of lines, the most elegant hands …" He was babbling. He forced himself to silence in the face of her disbelief. "Really," he finished. "So beautiful."

"Beautiful!" Goodness gracious! No one had *ever*—not even John. He'd called her "lovely", but in that tone of voice which meant "I care about you". This man—he had an artist's eye, and he thought she was *beautiful*? She couldn't doubt he meant it; every word and gesture was earnest.

"Of course!" he said. "The most beautiful woman I've ever seen."

Meg had the strangest feeling that the world was spinning around her and settling into something entirely new. His hazel eyes gazed into hers; he was so close she could smell him, an oddly masculine scent of paint and woodsmoke and wool.

"Oh." It was all she could say.

He bit his lip. "I've offended you. I'm so sorry. I know I'm *persona non grata*—"

"No, no, not at all. I was just … surprised."

Lord Ashham looked nonplussed. "But why? I can hardly be the first man to tell you how perfect you are."

Meg laughed, a little bitterly. "You are, I assure you. My … looks are not admired."

He muttered something in Italian under his breath and then said, "English men are all fools, then."

"You think Italian men would be any better?"

"But yes!" Suddenly, an accent made itself known in his voice—more a rhythm than anything else. "They would follow you down the street, kiss their hands to you. "A Botticelli come to life!" they would say. "An angel walks among us!" And they would be right."

She laughed again, without the bitterness. "What a circus I would cause!"

"A wonderful circus." He took her hand and kissed it, sending a thrill through her. "It is the ambition of my life to paint you."

Oh. The thrill she felt from the kiss was replaced by a sharp disappointment. What had she *thought* he meant? The beauty the painter saw wasn't the same as being seen that way by the man. She took refuge in propriety.

"I don't think my father would allow that."

Looking at his boots, de Courtenay made a face. "Don't I know it!" Now, he sounded entirely English. He smiled at her; surely that warmth was from the man, not the artist?

"I'm finished!" Violet announced, at the same time as Toby came racing up.

"There's people coming!" He tugged at Margaret's arm. "They shouldn't see you here."

"No, they shouldn't," Nicholas agreed. He cast a quick look at Violet's colour wheel. "Not bad, Miss Violet, but a bit untidy. Why don't you make another one at home, and keep the edges of each colour clean?"

"I will!" Violet declared. Then Meg took both the children's hands—or was taken by them—and dragged off. She cast a look over her shoulder.

"Thank you!" she said. And then ran.

JUST IN TIME, too, Nick thought, as a party on horseback came past on the lane to his left; the lane led down to the hamlet of Upper Foxbury, which made no sense at all, but there it was. England.

He bowed to the party, which had several ladies in it, and was resolutely ignored by all the fair sex, except for Diana, Lady Hindmouth, who smiled at him. Her husband wasn't there, but two of the other men nodded, as well, which was a start.

Step by step.

Step by step he'd build a reputation here which would allow him to stand in the open with Margaret Deveny without destroying her reputation.

CHAPTER 10

*M*argaret Deveny stared at herself in the cheval glass.

Beautiful?

To a painter? That was something—maybe *more* than something, more than being pretty and taking.

Her face was… not ordinary. That was true. But try as she might, she couldn't see herself through Nicholas de Courtenay's eyes.

His eyes… she felt again the thrill as he had kissed her hand. A new feeling; she didn't remember ever feeling that particular frisson with John. Nick's hand had been so warm; he'd forgotten he had taken his gloves off to paint, she suspected, since really he should never have touched her with his bare fingers.

A shiver went through her at the thought and her whole body seemed to grow warm.

This was a very bad idea. Nicholas de Courtenay thought of her as an artist's model, nothing more.

For a moment, she imagined that—being an artist's model in Italy, where men would kiss their hands to her in the street. A swift image of disrobing in front of Nicholas, in a room with flimsy, blowing curtains softening the southern light, to pose for something like "Spring" or "Venus reclining"… warmth bloomed in her belly and a blush swept through her whole body.

No more of that. The very idea was scandalous. Beneath her.

But how she wished she could run away to Italy and see the wonders of the ancient world herself!

Perhaps she could convince her father to visit Oxfordshire, where they had excavated that Roman villa. It made her laugh—she could just imagine the expression on her father's face if she asked! No, all her travelling would have to be done through books.

CHAPTER 11

It was just chance that took Meg back to the same coppice the next day. What else could it have been? Certainly it wasn't because she'd noticed the day before that his drawing had been incomplete. And this time, Violet was with Cook in the kitchen, happily learning how to make currant buns.

He was there. She watched him for a while, without him knowing, which felt strangely intimate. His hair was curly, his eyes narrowed as he flicked his gaze from trees to canvas and back again, over and over. She made a small movement and he saw her.

For a long moment they simply stared at one another, and then he said, "Stay there! Please! It's perfect."

Stunned, she stayed in place as his sketching grew furious, ochre dust flying around him. She was subjected to that same flick of gaze, over and over, assessing and surveying. It was both impersonal and deeply intimate. He saw her outline, her dress, her hair, but somehow it was as though he also saw *her* in a way no one had ever done before.

Finally, he sighed and stepped back, and only then did she realise that her back was stiff from standing so long.

"May I look?" she asked. Her voice was husky, as though she hadn't spoken in years, which was what it felt like.

Nick made a face, and then shrugged.

"I'm not happy with it, but why not? But stay there, I'll bring it to you."

So she wouldn't be seen with him. He was a kind man. So many young men of his class were casual about such things.

He hefted the canvas and brought it to her, turning it towards her with a shy smile. And there she stood, in faint ochre lines, her hand on the trunk of the sapling next to her, her eyes wide and considering.

She couldn't doubt now that he found her beautiful. This was a drawing of a vision, an angel …

"I think," she said with a catch in her voice, :that you are exaggerating my good features."

Leaning the canvas against the tree, he stood back beside her. She was conscious of his body, next to hers; his warmth cut through her muslin dress.

"Nonsense! I haven't caught your beauty at all well." That wasn't the voice of an admirer—it was the artist speaking. He was frowning at the sketch. "The proportions are not quite right. Your top lip is longer, and your nose doesn't turn up like that."

Meg began to laugh. Abashed, Nick rubbed his hand over his hair, leaving trails of ochre in the curls. "Sorry," he mumbled. "It's just—"

"I live with Violet," she reminded him. "I'm accustomed to the antics of artists."

Then he smiled, and she lost her breath.

· · ·

Dio mio, she was even more beautiful when she laughed! Dazed, he brought her hand to his lips, and her laughter died away, her gaze meeting his.

Delicately, deliberately, he kissed each of her fingers, turned her hand over and kissed the palm. Her breath caught in her throat, but she didn't pull her hand away. He shouldn't do this, he shouldn't.

With a huge effort, he let her hand drop. Did she sigh? Her mouth, that perfect, generous mouth, was partly opened, as though she searched for words. Finally, he cleared his throat, but before he spoke, she cut in.

"Have you been to Rome, Lord Ashham?" It was a shock. Not only the words, but the tone, which was that of polite small talk. He moved back instinctively, and bowed a little. She was putting up a wall, and he had to respect it.

"Yes, often, Miss Deveny." His sketchbook! He held up a hand in a sign to wait, and went to get it. "You can see here." He flicked to the back, to the sketches he'd done in Rome before he'd taken ship for England. The Forum, of course, an aqueduct, and the Colosseum—a nice angle, that, from down in the arena looking back up at the rows of stone seats, the arches at the top half-broken against the sky.

Eagerly, Margaret leaned forwards and went over each sketch carefully.

Her interest wasn't in the drawings, he saw, but in the ruins themselves.

"Ah," she said, turning over the pages devoted to the Colosseum, "There is the gladiator entrance, and there the animal pits, the emperor's platform ..."

She knew it all.

"You should go there," he said. It stopped her. Her eyes shuttered, as though she'd given too much of herself away.

"I've been maundering on," she said, trying for lightness.

"You *should* go there," he said. Her face filled with a kind of rueful humour that took his breath away. Beautiful, yes, but also clever, lovely, kind …

"Perhaps I will. One day." She handed the sketchbook back to him; he took her hand and pulled her against him, the book flat between them.

"*Cara*," he said. He wouldn't have kissed her if she'd moved away, but she looked up at him in wonder.

Their mouths met. So sweet, so enticing. Just for a moment, and then she tore herself away with a gasp.

"I should say I'm sorry. Prove that I'm not my father's son. But I'm not sorry." He took her hand again, and held it tenderly. "Unless I've upset you."

Those blue eyes were wide and her soft lips were reddened by his kiss. So tempting! But he *wasn't* his father's son. Remorse overtook him.

"I'm sorry. I *am* sorry."

She touched his cheek with her free hand. Astonished, he put his own hand over it, his heart beating fast.

"I'm not," she said. Then her whole face lit up with mischief. "But you'd best be careful or they'll be calling you the *Second* Baron, instead of the Fifth."

"The Second Wicked Baron …"

She grinned at him. And his heart turned over, just like that. Just like that, it was decided. This was the woman he wanted to take to wife.

"I must go," she said, dropping her hand and withdrawing from him.

"Of course. Perhaps I'll see you at the vicarage …" He bowed. It was formal, but he meant it. "I will be counting the minutes until then."

He'd be counting the *seconds*. Thank God Deveny had accepted his invitation. Time to start a serious campaign. For Margaret Deveny, he'd put down roots here and give up all thought of Italy. He would paint her for the rest of his life, and love her, and count no cost. They would make a life here, together.

Meg floated home. "Cara" meant dear, didn't it? Or darling? Something like that, anyway. Good Lord, she was acting as though she'd never been kissed before.

But she hadn't; not like *that*.

She'd enjoyed kissing John, and she'd been sure that their marital relations would be pleasant, but *that* … her whole body was alight with the memory.

It was as though she were tinder and he had put a spark to her. She had never suspected she could want someone so.

The Second Wicked Baron… was it possible he had been toying with her? Hazel eyes, so earnest, so tender… surely he had meant every word, every touch.

And what did that mean for her plans for Italy? Looking at his sketchbook had been like glimpsing her own future. Could she give that up for a pair of hazel eyes?

If they could repair his reputation with the parish, her life would be the life she had imagined for so long, with John: a wife, a mother, busy and happy and doing good works, as Adeline did…

Was that enough? For the first time, she wasn't sure.

CHAPTER 12

Sir Hugo Deveny was a plain man who liked pound dealing, Nick had been told. 'Bluff' was the word that came to mind: tall, solid and fit from riding to hounds, but acquiring a small paunch which would inevitably grow bigger—it was easy to see what he'd look like in ten years' time: greyer, stouter, but still energetic. One of those "backbone of England" types, long on loyalty, short on imagination.

No matter, Nick thought, as he welcomed Deveny. He was the father of the most beautiful girl in the world. Before anyone else in the parish, Nick needed his goodwill.

His nebulous feelings about Margaret firmed more every hour, it seemed; wherever he went on the estate, he couldn't help imagine her with him, as lady of the manor. Or remembering her lips under his, a promise of so much more.

Deveny had arrived at Foxchester Hall by horse: "No need to get poor Bill Coachman out for just me!" he explained to Nick as he handed his mare off to a groom and was ushered inside. He hadn't bothered to change for dinner, either; "Just us fellows, eh, no need to stand on ceremony!" But Nick noticed him assessing his own clothes, which were very correct indeed, being black satin knee breeches such as were worn at Almack's. First step to happiness: impress the father.

Deveny stopped short of the door.

"Now, young man, before we say anything else, there's a question I have to ask you."

"Yes, sir?" *Madonna mia,* had he found out about his meeting with Margaret?

"Your father …"A sneer twisted his face. "Your father refused to let the Hunt cross his land."

"The Hunt?"

This was humbug country for hunting, but foxes abounded, and cubbing was taken seriously in a county where lambs were a promise of future prosperity.

"Yes. We value our Hunt traditions here. Well, what about it, young man?"

This was easier than he'd thought.

"Of course, sir, I'd be happy for you to hunt over my land. I have no objections at all."

"Good! Well, shake on it." Nodding sharply, Deveny shook his hand. Second step.

The light was still good, since they were keeping country hours, so Nick took him on a tour of the repairs he'd made to the house, and they ended on the back terrace so he could point out the improvements underway on the land.

Deveny nodded judiciously at the stone wall repairs and the upgrades to the tenants' cottages, and was positively approving of the plan to drain the Forty Acre.

"We need dredging of the Long Cut next," he declared. The Long Cut was a canal which ran along the bottom of both their lands and which Nick's father had allowed to become overgrown with willows and pondweed. Dredging it would require a joint project between the two of them and Merryam.

"Let's discuss it over dinner," Nick suggested.

Dinner had been planned carefully to appeal to a middle-aged man who was kept eating healthily by his wife (Nick had inquired carefully of the chambermaid, whose brother was footman at the Devenys').

Beef, rich sauces, buttered lobster, roast potatoes, gravy, jellied eels, a capon or two, and claret to wash it down. Nick was careful to drink no more than two glasses. This was all about making a good impression.

He was careful, too, not to mention Violet or Margaret. They talked Land. Drainage, rainfall, the prospect of a good hay harvest, crop rotation using the Norfolk method, dairy cow breeding: "Jerseys, pfff!" Deveny said. "Suffolk Duns, my boy, Suffolk Duns are best suited for lowland country."

Nick found he enjoyed it. He'd been crammed by Moffat in the last few months and was oddly proud that he could hold his own in the conversation.

By Deveny's fourth glass, he was "Nicholas". By his sixth, he was "Nick, my boy."

Around sunset, Nick went to draw the curtains—but, alas, not quick enough. Deveny saw the procession of women leaving the house.

"What the devil?"

Nick swallowed down his humiliation. "The women servants, sir, all bar the cook. They don't stay here after dark."

"Can't blame them, no, can't blame them. Their reputations would be smashed to tinder."

"Yes, sir, I know. Although I assure you, I've never offered an insult to a woman in my life."

Deveny nodded, his lips pursed as though thinking was a chore. How had this man sired the clever Margaret?

"Whay you need, Nick, my boy, is a wife," Deveny said

solemnly. "Some high-rankin' lady. 'bove reproasch. Bring you back to Shociety."

"Yes," Nick said. "My mother wanted me to marry. She wanted me to go London. Do the Marriage Mart."

Deveny nodded heavily. "Yessh. Clever woman. No one round here will look at you. Y'r father—" He shrugged. "No good girl'll take you. The biddies'll say bad blood."

Bad blood. The epithet which would follow him all his life. Damn his father! He'd have to be respectable and upright all the other acceptable virtues in order to redeem his name … and even then, would Margaret think him suitable?

"*No* girl around here?" he prompted.

Deveny pursed his lips. "Might get someone at her last prayers. But the family'd have to cut her off. If my Margaret tied herself up to you, I'd forbid her the house. Couldn't have the influence on the young ones, y'see."

Perhaps his face changed, because Deveny patted his arm. "Plain speaking's best, eh? Not sayin' you're not a nice lad, but I'd have to think of what was best for Meg and Violet. Any father would."

His gut twisted. Only someone from far away would accept him; but, oddly, that would save him. If she were well-born enough. Be damned to that. If he couldn't have Margaret, he wouldn't stay here. What was rehabilitation in the eyes of the ton if he had to marry some stranger to get it?

He had to make the estate work. Had to do what he could for his tenants. *Had* to paint Margaret Deveny, even if he did it in secret. Thank God he had that sketch. But after that … Italy was calling. A place to put aside his hurt, because even if Margaret would take him, he couldn't drag her down. Cut her off from her family and friends.

She loved them too much, and they loved her. He wouldn't condemn her to isolation and loneliness. He cared for her too much, ridiculous though that was. They barely knew each other, and yet after drawing her in the coppice he felt he knew and loved her very soul.

Oddly, making the decision, even admitting how he felt, steadied him. It was done. He loved her, but it was best for her sake if she never knew that. Time to stop mooning over what he couldn't have.

Nick shook himself and brought his attention back to his guest.

By the time he rolled Deveny into Nick's own coach, Deveny's horse being led behind, they were the best of friends. But not good enough friends to allow him to call at the Devenys'.

He stared at the ceiling all night, wishing himself the son of anyone but the Wicked Baron.

HER FATHER HAD APPEARED late at breakfast, with heavy eyes but a jovial manner. Elspeth and the children had already finished up and gone, but Meg had waited.

"How was your dinner last night, Papa?" she asked as she buttered him some toast.

"Oh, fine, fine. Ashham's doing some excellent work on that land. And he's agreed to open his estate to the Hunt, so that's all to the good." He paused, and took a sip of coffee, which he preferred in the morning. "We'll have to decide whether to invite him to join in, of course. Well, we have a few months to take his measure."

"He seemed like a perfectly polite young man," Meg said. Keep it calm, keep it distant.

"Ah, you've met him—at the vicar's?"

She nodded.

"Yes, yes, that's all to the good. Give him some acquaintance here. Make it easier on his wife when he brings her home."

A chill went through her. "His wife?"

'He's got his head on straight,' her father confirmed. "Plans to go to London and come back with some highly respectable lady. Slide his way back in to the good opinions of the old biddies that way. They'll leave cards on the wife and it'll go from there. Should work."

Of course it would work. Having the Baron Ashham absent from parish society meant a hole in the social fabric. The local gentry would be delighted to have it filled in. And a respectably married man was quite a different thing to a possibly-reprehensible bachelor. Especially if the wife was Lady So-and-So.

If he was going off to London … had she imagined the warmth in his eyes, the tenderness in his kiss?

A shudder went through her.

Obviously, she had. She'd thought he meant what he said. What he did… but he was more like his father than she'd believed.

Meg pushed back from the table and headed for the door.

"Finished?" her father asked. "Get Veitch to send up some fresh coffee, will you?"

"Of course, Papa," she said, blinking back tears. This was her life now. At her family's beck and call, because she was good for nothing else. Except taking Violet to Italy, pretending to be an old, respectable widow.

How could she have *imagined* that a man like Nicholas de Courtenay could fall in love with her—just because she had fallen in love with him?

Time to put dreams away and live the life she'd been given until she could take charge of herself.

CHAPTER 13

*H*ay-making time.

Moffat explained it all to him most carefully, as they were inspecting their own hayfields, which were a week or two off ripe. In this parish, there was a set process for hay-making, since each of the major properties had a slightly different time when their hay was ripe, due to long- and tediously-explained landscape features.

Because of this, the parish harvested hay together, with all hands working as one: the Mundford property first, then the Merryams', then the Hindmouth's, then the Devenys', where the after-haying feast had been held for the last twenty years. The tenant farmers' fields were included as well. Hundreds of workers in the field, and no time wasted. His father, however, had opted out of the scheme, and not allowed any of his workers to join the general toil. The year he died, Moffat had kept to his wishes. But now, joining in the parish haying would be another step in his rehabilitation. Besides, it made sense, even if it meant his own fields were mowed last.

"Which means, my lord, that it's your job to put on the hay-making dinner," Moffat concluded.

He remembered the Hay Night dinners on the estate from his early childhood: nights of feasting and music and dancing, with everyone in high spirits from achieving, he now realised, that most important of agricultural pursuits: getting the hay in.

The dinners had stopped, he remembered, a couple of years before his mother and he had left the district. After his grandfather had died and there had been nothing holding back his father's excesses.

"Have you been following that tradition recently?" Nick asked. Moffat looked over his shoulder, choosing his words.

"Well, your lordship, your father..." So not only had his father stopped joining in the parish haying, he'd shorted his own workers of the proper feast after their labour on his land.

"No need to explain." He let his hand fall on Moffat's shoulders. "But do we need to let everyone know that we're going back to the old ways?"

Moffat took in a deep, considering breath and let it out.

"Well, now, if our people turn up at Mundford's on First Day, I'm thinking it will be plain to everyone."

"And First Day is when?"

"Mundford's steward thinks three days, weather permitting."

Nick nodded. "You'd better start ordering in food for the Hay Night Dinner, then. Assuming we have enough in the coffers to pay for it?"

Turning shocked eyes upon him, Moffat spread his hands. "Oh, m'lord, I'd *never* leave us short for Hay Night!"

Of course not. Nick bit back a smile. "Good man. Better

get me a smock, then. As I remember it, my grandfather always worked in the fields with the hands."

"Aye," Moffat said. "He did. Although your father thought it beneath him…"

"Less said about what my father did and didn't do, the better, don't you think? Get me a smock."

"Aye, I will." Moffat beamed approvingly at him. 'It'll be grand to see a de Courtenay mowing hay again, my lord."

And he had no intention of making an ass of himself over *that*. So he collared one of the oldest of the farm hands and a scythe and, and got himself a lesson on how to mow hay.

Because, as he remembered hay-making, the wives and daughters of the big houses brought refreshments to the workers, and he would *not* look clumsy in front of Margaret Deveny. She might be forbidden to him, but he would keep her good opinion if he could.

First Day dawned pink and blue—a perfect June day.

As they did every year, Meg and Elspeth took the children to the Mundfords', where the ladies of the house would join the cooks in the kitchen to make sandwiches for the workers. Adeline and her mama-in-law Phoebe were there also, of course.

It was the only time Margaret ever saw Lady Mundford dressed in less than the height of fashion, and that was only because it was "tradition" to dress simply, in a round gown of stuff.

Mind you, Lady Mundford's "stuff" looked like an expensive indigo-dyed cotton rather than homespun.

The children were shooed out of the kitchen and told to stay out of the way of the mowers. It was said without much hope of being obeyed. Toby would undoubtedly jump in and help, Michael would follow in determined imitation, and

Violet would find somewhere she could sit and draw the activity.

A chambermaid bustled in. "My lady!" she gasped, sounding scandalised. "The Wicked Baron's come with his people!"

The whole kitchen stilled. Margaret opened her mouth, and closed it again. It wasn't her place to tell the Mundfords what to do.

"Just like his grandfather," Phoebe Merryam said. "He was so reliable over hay-making."

For some reason, this simple remark took all the tension out of the room.

"He was?" Lady Mundford asked. She was from Suffolk, and hadn't known the old baron.

"Oh yes!" Phoebe nodded. "Every year, sure as sure. He was a great believer in tradition, the fourth baron."

"Hmm." Lady Mundford nodded, and dusted her hands off. "We should thank the sixth baron, then."

Meg couldn't help it; she trailed Lady Mundford out to the forecourt of the manor. She wasn't the only one, though. A whole host of people—servants and farm workers and gentry alike—wanted to know how the strict Lady Mundford would receive the Wicked Baron.

By the time they came out of the front door, however, Lord Mundford had beaten them to it. A stocky, homely figure, he was renowned in the district as being passionately devoted to his estate, so it was no surprise to anyone that *he* was welcoming with open arms all these extra workers, piled on several much-needed hay wains.

"Ashham!" he half-shouted. "Good man!"

Nick—the baron, Meg corrected herself—jumped down from the leading wain and shook his hand.

"First Day at Mundford's," he said. "How could we miss it?"

It was as simple as that. The men never even came up to the house—they walked off together to the fields, the wains following behind, creaking. Meg didn't think the two men had even noticed the women on the steps. Or, if they had, she smiled to herself, they had decided discretion was the better part of valour.

Lady Mundford took a sharp breath in and let it out again. "Well! I suppose that settles that."

And it did. Surprisingly for such an astringent woman, Lady Mundford adored her husband and treated his every decision as Holy Writ.

They went back to making sandwiches, but Meg was conscious of a tight ball of nerves and excitement somewhere under her heart. Just knowing Nicholas de Courtenay was out there was doing something very odd to her. She concentrated on slicing cheese and put that thought away from her.

But when it came time to carry the baskets of sandwiches out to the workers, she found herself scanning for the baron. Who was impossible to see in the crowd of smocks and dresses.

The men moved across the field in a staggered row—one sweep of a scythe between them. The women followed behind, raking the hay out for drying.

The sharp, clean scent of new-mown hay went right down to the bottom of her lungs, and the very air danced with fragments of hay, shining in the sun.

This is England, Meg thought. *The best of England.* But she wondered, with a quick thrill, what haying would be like in Italy.

Lady Mundford rang a handbell and work came to a stop across the fields.

Trestle tables had been put up in what was usually a sheep paddock, and the women deposited their baskets of sandwiches and fruitcake, as well as the large jugs of small ale and the innumerable tankards, only brought out for the haying.

And there he was, dressed in a *smock* of all things, laughing at something one of the men had said, his curly hair flecked with hay seeds.

Her cheeks felt hot, although the tables had been placed in the shade of the barn.

She picked up a basket and held it out to him, and he stopped short and just *looked* at her. Around them, noise and movement picked up, but they stood still, in a pool of quiet, eyes locked. Her heart beat faster than seemed possible; his face was blank, but his eyes were alive.

Then a man pushed past him with a muttered, "'scuse me, m'lord," to take a sandwich from her basket, and he started and said, "Certainly."

"Would you like a sandwich, Lord Ashham?" she asked, swallowing her nerves.

He coughed, throat no doubt dry, and she put the basket down, picked up a full tankard and took it to him.

His hands—deliberately?—closed over hers as he received it; he drank without taking his gaze away from her.

"Thank you, Miss Deveny." His voice was roughened a little, and the note in it sent a frisson down her spine. She went to move back, to get the basket, but he touched her hand—just a touch—and she froze, half-turned away. "I could look at you for the rest of my life and consider myself blessed."

She gasped and turned back. That had sounded *sincere*.

"I mean it," he said. His gaze caught hers and held them; the golden flecks in his eyes seemed to burn.

A couple of the workers had noticed they were talking and elbowed one another. Lord, she couldn't become a victim of gossip about him! It would be disastrous for both of them—and for Violet. Besides, he was going to London to find a wife. He had no right to be saying such things to her.

"I'm sure you can find your own lunch, Lord Ashham," she said clearly. He flinched, and moved back. Head high, she moved along the table, consolidating sandwiches so she could take a couple of empty baskets back to the kitchen. Deliberately not looking at him, though it was so *hard* not to look back, to tell him she hadn't meant it, it was only to stop the gossip …

The memory of his face, the way his mouth had turned in, hurt and confused, lashed her all the way back to the kitchen.

CHAPTER 14

Get a grip on yourself, man!

Nick forced himself to smile at the workers as he put the tankard back on the table and took up a sandwich.

Stupid to feel hurt. To feel as though something had pierced his side and gone straight to his heart.

"She'm a fine lass, milord." One of his own workers, old Jebediah Millar, was talking to him. "Miss Meg's the pick of the crop around here." Around him, the other men nodded sagely.

"Aye, she's a good 'un," they mumbled.

Damn. That's why she had pulled away from him; she'd seen the men watching. Relief flooded him, disproportionate to the situation. It was like taking a deep breath after gasping for air.

But how best to protect her reputation? Deliberately, he looked chagrined.

"Well, you know, lads, a lady like Miss Deveny isn't going to look at the Wicked Baron's son. I have no hopes there. I'm lucky she even speaks to me. But she's too much a lady not to."

They glanced at each other. A couple nodded. One shrugged agreement. No one corrected him.

Not one.

If even his own men didn't think he was worthy of Margaret, what hope did he have? Perhaps her withdrawal had been because of his presumption, not because of the watching men …the truth of that settled heavily within him. He had complimented her broadly, touched her with his bare hands. It had been an appalling breach of etiquette, though it had seemed so natural after their encounter in the coppice.

Of course she'd been appalled—by his lack of concern for her reputation, if nothing else.

He had to speed up his rehabilitation. She was out of mourning now, so she'd be swept up by someone much more suitable than he.

There had to be *something* he could do to make himself acceptable—to her, first, and then to her family.

The first thing, he supposed, was to treat her with a proper formality. He bit into the cheese sandwich. Damn these English and their "propriety".

If he followed his instincts, he'd snatch her away. He sighed and took a last bite. And ruin her forever.

"My dear," Lady Mundford said quietly, "be careful."

No mistaking that tone. Someone had informed the lady of the manor about that moment—that extraordinary moment—up by the barn. Meg stacked the last of the empty baskets back on the kitchen table, and turned to face her.

"I wasn't expecting it," she said simply. "I just went up to refresh the baskets."

Lady Mundford looked pleased. Perhaps she had thought she'd be rebuffed. But Meg couldn't afford gossip, and this might be a perfect opportunity to get Lady Mundford to think more deeply about Nicholas' situation.

"There was nothing one could object to," Meg continued. "Just a … a certain look in his eyes. He was perfectly polite." She sighed. "It's such a shame, really—I do feel sorry for him."

A blink and a tilt of the head. Lady Mundford was trying to work that out. "I don't quite …" she said.

"Well, it's so sad …" Meg let her voice trail off. "Through no fault of his own, he can't approach any young lady of quality and expect to be welcomed. No house of substance will receive him. He must feel very isolated. And he was accustomed to polite society in Bath, with his mother."

Just leave that there, she thought. Remind Lady Mundford that Nicholas had been brought up in England, not Italy, and by a respected lady, not by his father.

Lady Mundford took her arm as they walked back to the drawing room, where the other ladies had gathered for their own luncheon.

She paused in the doorway, holding Meg back.

"And if he *could* approach a young lady of quality, Margaret? Would he approach you?"

Meg laughed, quite spontaneously. "Oh, Lady Mundford, I shouldn't think so! A bluestocking like me, almost on the shelf! Hardly." She buried the memory of his voice, his gaze. Even if he *was* received back into polite society, he wouldn't be interested in her. Everything she was saying was true. No matter that moment in the coppice—he was going to London for a wife. "I imagine he'd find himself a nice young thing with a good dowry, probably from a titled family." Like your daughter, when she comes out, next year. It hung in the air, unsaid.

"But, this afternoon…"

Meg shrugged and moved into the room a little way. "Men look at women. That's what they do."

Lady Mundford raised her eyebrows, but tilted her head to acknowledge the truth of Meg's statement.

"I am concerned about the haying on the Foxchester estate," Lady Mundford said as she sat and poured the tea.

Mrs Birchleigh nodded agreement. "Should we go inside to prepare the lunches? That seems … inappropriate."

"We can hardly ferry food in," Adeline said. She sipped her tea delicately. "There are surely enough of us to be chaperone enough for any young women!" Her tone was judged so perfectly that they all laughed.

"Perhaps you're right. But he must not get the idea he has been accepted." Lady Mundford poured more tea, and Meg tried to forget that she would see him again tomorrow, and the day after that, and the day after that.

It felt dangerous. Days full of possibilities: the touch of his hand as she passed him his tankard, the warmth of his eyes as he watched her, the sight on him in the distance, wielding a scythe with surprising skill. She wasn't very familiar with desire, but she could recognise it rising in her at the thought; a warm, pulsing sensation that made her light-headed. Perhaps she should stay home tomorrow, and plead illness.

She knew she wouldn't. It might be a fruitless love, but she would take what she could of his company. The memories would have to last her a long time.

CHAPTER 15

As the days went past, the mowers kept up their steady forward march across the parish: first the Mundfords', then the Poulteneys', then the Hindmouths', then the Devenys'. By then, the tedding and stacking of the hay at Mundfords' had been done and the ranks of the women walking behind the mowers swelled, though some were still at the other estates.

Nicholas, deliberately, put his heart and soul into the work. He might not know how to ingratiate himself with the local bonnet brigade, but he knew how to make friends among men. He was everywhere he was needed, and he started each day with a discussion among the local landowners about the progress of the hay, the state of everyone's fields, and whether they would get all the hay in before the weather changed.

He kept quiet unless asked a question, and inquired of the older men about their local knowledge and greater experience. He was deferential and exquisitely polite. And he let them make all the decisions—for now. Once they got to his own land, he would speak up. They wouldn't respect him otherwise.

With the hands, he was bluff and manly and worked his arse off. He reflected, as he advanced along the meadows, on the commonality of country life across the world: they were ruled by the seasons in the same way in both Italy and England; young and old, rich and poor, caught up in the needs of the land. Unlike life in Bath, where the seasons were about Society and its rhythms.

He preferred this.

This golden light, diffracted by the shreds of chaff in the air. The sweeping curves of the scythes—how could you show that in a painting? The ruddy cheeks of the children who ran behind their mothers, helping to spread the new-mown hay. The scent of hay: fresh, sharp, but holding the undertones of the hayloft in winter, comforting and familiar.

And at lunch, there was Margaret. Stately, beautiful Margaret, so careful not to look him in the eyes. Had he really offended her? Or was she just being wary about gossip? It fretted him, all through the mowing.

On the last day at Devenys', at mid-morning teatime, her father sought him out, on a slight rise near the house. Mr Deveny had worked hard, too, and now looked puffed and tired. Nick passed him a glass of water Violet had run over to him, and the man drank thankfully.

"Weather's changing," he said. "Jebediah says so, and he's never wrong."

A spurt of alarm went straight to Nick's bowels. He *had* to get his hay in; the wellbeing of his people depended on it.

Deveny took a deep breath. "You can pull your people out now, of course, if you choose."

That would be the sensible thing. The thing his father would have done – had done, by not joining in the parish-wide effort, but getting his own hay in and too bad for everyone else.

If he let his people keep working Deveny land, and the rain came …

If his hay crop was ruined, he'd have to buy more. It would beggar him, at least for a few years. No going to Italy, no breaks from the constant demands of a country estate. He might not even be able to afford paints.

But if he pulled his people now, Deveny would be right to turn his back on him. And he would never see Margaret again. His very heart seemed to twist at the idea, and he thought, light-headedly, *Madonna mia.* His love seemed to have grown over the past few days, sending down deep roots.

"No, sir," he said slowly. "Let's throw the dice and try to get it all in, yours and mine."

Deveny let out a long sigh, and clapped a hand on his shoulder. "Good lad. I've sent word to the others to get the hay into their barns. They can ted it in shelter if they need to, after we've got yours in. They'll be with us tomorrow."

"Thank you, sir."

The next twenty-four hours went by in a blur for Margaret. Jebediah's prediction changed everything. There was no time for extremes of propriety when so many families' wellbeing was at stake.

As soon as they had finished in her family's fields, late in the afternoon, everyone went helter-skelter to Foxchester Hall, and she went with them—not just to brew tea and make sandwiches, but to gather and stack the hay behind the mowers with the other women and the older children. Everyone worked—even young Michael. Lady Mundford, Elspeth and Mrs Birchleigh took over the kitchen to release the scullery maids and the yardman. Phoebe was back at

Mundfords', supervising the barning of their crop. The rest of them headed for the fields, because Jebediah was never wrong.

They worked solidly for the few hours of daylight left. This hay couldn't be left to dry in the fields. It had to be stacked and put into haywains and taken to the big barn behind the stables—the barn being empty of livestock in summer.

In previous years, the gentry might have shrugged the danger off and left the fields to the hands; but the last two years had been disastrous for the countryside, and every flake of hay was needed. So it was *everyone*: all over the parish, every hand was drafted into getting the drying hay into barns. Shops shut, apprentices were released from their duties, and maids from their dusting. Most went to the properties they had already mown; but the mowers all came to Foxchester Hall. Even the vicar came, complete with his own scythe.

The few hours they had that afternoon hardly made a dent, and they were all back at first light.

The heat was terrific, even early on, and the air was heavy and humid. Meg's hair stuck to her neck and cheeks as she laboured alongside her own maid. It made her laugh; no lady's maid in London would allow herself or her charge to toil like this. But she exulted in it, too. This was *real*, unlike the tea parties and Assemblies. This *mattered*.

Nicholas was working like someone possessed. She had avoided gathering right behind him, since that was the place traditionally taken by the mower's wife, but she was in the same field, and he swung his scythe as strongly as any yeoman, and faster than all but the most experienced.

Her father was organising the distribution of the hay in the barns, making sure none of it would moulder or combust.

By lunchtime, clouds had begun to gather out at sea, and the wind was coming from the north-east, and picking up, pushing Margaret's sunbonnet back on her head. She angled her shoulder against it and kept working, though her back was on fire from the constant stooping and stacking, and every inch of skin was itchy from the tiny fragments of hay.

Instead of going up to the house for lunch, the mowers grabbed sandwiches in the fields. Margaret insisted on Michael going back; he was sun-pink and blinking with tiredness. But Toby refused, and Violet was nowhere to be found.

Throughout the afternoon, they worked. And worked. As each field was cleared, more mowers joined the next one, working from two directions.

They were doing well, but the clouds built and stretched across the sky, blotting out the sun. The heat built too, until every breath was a struggle. The wind rose.

With half of one field left to mow, the rain began to spit. The mowers left their scythes and joined the stackers, bundling swathes of hay together and throwing them up onto the wains. Meg found Nick beside her; it was more efficient if she picked and bundled and he threw, so that was what they did.

Nick stopped and looked back, and she followed his movement: a line of hard-driving rain was advancing across the fields.

"Go, go!" Nick cried to the drivers, and the wains took off for the barn, leaving a few stacks still on the ground. "Run!"

They ran, trying to outrace the rain, but all holding back so the wains got through the gate first, and the crowd of workers came afterwards, running hell-for-leather up the slight rise to the house and shelter.

"Toby!" Meg gasped. Nick stopped and looked. Toby was

labouring in the rear. Nick caught his hand and pulled him along, Meg by his side at the tail of the line.

"Everyone into the house!" Nick called out, but he followed the wains to the barn, and Toby followed him, so Meg went too. As all the workers disappeared through the kitchen door, the rain caught them, a slap of water full of the cold of the North Sea. Meg gasped with the shock of it, and with fear.

But it was all right. The last two wains had squeezed into the last space in the barn, just in time. Toby leapt around in the rain, yelling triumph.

Nick grinned at him and went straight to the horses to unharness them. The drivers jumped down to help and then led the animals across a covered walkway to the stables.

"We did it! We did it!" Toby chanted.

"We did, thanks to your help," Nick agreed.

"But it won't be much of a triumph if you catch pneumonia," Meg cut in. "Go on, go and get into some dry clothes. Or at least have something warm to drink."

Grumbling, Toby ran for the kitchen as thunder crashed overhead and lightning zigzagged across the sky, and the rain intensified until Meg couldn't even see the house through the deluge.

"Wait," Nick said, "it will calm down in a moment." He smiled, his eyes merry in a face brown from days in the fields. Warmth speared up inside her.

Her dress! It was wet through, which meant that the thin muslin was clinging to every inch of her skin. She shook it out, but it was a lost cause.

"Oh, don't," Nick said softly, moving closer. "It becomes you. I would love to paint you like that."

That warmth was spreading, and it was dangerous. And so was his voice, so low and deliberate. He was going to

London to marry A Lady. He didn't want her for anything other than a quick flirtation.

"There's more of your father in you than I thought." A flicker of hurt went over his face, and she relented. "A rake must be attractive, after all."

His smile changed, became more intimate, and he raised one hand to stroke hair back from her face.

"Attractive?" Just a murmur, but it sent every nerve tingling.

"Nick …" she said, protesting … something.

He moved even closer; she could feel the warmth of his body, radiating out through his wet clothes. They were both drenched; if he touched her, if their bodies touched, that warmth would strike through as if they were naked. Her breath caught in her throat. She'd never had this terrible sense of *anticipation* with John; nor the desire to simply lean into him and surrender.

His mouth came close to hers; his arm came around her shoulders, thrillingly warm. His breath smelled of hay. Meg let her head fall back on his arm and gazed into his eyes. In the dimness of the barn, they were darker, mysterious. Intense.

Nick leaned closer. His lips were light, brushing against hers, but her shiver went right to her toes. She raised a hand to his cheek, and he came closer still, his mouth coming down again…

"Look!" a shrill voice declared. "Look what I've done, Baron!"

They jumped apart as if the devil himself had confronted them.

It was Violet, jumping down from the hayloft onto one of the big piles of hay, sliding to the floor, waving a sketchbook triumphantly.

What had she seen? She seemed oblivious to any tension.

"Look!" she said, presenting the sketchbook to Nick.

It was a drawing – a detailed drawing of the hayfields, with the clouds rolling in from the sea. An extraordinary drawing for a ten-year-old. Each figure was recognisable – Meg could pick out herself, and Toby, and Nick, and a dozen others, simply through the way they stood or the tilt of their heads.

"Whoooo…" Nick let his breath out in a long stream. "You have been busy."

"There's others," Violet said. "But this is the best."

Nick nodded. Astonished, Meg could see that his attention was entirely on the sketch, as though the last few minutes had never happened.

"I can see that being high up suits you," Nick said. "The extra distance has given you a better sense of perspective. The relationship between foreground and background is much better."

"That's what *I* thought!" Violet crowed. She put her hand in his and tugged him towards the house. The rain had died away, and Meg hadn't even noticed. She glanced at Nick, to find him looking at her with a wry smile. She smiled back. She wasn't *quite* sure what had happened between them, but she was sure she was happy about it.

"Tuck the book under your pinafore," Nick said to Violet. "And go ahead. We'll be in in a minute."

"All right," Violet said. "But you'd better not let Papa catch you kissing."

She ran off, her boots splashing in the kitchenyard puddles.

"She saw," Meg said. "Good God, she has no discretion at all! She'll tell everyone!" The entire middle of her body seemed to be sinking into the floor; she could barely breathe.

"Not young Violet. She's got more sense than that." Nick

kicked the ground. "But … just in case she does … perhaps we'd better be ready to announce our betrothal."

Meg watched his bootheel dig into the mud. She was *not* going to say, "Betrothal?" like a ninny. He was talking about being forced into marrying her.

For a man like Nicholas, no doubt a kiss meant nothing. Especially with a spinster like her. But to be *caught*… horrible to marry because they'd been *caught* in an action he took so lightly.

It was an unfortunate time to realise her love for him was so deep, but there it was. Warm enough to sear her to the core. She couldn't allow him to be sacrificed on the altar of respectability. She didn't *want* him like that. She didn't want to be… to be settled for.

"I have no appetite to be compromised into marriage," she said. "Besides, I'm going to Italy with Violet. I can always do that earlier than I'd planned."

"Italy?" Astonished, Nick stared at her. *What on earth?* Margaret put her nose in the air.

"Why not? She needs tuition, and I can pose as a widow. It will be entirely respectable!"

He began to laugh, leaning back against the wain for support. "Oh, Margaret, my darling, what do I care if you're respectable? I'm the Wicked Baron's son! If you ruin yourself, that just makes it easier for us to marry!"

"Easier?" The clouds were shredding, moving off to the west, and the golden light of evening began to break through, so he could see her better. Her voice was uncertain, and her eyes huge and blue.

The whole world smelled of new beginnings. Surely they could have one?

He reached for her hand, slowly, to give her time to move

away. That dress; it was positively indecent, but that wasn't why his heart was beating so fast. He'd watched her for days, especially the last day, working together. Her strength, her kindness, her intelligence … and her beauty. If she wanted to go to Italy… that meant she was prepared to leave her family behind. He wouldn't be robbing her of anything she valued, even if she was ostracised. They could go to Italy together, if they had to; or stay here and brazen it out until the county came around. The Merryams, at least, would receive her. And she wasn't a girl. She could make up her own mind.

"I would like to marry you, *cara mia*." He took one hand, and then the other. "Do you think you would like to marry me?" Her lip trembled and her eyes filled with tears. "Ah, I'm sorry. I'm a brute for even asking you. I'm not fit to be a husband or a father. Not with my heritage. Forgive me, *cara*."

He kissed her hands and let them go, but she grabbed them back. "You would be a good father," she said earnestly, "because you are a good man."

They stared at each other for a long moment, the tension thick between them. A good man. If she believed that, all things were possible … some deep knot untied inside him. Perhaps he *wasn't* like his father, in any way. Margaret took a deep breath.

"Do you *really* want to marry me? Not just because you may have compromised me?"

He clasped her hands more firmly. "Of course. How could I not? I told you, you're the most beautiful woman I've ever seen, and I could happily gaze at you my whole life."

THAT WAS TRUE. He *had* said those things. Before all this. Could he really mean them, though, about a lanky Long Meg like her? Oh—it was only her father who had said Nick was going to London. *He* never had. Her heart began to beat faster.

His mouth curled in a smile which troubled her blood. "*Cara mia*, if you go to Italy, I will follow you there, and kiss my hand to you in the street, and serenade you beneath your balcony like a lovesick Romeo, and beg you earnestly, every day, to become my wife."

Oh my.

"We have to go in," she said uncertainly.

"You have not answered my question. I want to marry you. Do you want to marry me?" Half-dazed, she nodded, and he moved closer. "You have to say it out loud," he whispered in her ear.

"Yes," she breathed.

This time, his mouth was hot and demanding, but she was ready for it, curving her body into his willingly, cool flesh leaping into warmth and life as they touched.

She pulled away reluctantly, and his mouth travelled down her neck in a most distracting way.

"Nicholas. Nick. We have to go in."

"That would be an *excellent* idea." The voice was cold, and clear, and cut through her. Lady Mundford stood in the doorway, glaring at them. They sprang apart, aghast.

Nick bowed—why? And then he, deliberately, reached out and took Meg's hand. "You can be the first to congratulate us, Lady Mundford."

She blinked. She was *surprised*. Damn her, she was surprised—was that an insult to her, or to Nick?

Lady Mundford swallowed whatever she had been planning to say.

"I see. I might congratulate *you*, Lord Ashham, but do you truly expect me to congratulate Margaret?"

Margaret moved forwards and planted her feet. "Nicholas

is a fine man, Lady Mundford. If the parish won't accept us, we'll go to Italy and live there. And be happy."

"Without your family? Cut off from everyone you know?"

"If that's what I have to do." Nick made a sound of protest, and she smiled reassurance at him, although her heart was twisting within her.

The woman's mouth twitched with something between annoyance and resignation.

"I see." She looked at Nick. "And you, Lord Ashham? Do you have anything to say?"

He came forward and took Meg's hand. "Lady Mundford, what can I say except that I'm not my father? And I will spend my life proving that to Margaret."

She assessed them both, and then sighed. "It would really have been much easier if you'd waited even a *little* while."

"I've waited long enough, Lady Mundford," Meg said. Lady Mundford blinked, and then sniffed.

"Very well then." She turned on her heel and walked back to the house.

"What does that mean?" Nick demanded. ""Very well"?"

"I suppose we'll find out when we go in." It could be a disaster. It could be the scandal of the decade. They would only know if they confronted it.

Nick kissed her knuckles. "I would not ask you to give up your family."

Meg shivered. "With luck, I won't need to."

"At the very least, *carissima*, we are together now."

Smiling, she touched his cheek. "So we are." But would she be allowed to have both Nick *and* her family? Time to find out.

CHAPTER 16

Nick had left instructions in the morning, and he was pleased to see they had been carried out: the ballroom had been turned into a feasting hall, with the long trestle tables normally set up outside for the workers put up here, covered with cloths, and laden with food and drink. The workers were digging in heartily.

The gentry were at the high tables, of course (although not literally high, they were set apart from the workers' boards and were actual tables rather than trestles).

Margaret had been whisked off by his housekeeper to get dry clothes; apparently her maid had brought extra, anticipating a party. His own valet had provided a dry jacket.

So he walked to the high tables on his own, which was just as well. No need to start the gossips going. He had placed Mr Deveny, deliberately, at his right hand, and the man nodded quite convivially to him. Nick found himself praying that Deveny would accept him as a son-in-law. He didn't seem to suspect anything; had Lady Mundford actually held her tongue?

"Nice spread," Deveny said. Around the table, heads nodded and glasses were raised his way.

Was this all it took to be accepted? Food and drink?

But then, down the table, Lord Mundford stood and tapped a spoon on his glass. Silence fell. Oh Lord, what now?

Mundford cleared his throat. Beside him, his wife looked up and nodded, a clear signal to the assembly that she endorsed what he was about to say. Nerves clutched Nick's guts. Was he about to lead a walk-out? To say, thanks for the food but don't think it entitles you to our friendship? To damn Margaret in the eyes of her family and neighbours? He'd never felt so helpless.

At the back of the hall, Margaret appeared in the doorway, a willowy vision in white. She put her hand on the doorframe, and for a moment his artist's eye was entirely caught by her. Then Mundford began to speak.

"As many of you may know, this is the first time I have crossed the threshold of Foxchester Hall for more than thirty years."

A whisper went round the room, and many heads nodded sagely.

"I had thought never to come here again. And, despite the feast spread before us, I would *not* have crossed the threshold had the prior owner been the host."

He turned to Nick and half-bowed. "Ashham will forgive me for speaking plainly, I am sure—it does none of us any good to ignore the situation." There was a slight question in his voice, so Nick pushed down a surge of anger.

"Of course," he said. "I have no illusions about my father."

Deveny patted him on the arm. "Good man."

"I am pleased to hear it," Lord Mundford said. "But I am even more pleased to see with my own eyes that we have a proper man in charge of Foxchester Hall again. Ashham, I'm sure I speak for all here that your hard work over the last few days, your generosity in allowing your own men to keep mowing for others, despite the risk to your own crop, tells us that you are your grandfather's heir, not your father's. And this—" He gestured to the room, the tables, the food and drink. "—this tells me that you respect tradition, and will prove a fine addition to our parish. To Lord Ashham!"

The company surged to its feet. "To Lord Ashham!"

So this was what it was like, to belong. Warmth rose within him of a kind he'd never known. These were his people; this was his place. Forever. Lady Mundford was smiling at him, only a touch sardonically. He touched his heart and bowed his head, and she smiled more deeply.

He sought out Margaret, standing at the back still. She was smiling. She looked—yes, she looked proud. He smiled, too, and came to his feet.

"Ladies and gentlemen, I was born here, and though I've roamed far and wide, I've come to realise that this is my home, and I'm glad to be back." There were cheers from the floor. "But though I very much treasure Lord Mundford's words—" He bowed to Mundford. "I think there is someone else here who deserves a cheer more than I. Jebediah, whose warning allowed us to act quickly and save our bacon! To Jebediah!"

The very old man, seated at the table nearest them, rose to his feet and bowed, stately as a courtier, as the whole room erupted in cheers. What a face! He would make a wonderful Moses, old and sere, looking back on his life.

Nick tucked that thought away as he sat down, and the assembly quietened. He turned to Deveny. Seize the moment. He spoke quietly. "Since I'm *persona grata* again, sir, I wanted to have a word with you at some point. About Margaret."

Deveny blinked, seeming totally surprised. On his other side, his wife leaned forwards. "That's an excellent idea, my dear."

Margaret was making her way towards them, to the seat next to her stepMama which had been kept for her.

"Well!" Deveny harrumphed a bit, but under the surprise Nick could see a quick calculation happening. "I daresay that would be … acceptable."

With that approval buoying him, Nick leapt to his feet and handed Margaret to her chair. Around the room, a buzz of comment started, but it didn't sound hostile. He hoped.

Margaret looked up at him and smiled, as though she didn't care if people were gossiping.

"Oh, let them announce it now, Hugo!" Mrs Deveny said quietly.

"You've *asked* her?"

"I'm of age, Papa," Margaret interjected in a whisper.

Deveny frowned at him.

"Honestly, sir, it only just happened. Five minutes ago. We haven't been sneaking around behind your back. But I knew it was Margaret for me the first time I ever saw her."

"And it's an excellent match," Lady Deveny added.

"*Please*, Papa. I would so like to have it all out in the open."

That was Margaret; not a shred of artifice or dishonesty in her. Perhaps his feelings showed in his face, because her father shook his head as though despairing, and said, "Very well. But *I'll* make the announcement."

No sooner had he stood and made that announcement than Violet streaked down the hall from the children's table, shrieking, "Now you can teach me painting!" She threw herself into Nick's arms as he stood up, and he swung her up in the air and then placed her firmly down.

"Yes, sister Violet, I can teach you to paint." Violet spun in place with joy until she became giddy and fell over.

Even Lady Mundford laughed.

EPILOGUE

"Madame Antiquarian!" Nick's voice came from over her shoulder. Meg straightened and smiled at him, only then becoming aware of how her back and knees ached.

Nick and Violet tramped up the hill to her, sketchpads in hands, with the watercolour box slung over Nick's shoulder. Meg brushed the last of the dirt off her skirt and waited for them.

Behind Nick, a line of local women carried baskets of excavated dirt on their heads over to the sieving stations the French antiquarians had set up. It had been such a thrill to discover actual excavations happening at Pompeii, and even more of a thrill to be allowed to participate. She had learned so much—had become a proper antiquarian. There were several sites at home she was itching to dig out, now she had learned how.

"Look!" she said as Nick and Violet reached her. She

spread out her hands, showing them several large shards of pottery she had dug up only minutes before.

"Impressive!" Nick said with a grin.

She shook her head at him. "Well, what do *you* have to show for *your* morning's work?"

"Here, look." Violet quickly opened her sketchbook. A study of the Bay of Naples, a quick watercolour sketch. It really was very good. The lessons Violet had taken in Florence and Rome were bearing fruit.

"It's good," Meg said.

"Not good enough." That was Violet, always pushing herself to be better.

"And you, sir?"

Nick smiled, the smile he reserved only for her. Warmth bloomed inside her. Would she ever get used to being loved like this? And desired?

"A gift for your birthday," he said. The drawing—it was more than a sketch—was a portrait of Violet. She was painting, her face in that calm, almost blank expression she had when she was deep in the creative moment. It was masterful, capturing Violet's mien and posture exactly, but showing it with enormous affection.

"Oh, Nick!" Meg leant her head on his shoulder.

"Now *that* is good," Violet declared. "You're getting even better than you were."

"Praise indeed!" Nick laughed at her and Violet stuck out her tongue. Meg was caught between a laugh and a groan. It was good that she was still a child and not adult before her time, but to do such a thing in public!

"Will I ever make a lady of you?"

"It seems unlikely," Nick teased.

"Does an artist have to be a lady?" Violet shot back, and the two began a familiar wrangling.

Meg handed her shards and work gloves over to a foreman

and waved goodbye to the other diggers. Arms linked, the three of them began to walk down the hill towards the Herculaneum Gate. Towards the village, and the small house which they were calling home right now. She sighed with contentment. Home was wherever Nick was, and that was all she would ever need.

Nick paused for a moment, and Margaret and Violet stopped with him. The Bay spread out below, blue and beautiful, while the high Italian sky arched above them. There were fields between them and the water, and houses on the Bay itself, and the world smelled of fresh dirt and autumn woodsmoke, of paint and lemons.

How lucky a man he was!

And soon, he'd be even luckier. Margaret had laughed at him when he'd suggested a woman expecting a baby shouldn't labour in the earth; they'd come to a compromise with her only digging in the morning, before the sun became too hot.

He exchanged glances with Margaret, and she nodded. Time to share the news, both good and what Violet would undoubtedly think was bad.

"We'll be leaving this soon, and going home," he announced to Violet.

"Oh, no!" she cried. "But why?"

"Call me old-fashioned, but I'd like my first child to be born on the land of his ancestors."

Margaret laughed. "That *is* very old-fashioned!"

Violet gaped at them. "A *baby*?"

Margaret hugged her. "A baby."

"And we should get to the Channel before the winter storms hit. We'll sail to Marseilles and then buy a carriage to take us across France. So you'll see some more sights along the way, Vi." Nick ruffled her hair.

She sighed, kicking the stones on the road glumly. "I suppose I can't complain."

"I'd advise against it," Margaret said dryly. "You've had a good year."

"And I have learned *so* much!" Violet switched moods as quickly as ever, and hugged them both. "*Thank* you! Now, when I get home, no one can refuse to teach me!" She ran ahead of them onto the road down to the village, the ribbons on her hat flying.

"And I shall become a British antiquarian," Margaret said with satisfaction. "I think I'll start with the bottom of the Long Forty. We used to find bits of pottery down there when we were little."

Nick began to laugh, and Meg drew back, hurt.

"My bluestocking wife!" he chuckled, but there was only love in it, and she relaxed. "You should write a monograph."

"I *will*," she said, putting her nose in the air in a parody of a huff.

"Good. You write it, and Violet and I will do the engravings of all the treasures that you'll find."

Nick would always back her. Happiness spiralled within her, different joys all combined to make her dizzy. Nick leant forward and kissed her quickly, to cheers from a passing mule driver. "I am pleased to have a clever wife who will become an authority on Roman Britain."

She had thought no further than a small excavation, but at his words her world expanded.

"I *shall* become an authority on Roman Britain. *You* shall become one of England's great painters."

He let out a shout of laughter.

"Yes! And then we'll both be cast in the shade by Violet, who will become one of the *world's* great painters!"

"I wonder what our child will be?" she mused, tucking her hand into his arm.

Nick raised her hand and kissed the dusty knuckles. "Loved, my darling. Our child will be loved."

And so she was.

BUILDING A HOME

BUILDING A HOME

A formal invitation to afternoon tea with the Dowager Countess of Merryam at the Dower House *sounded* rather daunting—unless one knew the Dowager Countess.

Knowing the countess, Felicity Simons sailed into the Dower House drawing room with full confidence that she would have a lovely afternoon.

The dowager, Phoebe Merryam, rose to greet her, holding out both hands and smiling, looking more like a Diamond than any dowager should. Felicity took her hands and they kissed cheeks. The new countess, Adeline Merryam, sat on a sofa and smiled up at her, obviously not getting up due to her advanced pregnancy. Felicity dropped her a curtsey.

Lady Faulkes came in after her and there was another round of greetings. She, too, was expecting. A pang went through Felicity as she saw them exchange glances of shared experience. Pregnancy was something she was unlikely to experience. She should just accept that.

"My dear, how well you look!" The Dowager sat on

another sofa and patted it invitingly. Felicity sat, ready to hear and give whatever gentle gossip was available in Little Foxbury.

After tea and a discussion of the new church choir leader, Phoebe twinkled at her with that mischievous smile which was all her own.

"Now, my dear, I've brought you here with an ulterior motive."

"Ahah!" Felicity raised her eyebrows with real curiosity. Whatever Phoebe's motive, it would be interesting.

They all laughed. "Yes, indeed," Adeline, Lady Merryam, said. "Who knows what it could be, when it's my mama-in-law organising it!"

"It could be *anything*," Diana, Lady Faulkes agreed, laughing.

"Pish," Phoebe said. "It's about the architect for the new school."

"Oh, had the committee chosen someone?" The women present were all on the committee, as were Lord Faulkes, Lord Merryam and Lord Ashham, a local baron.

"Yes, indeed, and I think well chosen," Adeline said. "A Mr Grey."

"He's been designing lock keepers" cottages for the Stratford-Upon-Avon canal." Diana took a sip of tea and put her cup down. "Just what we want. Someone who's not too obsessed with grand buildings."

"Someone *sensible*," Phoebe said firmly. "Which he does seem to be. He's done fine work on that orphanage of Tony's in Soho."

Why were they telling her this? "Where do I come in?"

Phoebe smiled at her. Hmm... that was the "surely you can do this thing" smile. She'd seen it before, whenever she was being asked to contribute time to a town project.

"He's done the basic drawings, but now the land's been

formally passed to the town by Lord Ashham, he's coming back to refine the detailed drawings and supervise the builders. He needs somewhere to live while he's working on the project."

Somewhere to live?

With her and Joshua?

"I'm not sure Joshua..."

Her brother was the kindest of men, but he was also *not* sociable.

"He plays chess," Phoebe said. "He gave me a good game, when he was here last."

Ah. That did change things. Phoebe Merryam was an excellent chess player, and Joshua's favourite opponent. Not that they played often, because the dowager countess spent half the year in London and quite a lot of the rest in visiting friends.

"We offered him a bed," Diana Faulkes said, "but he felt it was too far from town. He wants to be at the site bright and early, when the workmen arrive."

Adeline shrugged. "We all have the same problem, since we all live outside the town."

Indeed they did. On large estates with very large houses, which could include the odd architect without a ripple. In their small townhouse, however, a lodger would cause a tidal wave.

"I'll ask Joshua," she said. "But you know what he's like..."

Smiles all around. Joshua Simons was an excellent doctor, a learned and committed physician. He was also absent-minded, liked his solitude, and made friends very very *very* slowly.

They had been here five years now, and he would still have found this afternoon tea difficult, since it didn't have a clear purpose or set time limit.

His patients adored him. Every single one of them *knew,*

down to their bones, that the doctor would stop at nothing to help them.

"Perhaps if I suggest this is a way of helping the town..."

"That's the way," Phoebe said. "Or just don't tell him. It's quite likely he wouldn't even notice unless you pointed it out to him..."

She had to laugh, because it was true, but the laughter came with a small ache. She loved her brother. Of course she did. He did *need* her so much, though. Without her, she wasn't sure he'd even remember to eat.

That was *her* contribution to Little Foxbury. To keep its doctor hale and hearty and fit for duty.

"I think we can do better than that."

The ladies smiled and conversation went on.

As Felicity was driven back to Little Foxbury in the Merryam brougham, she pondered on exactly how to disclose to her peace-loving brother that they would be having a long-term house guest.

Please God he was as good a chess-player as Phoebe thought.

Andrew Grey assessed his new lodgings. The house was typical of this city; a century old, it was two floors plus four dormer windows. Fake plaster stonework over brick on the ground floor, plaster above, tiled roof, classical pilasters either side of the front door, which opened straight onto the street. He expected it would be a four-room ground level, with sculleries attached at the back, four or five bedrooms above, and then attic bedrooms for servants and storage. A good, solid, workmanlike house, with plenty of four-paned windows to let in the northern light.

The room on the right of the door had blinds rather than curtains—no doubt the doctor's office. On the left, there were drapes in a soft turquoise. The doctor and his sister, arranging their parts of the house to suit themselves.

He adjusted his shirt-points and cravat before knocking on the Simons' door. Ridiculous to feel nervous. He'd lodged all up and down the country, in inns and private houses, but the dowager countess had emphasised what a favour the Simons were doing him and how kind Miss Simons, in particular, was being. There had also been an odd emphasis on "not bothering the doctor". Perhaps the man was a martinet.

Oh, well, if it didn't work out he'd just have to stay at one of the inns, despite the racket and stable-yard smells.

The door was opened by a maid, an older woman with a pleasant, rounded face. A pianoforte was being played softly inside, with considerable skill.

"Mr Grey to see Dr Simons," he said, and then realised that she might think him a patient. "And Miss Simons."

"Don't you worry, we're expecting you," she said. She turned to call over her shoulder. "Dan! Get Mr Grey's bags."

As she led him into the house, past a line of chairs where patients must wait, a boy of about twelve slid out and grabbed his two valises—one full of the tools of his trade, the other his clothes—and took them up the stairs on the right.

"I'm Molly," the maid said. "The scullery maid is Bridie. Dan's the yard boy, but you won't see much of him."

He smiled at her. Obviously this house didn't insist on a "proper" distance between servants and residents. A good sign.

Molly showed him into the left-hand room; the drawing room, where a young woman was seated at a grand pianoforte, her hands poised over the keys, her rather beautiful eyes raised to the door. It was like a scene out of an old master. The lovely pianist, more a young woman than a girl, the light falling over her shoulder and, behind her, a mirror which showed her straight back and beautifully braided dark hair.

His heart thudded and seemed to stop. Then it stuttered to life as she rose, smiled, and came towards him. She dropped a slight curtsey, her posture composed and controlled. He bowed.

"I'm Felicity Simons," she said. "Welcome to Little Foxbury, Mr Grey."

"I'm delighted to be here, Miss Simons. Thank you very much for having me to stay."

And thank God that the Earl of Merryam had negotiated his room and board, and paid for it upfront as part of his fee. He would have been quite unable to discuss that with this goddess. The fee had been merely enough to cover the extra food he'd consume, he'd been told. The dowager countess had insisted on paying against Miss Simons' wishes, apparently, and he was so glad. He didn't, at least, have to feel like a leech.

The room was quietly tasteful, with both modern and antique pieces, including a large chess set. The turquoise colour of the curtains was picked up with sofa cushions and a cream and turquoise Oriental rug. The wall opposite the windows was covered in bookshelves, filled with books which looked well-read. The whole effect was both comfortable and peaceful. Nothing overwhelming.

"It's our pleasure," she said, going to the door. "My brother is in his consulting room with a patient. Allow me to show you to your room."

He followed her mutely up the stairs to a back bedroom, where she opened the door and let him go through first. Although it faced south, it was big and airy, and had two large windows, so it was light enough. She'd set up a desk for him in the corner by the windows. It wasn't the normal bedroom secretaire, but a solid table big enough to lay out his plans.

"How kind of you to give me a workable desk." Easy to sound grateful; the size of the desk showed a real thoughtfulness.

"I thought you might prefer somewhere private to work."

Miss Simons was so composed, but when he smiled down at her, she blushed slightly and moved back from the door.

Of course, how rude of him. It was unusual for a single woman to be in charge of a household, and definitely not appropriate for her to be in his bedroom.

Dan had put his bags at the foot of his bed. Andrew moved over to them and turned back to smile at Miss Simons.

"Molly will bring up some hot water for you," she said. "If you'd like to join us for afternoon tea, it will be at four. Our meals are often a little hard to predict, since they tend to work around my brother's emergencies, but we'll try to keep them to a more standard pattern while you're with us."

"Please, don't change anything on my behalf. I'm happy to eat whenever is convenient to you."

For the first time, she smiled with her eyes as well as her mouth. Those eyes were a warm hazel, with touches of gold. Her face transformed and his heart stumbled again.

"You're very kind."

Molly came from behind her with a ewer of steaming water and Miss Simons excused herself, leaving him dazed and feeling as though he'd fallen not on his feet but on a featherbed.

What a woman.

Good Lord! What a smile he had!

Felicity wasn't at all sure she should be sharing a house

with a man who made her pulse speed up so. Mr Grey wasn't classically handsome, but he had a good strong face and such kind eyes. She'd been worried he'd be pushy and too particular, and instead he'd been just…lovely.

Joshua's patient was letting himself out as she came down the stairs, so she went in to the office.

"Our new housemate has arrived." She leant back on his big cylinder desk and looked him over as he made notes on the patient's card.

Not too tired. Good. He must have had enough sleep last night. A nice change, because it was baby season. Late summer always was…nine months from the cold winter night and festive cheer of Yuletide.

Occasionally she was aware that she had far more knowledge of the, the *realities* of life than most unmarried women. Live with a doctor long enough…first her father, now Joshua. She had become accustomed to stories about childbirth and venereal diseases, and they had become accustomed to her listening.

"Hmm." Joshua was reading over his notes, not paying attention. As usual.

"He has pink hair and purple eyes."

Nodding absently, he kept reading. And then, like clockwork, her words filtered down to the "pay attention" level of his mind. He looked up sharply. "What?"

"Our new housemate has arrived."

Joshua grinned at her. "One day, you're going to say something outrageous like that in front of other people, and they'll think you've run mad."

"One has to find one's amusement where one can," she said airily. "Tea at four. You can meet him then."

She went out and closed the door behind her as Molly answered the front door and let in Mrs Shelby and her son Mortimer, whose forehead was bleeding. Another escapade which had ended in tears. That child was going to kill himself one day.

"What was it this time?"

Mrs Shelby threw her eyes to Heaven.

"A donkey."

Of course. If there had been a donkey, Mortimer Shelby would try to ride it. He and Dan were thick as thieves, and there was nothing to choose between them for derring-do. Dan, at least, had a job to keep him occupied. Mortimer was unlucky enough to have a family just too well off to need him to work, but not well off enough to send him to boarding school.

The Dame School didn't take students over twelve. The new school…had they discussed what would happen with boys like Mortimer?

"You need to get him an apprenticeship," Felicity said. Mortimer's face brightened.

"Saddlemaker, Ma! Mr Brown said he'd take me on."

Mrs Shelby looked down at him with exasperation. "Your da would never let you go to a trade when you have the shop to inherit!"

"Perhaps he would, if Mortimer was interested in it."

"I am, Ma, honest I am! I like making things! Johnnie can have the shop." He paused. "Saddles aren't the *most* interesting, but it'd be better than a shop."

Mrs Shelby just sniffed.

Joshua came out and allowed them in.

Felicity continued to her drawing room and sat at the piano, but couldn't bring herself to play. Her mind was whirling, and her heart seemed to be jumping around. She was far too conscious that, on the floor above her, Mr Grey was washing.

A lady had a disciplined mind, and didn't allow herself to even *think* of improper things.

According to her grandmother.

A woman who had had ten children, so she must have *done* improper things, even if she didn't think about them. Or were they *not* improper, if done with a husband?

If only her mother were alive. She had died in childbirth with a late-in-life baby when Felicity was fourteen; Father still lived in Manchester, but they rarely saw him since she'd chosen to live with Joshua instead of him. He accepted that it was necessary, but he didn't like it, and neither had her Aunt Almeria, who kept house for Father.

Almost four.

She went out to the kitchen to help Molly with the tea.

"A plum cake!"

"Well, it do be an occasion, like," Molly said, putting on her "country-woman" accent.

"Mm-hmm." They grinned at each other. She was such a treasure, Molly. Never upset by Joshua's odd hours and skipped meals. Always willing to get up early to make him bacon and eggs.

Felicity took the late night extra meals, Molly the morning. It had worked for three years now. Having someone else in the house now made her nervous.

It would be all right. Surely.

As long as Joshua didn't take Mr Grey into dislike.

"So, they tell me you're a chess man," Dr Simons said. He was as tall as Andrew, and rangy, with untidy brown hair and dark eyes. Fairly blazed intelligence, which must be reassuring to his patients. "Are you?"

Andrew blinked at him.

"Yes." He shrugged. "I haven't had much chance to play lately, though, so I may be a bit rusty."

"Let's see then."

Biting back a smile, Andrew joined him at the board—Simons had given him white, which was the polite thing to do for a guest.

No need for small talk, apparently. Something of a relief.

He moved his first pawn.

SHE CAME BACK into the drawing room to find Joshua and Mr Grey at the chess board. Just like that.

"Tea?" she asked, and Mr Grey looked up and smiled at her, while Joshua simply nodded.

She wasn't sure if she was annoyed or relieved by not having to make conversation with Mr Grey. On the one hand, she'd like to know more about him. On the other…he was dangerous to her peace of mind.

She poured tea and Molly took it to the men, along with slices of the plum cake. Both men were focused on the board, and both absent-mindedly thanked her and ate and drank without looking up.

Peas in a pod. She went to the piano to test a theory. Yes, just like Joshua, Mr Grey didn't even notice her playing softly while they were staring at the board.

But when the game was over—Joshua had won, although not by much—Mr Grey joined her in the conversation setting while Joshua fished the latest medical journal out of his capacious pocket and started reading. A chess game was all the acknowledgement their guest would receive, apparently.

Mr Grey didn't seem to mind.

He conversed like a sensible man, and even asked questions. "Your own work? You're a pianist?"

Her breath caught. He had heard her playing, but to call it her *work*…that showed a level of respect she hadn't previously received. Not from anyone.

"No, no. I teach pianoforte," she said. "To children and young women."

"And perform, surely? You're very good."

He *had* been listening! Somehow, her heart was fluttering and her whole body was warm.

"My father didn't believe in women performing in public," she said.

"Ah. It's not an uncommon prejudice, even with proper recital halls being built now."

"No, not uncommon. I'm not sure I want to perform, honestly. I just enjoy playing, and I quite enjoy teaching."

"Perhaps you can give music lessons to the school-children."

She waved that idea off, but it was an interesting one. She might come back to it one day.

"Tell me about the school."

"Two classrooms, with big windows, and a door between them, which does away with the need for a corridor and allows us to have twice as many windows directly into the classroom."

"A junior and a senior room?"

"That's the plan. In one class, young ones to around ten years of age, and then the seniors would be ten and up, depending on the level each child reached. Where a student shows exceptional promise, the baron has set aside extra money for tutoring past fourteen."

"That's very foresighted." The new heir to the title of Lord Ashham was the exact opposite of his hated father, who had been known locally as the Wicked Baron.

"He wanted to get everything sorted before he and his wife went to Italy, they tell me."

Italy! She envied the girl who she still thought of as Meg Deveny. Travel…no hope of that, being tied down to Joshua and Little Foxbury.

A knock at the door brought Molly from the kitchen, and then she stood in the drawing-room doorway.

"It's Seth Norling, sir. His wife's in labour."

Joshua hoisted himself up, while Molly called back, "Dan! Dan! Bring the gig around!"

Felicity rushed to the kitchen and wrapped two of the pasties that Molly always kept ready in a linen napkin and put them plus a canteen of water into the calico bag used for the purpose.

She came to the hall and handed it to Joshua as he left his office, his doctor's bag in hand, and stood for a moment at the door watching Dan drive him off, Norling standing up behind the gig on the footman's step, hanging on grimly.

THE HOUSEHOLD HAD SWEPT into well-practised action. Andrew stood at the drawing-room door, bemused, as Molly helped Simons into his great-coat and Miss Simons opened the door for him.

Outside, he could just see a gig with a pony, with the boy Dan driving. Odd.

As Miss Simons closed the door, she caught sight of him and was startled.

"I'm sorry! I didn't mean to pry."

She laughed a little breathlessly. "No, I'm sorry for just abandoning you. But when a woman is in labour…there's no time to waste."

"There's no midwife?"

"There *was* a midwife, but she died, and unfortunately there's been no one to take her place. So Joshua is it, although the men of the district aren't pleased to have a man-midwife look after their wives."

"A doctor is different, surely?"

"Perhaps in London, but in the country, birthing is still very much seen as a woman's responsibility."

As if recollecting her manners, she waved him back into the drawing-room.

"The boy—Dan, is it?—he drove? He seems young."

"Twelve. But more than capable. And yes, he drives Joshua."

She flushed a little as they sat; was that embarrassment?

"My brother, I'm afraid, has absolutely no sense of direction. It's fine when he's coming home, because the pony will find the way. But going to a strange place…he'll end up in Norwich, or taking the wrong turn off a cliff! When Dan was younger, he'd go with Joshua and tell him when to turn, but he loves to drive and he's quite a good whip, so he took over." She smiled impishly, and his heart seemed to clench. "I'm ashamed to say it, but it's much easier for me to sleep at night, knowing Dan is with him. He's such a sensible boy, and he sleeps while Joshua is with his patients, so it's not as though he gets too tired. The gig has blankets and so on in its luggage box."

"Dan's parents don't mind?"

"Oh, no! They're delighted that we give him so much trust. And they have twelve children, you know, so it's a help that we clothe and feed him as well as pay him. They know he's safe with us. Joshua would never let anything happen to him."

Andrew had a strong and sudden sense of having walked into a fully-developed, well-run organisation, a place of light and warmth, where there was no room for him. As if he'd walked into a bustling restaurant with every table full. It filled him with an aching loss.

He loved his job, and had high ambitions, but he had no home. Was unlikely to have one for years, travelling as he did from site to site all over the country. Perhaps when he was fully established as an architect and could afford an office in one of the big cities. London or Birmingham. Only then could he even think about a wife and family, and building a home like this one.

One day.

THE NEXT MORNING, Mr Grey set off early—Molly had prepared bacon and eggs, as usual, for Joshua and simply doubled the amount for Mr Grey. They tended to plain food, because Joshua had a dislike of fancy sauces and anything that smelled too strong. No kippers for breakfast. Mr Grey had tucked in heartily while Felicity had her normal boiled egg. So that was all right. Not a fussy eater.

Felicity watched him walk north towards the school site, which was on the border of Lord Ashham's lands. The old gatehouse would be renovated to be the schoolmaster's house, but the school itself was being built from scratch.

As he turned the corner, striding out, a small figure darted out from the alleyway and followed him. Mortimer. She couldn't help but grin. Poor Mr Grey. He'd be peppered with questions all day, unless he was stern with the boy.

She rather hoped he wouldn't be…but also hoped he'd be able to do his work.

Perhaps she should stroll down in a little while and make sure that Mortimer wasn't annoying him.

A BEAUTIFUL SEPTEMBER MORNING, a fresh site, a good crew of workmen and nothing he had to think about because when he was finished, he'd just stroll back to a lovely house and have his dinner, looking across the table at the most beautiful woman he'd ever met. Molly had even given him a pasty for his lunch.

Life was good.

Even with Mortimer Shelby bombarding him with questions.

Mind you, they were quite good questions.

"Why are they digging down to put the foundations in?"

"Why are the foundations stone instead of brick?"

"Why are the doorsills stone?"

The building team foreman told him "Off with you!" but he remembered his own days as a youngster home from school, hanging around building sites and, yes, asking questions, so he tolerated the boy.

Mortimer was particularly fascinated by the stonework. What type of stone? Where did it come from? How did you cut it? Andrew and the stonemason answered some, and ignored others, but that didn't deter the lad.

Andrew had his reward when lunchtime brought Miss Simons to the site, with a can of soup for him.

"Off you go home, Mortimer," she said. "Your mother's looking for you."

The boy kicked at a stone in disappointment, but headed off obediently. Miss Simons, obviously, was an Authority to him.

"Did you come especially to save me from him?" he asked her. Her eyes danced with amusement.

"I thought you might be growing a little tired of questions."

"He's a bright lad."

"He is. And not being helped by his mother's pretensions to gentility."

"The school will give him something to do."

"He'd be better off working with me," the stonemason, Dodds, said. "He's got an eye. Saw straight off that the back door sill was on the seam. Thought it might crack. It won't, mind, but it showed he's a thinker and a noticer, which you have to be in this job."

"Would you take him as an apprentice?" Andrew asked.

"Weeeelll… tell you what. I'll take him on for this job, just to try him out, like. If he's good enough, aye, I'll take him on."

Miss Simons smiled so blindingly that Dodds blushed, despite being old enough to be her father. Andrew was torn between laughing and envy. He wished she'd smile at him that way.

JOSHUA TOOK a sip of his lunchtime soup and then paused. "I don't quite like the way that man looks at you." His voice was, well, *timid* wasn't the right word. Uncertain?

So he should be. Her life might revolve around making sure *his* life ran smoothly, for the benefit of Little Foxbury, but that didn't mean he had any real authority over her.

"So no man can look at me with admiration?"

He had that look on his face. The one where he knew that he wasn't good at understanding people. Bodies, yes. People, no.

"Am I over-reaching?" As always, Joshua was humble. A rush of tenderness came over her, and tears pricked her eyes. How many men would react so? Doubting themselves? She was being mean.

"I think he does admire me, yes," she said. "But is that so bad?"

He put his spoon down, as if he'd lost his appetite.

"It is if he marries you and takes you away."

There it was. The thing unspoken between them: that his well-being relied on her continuing as a spinster.

"I won't leave." She made her tone as certain as she could.

He nodded and picked up the spoon again, eating with enthusiasm.

She had lost her own appetite completely.

"A letter for you, Mr Grey." Miss Simons held out a thick envelope, which had been franked by a meticulous hand. The Duke of Rippingdale? What on Earth?

"Thank you, Miss Simons." He took the letter and sat on the sofa to open it. For some reason, he felt quite at ease, reading his correspondence in front of her, although it would normally be considered quite rude. The last three weeks had been delightful; an even, measured pace to his days. He was working hard, sometimes even physically helping out the men on site, excited to see his school taking shape. And in the evenings, it was back to the house, to a plain, delicious dinner, a game of chess with Simons or an evening of conversation with Miss Simons. Or both, if the doctor was called out.

He could live like this forever.

The work here would end, however, and this letter might be the answer to where he went next.

Yes. It was an invitation to Rippingdale, to discuss creating a village school there.

Satisfaction and pleasure went through him on a wave. He was becoming *known*. Just as he'd hoped. With the payment for the orphanage he'd just finished, and this school, and the Rippingale school, he was amassing a nest egg to set his own office up. A few more commissions…

"Good news?" Miss Simons asked—no wonder, he was grinning like a fool.

"Yes!" He explained about the possibility of a commission, expecting her to be pleased for him. She said all the right things, but her manner was subdued.

He didn't dare hope that it was because he would need to

leave, though the thought of leaving her was a knife in his gut.

What good was it if she liked him? He couldn't offer her anything. Not a home nor security nor a family. Not yet.

He was struck by envy of Joshua Simons, who came home every day to this perfect home.

"Your brother is very lucky!" he said impulsively. She blinked those beautiful eyes and sat back in her chair.

"He does a great deal of good work in the world." Her voice was soft. Explanatory, almost.

"He *can* do that work because you've set this house up around his needs and the needs of his patients. The chairs in the hall, Dan, Molly having food ready for them, even this room is as much library as drawing-room. And you, always here, always ready, alert to everything, managing everything. All to give him the home he needs."

She swallowed. Had he said too much? Was he quite mistaken? His palms grew sweaty.

No one had ever *seen* her so clearly. Phoebe and Diana and Adeline *knew* she kept house for Joshua, but none of them knew the details. Why should they? No one—except, perhaps, Molly—had *understood*.

She swallowed around a lump in her throat and blinked back tears. It was a woman's lot to serve, whether she liked it or not, but so often that service was invisible to men. Taken for granted.

"I'm glad I can help him." It was all she could find to say, but she meant it.

They had both relaxed back into their chairs. Molly brought in more tea, and they stayed there, talking about music and the architecture of recital halls, and from there to his work and his travels around the country.

"I would like to travel," she said on a sigh, after hearing about Edinburgh.

"I wish you could come with me, then." He said it without thinking and knew he'd turned scarlet. An outrageous thing to say to a young lady. "If-I mean, if…"

"It's all right, Mr Grey." She bit back a smile, but when she saw that he was smiling, she let it out. "It was a nice thought, if an impractical one."

"You could come if you were my wife." That came out without his volition too.

Dead silence. They stared at each other in mutual shock.

"Or…or if you were, um, the wife of someone who travelled," he stuttered.

Her whole body tensed. "I'll never marry."

He sat straight up. "No! What a waste that would be! Why not?" She just stared at him Could he get his foot any further into his mouth? "I'm sorry. Again. It's none of my business."

"No. It's not."

Perhaps he looked forlorn, because she softened a little. "My brother needs me too much. I can't abandon him."

THERE. She'd said it. The first time she'd ever said it aloud. She'd never marry, because Joshua needed her too much. And for the first time, she felt her heart crack across at the thought. Because Andrew Grey was looking at her, and he was everything she'd ever wanted in a husband.

But now he'd nod, and look wise, and commend her selflessness.

"What nonsense!" he said. He seemed almost angry.

"It's not nonsense! You said yourself that I'd set this house up to help him—"

"Yes, of course. But he could get himself a wife of his own to do that."

She shook her head, an old pain piercing her. "No. Joshua has no interest *at all* in marrying. He's a bachelor to the bone."

Mr Grey was a man of the world. It didn't shock him. On the contrary, he just shrugged. "Well then, your husband will just have to live with the two of you."

Felicity felt as though a bucket of cold water had been thrown over her. He said it so *simply*, as though it were nothing, an obvious course of action.

"No man would—"

"*Any* man would, if it meant having you to wife!"

Somehow, they were both on their feet, staring at each other.

"You're not serious!"

"I'm deadly serious. I'd marry you tomorrow and be glad to welcome Joshua as part of the package!"

She plumped down, all the air taken out of her, limp as old lettuce.

He followed, but he sat next to her on the sofa, instead of in the chair opposite.

"You've only just met me." Her voice was weak.

"I knew the moment I saw you." He took her hand; it trembled in his. "A goddess, I thought. It was ridiculous, but I knew."

Her head was swimming. "We can't—"

"No, of course not. We have to take it a *little* slowly. Still, I'm courting you, Felicity Simons. I want to make that clear."

"Joshua—"

"Joshua and I are already friends. Couldn't you see that? And I saw the way he looked at you, so apologetically, as he left. He'll be delighted to have someone here to keep you company. As *I* would be delighted to know that my wife has company and support while I'm away working. And you could come with me on the initial trips, the ones to meet the clients where I don't have to stay for long. Joshua will survive without you for a few days at a time."

She looked up at him, at warm brown eyes and a tender smile, and it was as though she were turning to chocolate sauce inside. Hot and smooth.

Could it be that simple?

"Courting," she said. They could take their time. That was the way. Get to know one another.

"Courting," he agreed, with a smile that lit up the whole room.

Oh my goodness.

COURTING! He crowed inside with jubilation. She'd agreed!

He would make Joshua *love* him! They would be the best of friends. And then…then when he left, he'd have someone to come home to. This wonderful, kind, alluring woman. All he could ever hope for.

He raised her hand to his lips and kissed her knuckles, and thrilled to her intake of breath.

"But not for *too* long. Perhaps an October wedding?"

THE WEDDING WAS IN NOVEMBER, because the building of the school had run over time.

As a beaming Joshua walked her down the aisle, the pews on either side were filled with their friends and, increasingly, their patrons.

The high-and-mighty of Little Foxbury apparently needed gatehouses, workers' cottages, even stable-blocks.

Felicity suspected that at least some of these projects had been invented so that her husband could stay with her for the first year of their marriage. People were so kind.

Diana and Ned Faulkes sat with their four children,

smiling at them. Adeline, next to Tony Merryam, cradled her own baby daughter.

Phoebe Merryam winked at her as she went past, and Felicity had to fight not to grin. Phoebe claimed that she had *known* they would fall in love, and honestly, it would be just like her to have planned the whole thing.

There was Andrew, standing at the altar in a sharply tailored coat and a blindingly white neckcloth, staring at her as though she was the centre of the world.

Her kind, gentle, clever Andrew.

He took her hand. Guided by the vicar, Mr Courtney, they said their vows, and there they were, in front of the altar, husband and wife.

THEY SAT on the chairs put on the side for them, and the vicar moved into the Communion service.

Felicity was his! Andrew couldn't quite believe his luck. He exchanged grins with Joshua, who had become a brother to him too.

The church was full of friends and patrons, all of them brimming with goodwill towards him and *his wife*!

He pressed Felicity's hand and they smiled tenderly at each other. He was the luckiest man in the world.

He had found, not only a home with Felicity and Joshua, but friends and a place to belong in Little Foxbury.

ABOUT THE AUTHOR

Elizabeth Leydin writes award-winning, sweet, clever Regency romances: she's been a fan of Georgette Heyer her whole life, and it shows! Originally publishing as Pamela Hart, she decided that the Regencies needed their very own pen name, and chose her great-grandmother's name.

Sign up for Elizabeth's Substack blog, 'Corsets & Coaches', where she shares true-life Regency stories and tidbits, as well as news about her latest releases, or watch her "This Week in the Regency" videos on Youtube.

www.ingramcontent.com/pod-product-compliance
Lightning Source LLC
Chambersburg PA
CBHW071728190726
48292CB00003B/658